Courting the Duchess

Spy Society, Book 1

Kelsey Swanson

ARE YOU SIGNED UP FOR DRAGONBLADE'S BLOG?

You'll get the latest news and information on exclusive giveaways, exclusive excerpts, coming releases, sales, free books, cover reveals and more.

Check out our complete list of authors, too!

No spam, no junk. That's a promise!

Sign Up Here

www.dragonbladepublishing.com

Dearest Reader;

Thank you for your support of a small press. At Dragonblade Publishing, we strive to bring you the highest quality Historical Romance from some of the best authors in the business. Without your support, there is no 'us', so we sincerely hope you adore these stories and find some new favorite authors along the way.

Happy Reading!

CEO, Dragonblade Publishing

For my husband.

Love is work, but it's so worth it.

Prologue

London, March of 1815

TOO LATE, ALAINA realized that being considered that Season's Diamond of the First Water meant leaving behind everything she knew and loved. Not only had she abandoned the schoolroom for the ballroom, the watchful eye of her governess for the judgmental gaze of society, and exchanged ribbons and bows for glittering gems designed to attract and impress, but she'd somehow managed to snag the hand of the most eligible bachelor on the marriage mart—the young Duke of Morton; a man who'd inherited his title just six months prior and (much to the shock and dismay of titled mamas everywhere) foregone the sowing of his oats alongside his peers and, instead, gotten engaged unconscionably young. Sterling St. John had begun courting her shortly after their first dance at the annual Aldborough soiree. After they'd shared one waltz, during which Alaina had been immediately drawn into his glorious hazel eyes and gentle smile—much like every woman of her acquaintance, young and old—he'd sent her mother into a hyperventilating excitement when he'd arrived to call the following morning with an outstanding bouquet of lavender hothouse roses.

The ensuing courtship would be considered by most to be a whirlwind of romance—a love match, to be sure. For who could deny the obvious affection noted by the jealous stares of debutantes and matrons alike when the couple were spotted enjoying ices at Gunther's, strolling in Hyde Park, and dancing at each event thrown that Season? There were some invidious whispers speculating about what had attracted such a young man (and a duke at that!) to marry so young. Of course, the only daughter of the Earl of Brendt was considered a catch. She was well-bred, biddable, fit society's traditional standards of beauty with her pale skin and coloring, possessed a lithe young figure proportioned just right for bearing many sons, as her ancestors had done for centuries; she was educated in all the respectable arts and running a household, and she came with an enviable dowery. Despite all of these attractive lures, many men of the duke's station would enjoy at least another decade of hell-raising before settling down enough to begin the oft-tedious duty of marriage and procreation for the sake of the title—even if said prospective wife was one such as Alaina. Those same wagging tongues would go on to wonder if the duke hadn't been enchant-ed by Alaina's almost ethereal beauty and impeccable breeding, but that the perfection of it would wear off quickly and the young buck would certainly regret his decision. This ponderance was mentioned so often in the gossip rags that it eventually ate away at Alaina's fledgling self-confidence.

In her own opinion, Alaina felt their courtship had been quite customary. The duke had brought her small gifts of books and sweets, dined with her family, and demonstrated an appropriate degree of attention. She'd gradually moved past her general awe that she'd attracted the attention of this well-bred, stunningly handsome young man and had come to know him enough that she learned he abhorred peas and enjoyed anything containing copious amounts of sugar. He found most popular literature unpalatable, though he loved histories and even the theater—to which he took her several times, drawing the envious gazes of all those in attendance as they shared his private box with her mother acting as chaperone.

She had developed an inevitable tendre for him, allowing him to steal several kisses as they'd snuck off to verandas and behind hedges at various parties and society gatherings. His touch sent her heart to fluttering and, though she was untried and untested, even she could sense the restraint behind his cautious caresses and gentle tasting of her lips. Her physical reaction to him was all well and good, but how he made her feel with his actions—when he inclined his head to listen to her speak, or laughed along at one of her witty comments—was the tipping point for her young, untried heart. By the time the Duke of Morton proposed to her, she'd been head-over-heels for the young man. The confession of his growing feelings toward her and her stammering reciprocity were elevated by the promise he made to care for her for the rest of their days. Alaina retreated into that dreamy, glorious moment often in the months it took to plan the wedding her mother deemed necessary for a marriage of this caliber; she took solace in the knowledge that she would have him as her partner in all things. She would have him all to herself, and he, in turn, would have all of her. This never failed to make her heart pound.

Now, Alaina's heart leaped into her throat for an entirely different reason. With the reciting of their vows earlier that morning, all pretense and dictates between them were abolished. They were man and wife.

Heart clogging her throat, Alaina dismissed her maid with a gentle wave; she didn't trust her voice to be steady enough to speak. She met her reflection in the mirror of the unfamiliar dressing table as the door clicked shut behind the young servant. Her long blond hair had been plaited neatly and draped over the shoulder of her white silk dressing gown. Her belongings had been transported and unpacked in her new room at Morton House—the Duchess's Suite. *She was a duchess.* She wondered briefly how long that realization would take to sink in and sit well with her…how long it would take for her to accept her new name and identity.

She hadn't even celebrated her nineteenth birthday and yet she'd managed to attain a social stratum the likes of which most wouldn't dare to dream after. She could only hope that she was up to the task.

Alaina attempted a bracing breath to calm her nerves, but it did little to assuage her apprehension. Instead, she closed her eyes and slowly counted to ten.

Then twenty.

"All will be well," she whispered to herself over and over again, as if forming and then hearing the words would somehow make her feel their truth. Unfortunately, they had the opposite effect and lost a sliver of their meaning with each repetition.

Her mother had visited her room the night before the wedding to advise Alaina of what would be expected of her as a wife. The conversation had been as uncomfortable as it had been uninformative. All Alaina had really learned was that she and her new husband would share a bed the following night. She would be expected to allow him certain "liberties" with her person…which would involve some sort of fundamental physical differences between their female and male bodies. If she was lucky, then Alaina wouldn't have to endure too much of these attentions and she'd produce an heir and a spare for the dukedom without too much bother. This, somehow, did not manage to produce much excitement in Alaina's imagination. On the contrary, she found herself far more nervous than before her "initiation" to the guarded world of wifehood.

Still, something made her hope that it couldn't possibly be as unpleasant as her mother's stilted, awkward words had made it out to be. If it involved more kisses from Sterling, then she just might be able to endure it. Maybe.

She knew from even her limited experience that he was more than a passable kisser, and she could not deny that she enjoyed how he held her. She thought she just might be able to survive most anything so long as he was there to guide her with his infinite patience.

She opened her eyes once more and straightened her posture, meeting her own blue gaze with steady determination. "This was what you were born to do," she told herself in a tone more confident than she felt. In her marriage, she'd managed to achieve one of the highest echelons. She would be one of the most sought-after matrons and she'd have the wealth and power to exact real change with whatever charities and societies she decided to patronize. Her children would be secure in their place in the world. She had a husband whom she found to be attractive and kind and polite. Even if it wasn't the true passion and love match the gossips suspected, she cared for Sterling and believed he'd formed some genuine feelings of affection for her. She'd certainly caught him watching her often enough, and she didn't believe she'd imagined the embers burning in his arresting hazel eyes the moment before they'd kissed at the conclusion of the marriage ceremony.

A niggling, insecure part of her mind refused to completely dismiss the naysayers who cruelly insinuated that her young husband would regret this marriage—that he was still too young to be of a family mind and would quickly grow bored of his inexperienced wife barely out of the schoolroom. Despite how confident a woman of the *ton* was, she was not immune to the fork-tongued vipers. Once a juicy bit of gossip was planted, it spread like poison ivy throughout the elite and inevitably took root in the hearts of its subjects. Though she'd never spoken to Sterling expressly about these murmurs, she'd noticed he seemed to show her special attention whenever it happened to be mentioned in an edition of the *Tattler* or another cheap tabloid. It was, Alaina was sure, his way of reassuring her without repeating the hurtful words. The image of his handsome smile bolstered her as she took one more steadying breath.

Alaina spared a glance at the gilded clock atop the hearth's carved mantle. It had been more than an hour since she'd retired. The adjoining door to her new husband's room remained closed, but, surely, it wouldn't for much longer. Refusing to be caught staring at the barrier, she rose and wrapped herself more tightly in her dressing gown. She fought the intense, unladylike urge to pace and, instead, strolled to the tall windows on the far side of the room. *A woman does not pace. She does not fret. She does not fiddle with her clothing. A woman of good breeding is the epitome of serenity and poise.* The familiar words jangled in her skull like the coins in a coffer. It would seem her mother's nagging about her behavior wouldn't leave her head, even on her wedding night.

A cushioned seat had been built into the alcove of clear, glass-paned windows. She'd felt a warm rush of delight upon spying the nook, imagining herself tucked up there many a morning or night as she enjoyed reading one of her books. A little thrill traipsed across her skin when she realized that she'd no longer be forced to read only what her mother deemed "respectable literature." She hoped Sterling might take her on an outing to the bookstore later in the week where she fully intended upon spending an obscene amount of money on any and every book which caught her fancy. One thing her mother hadn't counted on as one of the draws to Alaina's new life was her hopeful goal of freedom. She would be a woman, no longer a child requiring a chaperone or parents to hold her hands in the world. She ached to stretch her wings and discover new and wonderful things, starting with expanding her mind above the small world her mother had curated for her. She prayed it hadn't been naiveté when she began to hope that Sterling might just hold the key to a new world for her.

Darkness had fallen, but London was far from quiet. Alaina peered out the impeccable glass into the evening. Outside, the lamplights had been lit and the echoing clop of horses' hooves and the rumble of carriage wheels echoed up against the sides of the sprawling Mayfair Townhouses. Her parents' London home was several residences down the cobbled street and across the way. She wondered if she'd be able to see the familiar white columns if she opened the window and poked her head outside on a warm, clear day. It was strange to think that she'd moved mere minutes away when it felt like she'd been deposited miles from her old life…and that she felt so hopeful about it.

The rhythmic ticking of the clock was the only sound as the minutes crawled by. There were no footsteps, no creak as the adjoining door was opened to admit her husband—though she doubted any hinge would dare to squeak in this ducal household. The staff to whom she'd been introduced several hours earlier seemed far too efficient for such a thing to occur.

Unable to resist the temptation of her new perch—and far too nervous to be found waiting in her bed—Alaina made herself comfortable on the cushioned window seat and tucked her bare feet beneath the hem of her nightdress. She leaned against the alcove's wall and stared unseeingly at the flickering lights below, mesmerized by the sway of carriage lanterns as they plodded along and carried their wealthy inhabitants to that night's entertainments.

It had been a long day.

Scratch that.

It had been a long three months.

The planning and fittings and stress had worn her to the bone. The wedding, her mother had said, was expected to be the event of the year and it would be Alaina's first true test as a duchess. Her mother hadn't been wrong.

It felt odd that all those weeks of planning had come down to only a few hours in the actual execution.

And now it was over, and she felt drained in body and soul.

"I'll just close my eyes for a moment," she muttered as she settled in. The seat was comfortable, the room was warm, the hour was late. All of this conspired against her resolve to await her husband. Finally, despite her best intentions, Alaina's eyes fluttered closed, and her head tilted to the side to rest gently against the cool glass.

IN THE COBBLED street several floors below, the duke's prancing bay stallion was brought forward from the stables by a liveried groom. A man dressed in simple black clothing and sitting astride a midnight gelding leaned down to take the reins from the servant. "Are you ready?" he asked in a tone barely above a growl.

A lean young man with chestnut hair and piercing hazel eyes dismissed his groom and looked up into the rider's face. Every muscle screamed at him to turn around, stride back into his Townhouse, and bar the door—to forget he'd ever agreed to this assignment—but he did not. Jaw set in a firm line, teeth clenched so tightly they squeaked together, he tugged on his fine black gloves and mounted his steed in one swift, confident motion. His heavy woolen greatcoat settled behind him on the horse's haunches as he gathered the reins.

"Would you be ready if you were in my position?" he replied in a clipped tone, bitterness shading his words.

"I cannot say that I've ever had anything to lose before, let alone something so dear as a wife."

His eyes snapped up at the other man's cool nonchalance. He hadn't known Oliver Black long, but he'd learned early on to expect bluntness the likes of which was rarely ever directed at a duke. The response shouldn't have surprised him, but the word "wife" ignited a flare of anxious fire in his gut—not because he had a wife, but because he was set to ride away from her mere hours after their ceremony…and without having the opportunity to share her bed.

As if reading his mind, Black said, "It's only a year. You'll return soon enough and be able to get on with your life."

Sterling knew this already, had walked into the agreement with open eyes, but that had been mere weeks before he'd met Alaina. His senses of honor and desire had been embroiled in a bitter war for months before, once again, his youthful impulsivity won out and he proposed to the only daughter of the Earl of Brent in her first Season. The idea of being parted from her had made him uneasy, but leaving her behind to seek out another potential match was unacceptable. Though his head knew it was unfair, he couldn't stomach the thought of her with someone else. He'd formed feelings for the beautiful, intelligent woman and knew that the only way to ensure she would wait for him was to marry her and make her his duchess.

And he'd had every intention of wedding her, bedding her, and then returning to her side as soon as possible...but his conscience stood between him and her bedchamber. Wasn't it bad enough that he'd married her without telling her he was obligated to make a lengthy trip to the Continent? How could he do that and potentially leave her with a babe in her belly; to experience pregnancy and childbirth without him? That was, apparently, where he drew the line.

Sterling's hazel gaze flicked up to the single glowing window above. A small, curled form was silhouetted against the dim candlelight and his heart emitted an involuntary throb.

He hesitated for only one moment more before his eyes hardened and he looked away, nodding to Black and kicking his horse into motion. He'd woken that morning knowing nothing in his life would be the same...he hadn't realized, however, how long it would be until he felt home again.

Chapter One

Eight Years Later

"I HAVE NEITHER the will to live nor the strength to battle my demons any longer. This cruel world has handed me too many misfortunes; this poison shall be a kindness!" Alaina raced around the blue drawing room of Morton House as she continued her stirring reenactment of Lady Blye's death scene from a popular, preposterously dramatic new novel written by one M. Alice Lowe and lately adapted to the stage by one of the leading London acting troupes at The Mask & Lyre theatre.

Alaina pivoted from foot to foot as she also assumed the roles of Lady Blye's maid and her (slightly mad) best friend, Lady Mane. The other women in the drawing room—Alaina's close friends and fellow members of her ladies' Reading Society—either sat in awe or giggled helplessly at her dramatics, depending upon how recently they'd been initiated into the club (and the duchess's antics).

"Here!" Alaina shout-whispered to one of the ladies, frantically gesturing when she'd forgotten her mark. The young woman jumped and launched into her lines, grateful for the reminder as she'd been too enthralled by the sight the duchess made. Alaina nodded approvingly, her smile beaming as her guest delivered her lines with a heretofore unwitnessed confidence. Her heart swelled with pride, and one glance around the room told Alaina that she was not alone in this. It was always rewarding when one of their new members found enough confidence in herself to stand up and use her voice.

Their group had voted to devote this month to the reading of plays, the latest of which happened to be quite the bloodbath. Many similar societies of the female elite largely stuck to discussing tamer popular novellas or political, spiritual, or moral treatises. What made the Duchess of Morton's Reading Society so sought after was the broadness of the reading material, how they didn't stray from what was considered more controversial (and, perhaps, "inappropriate") topics. Criticism of the Reading Society was a common undertone throughout the *ton*, though, to be honest, even those critical women secretly longed to be in the close circle of the confident, outspoken, occasionally eccentric Duchess of Morton.

Following her disaster of a wedding night, Alaina had remained in mortified isolation for a period of six months before she reminded herself that, regardless of what the tabloids said, she was a duchess. And, with that, came the power to do as she pleased. The process had been gradual and, at times, rather painful, but she'd eventually become the woman her heart told her she needed to be; she also became the friend she'd always wished she'd had. Part of this mission of self-exploration entailed the creation of her Reading Society. Initially, she longed for a place where women would be free to read and discuss literature without their families' censure. When she discovered more women than she also sought a refuge from the *ton*'s judgmental gaze and the freedom to be themselves, the Reading Society evolved into a haven for anyone who felt out of place or longed to find true companionship and camaraderie in a world often filled with duplicitousness. Alaina, the mother hen of the group, took women of all ages and possessing a broad variety of interests beneath her wings, sheltering them with her name and power and opening her home to each and every one of them who needed it. This, of course, was not always embraced by the rest of Society.

Much to the shock of matrons of the *ton*, the past several years bore witness to a dramatic change in Alaina's personality and role. Gone was the soft-spoken young debutant and, gradually, in her place blossomed a woman who knew her mind and was unafraid of voicing it—often to the dismay (and secret admiration) of many. She came to be known as the perfect example of how a woman might change after discovering the freedom of marriage (causing the simultaneous chagrin of titled husbands and great envy of unwed chits everywhere).

Of course, as some papers so boldly outlined, said freedom was directly correlated to the length of time one's husband has been absent.

In Alaina's case, that was precisely eight years, nine months, and thirteen days.

She hadn't seen or heard directly from her wayward husband since she'd retired to her bedchamber the evening of their wedding and fallen asleep waiting for him to come to her. Even after all these years, the memory still needled a raw part of her heart, though she'd taught herself to view it differently: There was something to be said for how a woman might discover her mind, hobbies, and passions when her husband hadn't made his face known since their wedding day. As she saw it, she could either wallow or she could make her own way, and she'd chosen the latter (after allowing her battered and bruised heart some time to indulge itself in some sorrow, of course).

Alaina made a little excited bounce on her toes as the other woman finished her rousing monologue. It was a job well done and she couldn't have been more proud of her friend for her bravery and poise. Now, it was Alaina's turn to finish the play.

Collective gasps and titters rose from her audience as Alaina hiked up the skirts of her terribly fashionable lavender gown and leaped up onto an unoccupied cushion of a sofa, baring trim, stocking-clad calves. She faced the room as bold and passionate as a Roman senator during a stirring campaign, pressing her rolled manuscript to her bosom. A couple of artful golden curls escaped her coiffure and teased the skin of her pink, passion-tinted cheeks. Her bright blue eyes sparkled with glee as she finished her dramatic reading, pantomimed tossing back a draught of poison, pressed the back of her hand to her forehead, and finished it all with a dramatic backward dive to the sofa in a glorious flurry of skirts and petticoats.

Though her eyes were closed, there was no mistaking the rustle of a dozen skirts as her friends rose to their feet and clapped, enthusiastically cheering on her performance. The grin on her face bloomed unbidden as she enjoyed their accolades. She rose to make a humble curtsy and begin the discussion of the scene when the applause was abruptly strangled, leaving only a single loud, slow clap. One glance at the confused faces of her friends told Alaina something was certainly amiss. Their various eyes were fixed over her shoulder and furtive whispers shot back and forth. Alaina frowned and turned to locate the disturbance.

A very tall, very handsome, very well-dressed man had entered the drawing room and leaned one insolent shoulder against the doorframe. He caught her eye and wrapped up his mocking applause.

His chestnut hair was brushed back from his face, though more wild and windblown than artfully designed, indicating he'd arrived on horseback. There was something familiar about the fullness of his mouth, the breadth of his shoulders, but the hardness of his stubbled jaw and the coolness of his gaze made her feel as if she surely would not have forgotten this man had they been introduced.

She dropped her manuscript to the sofa and straightened her posture. "And who, may I ask, are you, sir, to enter my home unannounced and unwelcome? Where is Maxwell?" she asked, frustrated that her elderly butler would have allowed a visitor to enter without at least calling upon the footmen to prevent such a thing from happening. Unless he had been unable to do so... Her pulse quickened as she hoped fervently the butler hadn't been harmed.

The newcomer's mouth tilted in an approximation of a smile; indeed, it might have been closer, but there was no mirth there in the slightest. He righted himself and crossed his arms over his broad chest, further accentuating the narrowness of his waist and the strength of his legs in their immaculately fitted tan buckskin breeches.

"I must compliment your performance even if I don't necessarily find the gruesome violence to be appropriate for well-bred women." His voice set off a bell in the cobwebbed halls of her memory, shaking loose something she'd long locked away. Though he referred to all the women in the room, his eyes never left hers.

Those hazel eyes.

Alaina refused to be unnerved. The bellpull was to the left of the doorway and there was no doubt the intruder would, if he so wished, be able to stop her before she could get near enough to use it. She could scream, but there were a dozen other women behind her, waiting nervously and mostly silently for her lead. She refused to show weakness—not even in front of her friends.

She crossed her arms over her chest and adopted the same strong stance as the uninvited guest. It immediately bolstered her nerves with a strange sort of power, drawing steel into her spine and cold fire into her veins.

"I shall ask you one more time," Alaina began, secretly proud that the strength of her voice did not waver. "Who are you and what are you doing in *my* home?"

After another second of unnatural immobility, the man's face split into a wicked half-grin. One of his powerful brows rose imperiously as he uttered words Alaina's mind at first refused to process: "Aren't you the least bit excited to welcome your husband home, darling? I'd take greater offense at your lack of recognition, but it *has* been a spell."

The world paused around her...her heart halted its rhythm. Her eyes frantically searched the man's face for any sign of falsehood. But...

Those eyes.

It was at that moment that she realized what had seemed so

familiar about him. The dust was swiftly wiped away from the looking glass of her memory. She had been living beneath those intense hazel eyes for the last eight years. They were the eyes of the Morton Dukedom. Piercing. Intelligent. Hawklike in their ability to make one feel as if he were laying bare her soul.

Generations of men in that family had possessed those eyes, and the London Townhouse's soaring portrait gallery filled with several centuries-worth of paintings to prove it. After she'd first stumbled upon the gallery sometime following her husband's secretive and hasty departure, Alaina had done everything she could to avoid the room. She couldn't bear to be judged by those ancestors as the one duchess who couldn't seem to even entice her husband stay long enough to consummate the marriage, let alone produce a legitimate heir. She recalled once wistfully thinking how she never would have married Sterling had his own hazel eyes been as cold as theirs; he'd only ever looked upon her with a fondness that had warmed the intensity of his mercurial gaze. But now…

Sterling?

The sounds of the world crashed over her all at once as her guests frantically gathered their papers and belongings—some taking longer than others as their morbid curiosity won out, and they none-too-subtly glanced between Alaina and this man who claimed to be the long-lost Duke of Morton.

Alaina silently cursed the situation ten times over and donned a well-practiced mask of impassivity to hide her humiliation, her panicking heart and roiling stomach. Not only had she not immediately recognized her wayward husband, but she had demonstrated said fact in one of the most mortifying ways possible: in front of a room of Society women. She loved them all dearly, but she didn't doubt that at least a few might innocently let the incident slip.

Even more embarrassing, his first glimpse of her in nearly a decade had been her flopping around like a beached whale…

What an impression to make upon one's spouse after an

eight-year absence.

This man who claimed to be her husband didn't watch the guests leave. Instead, he simply stepped to the side to allow her guests to pass with hasty curtsies, and those intense eyes of his bore into her from across the room. Alaina fought the childish urge to fidget under his scrutiny.

So much for his eyes being warmer and more inviting than his ancestors'.

Time had changed her husband in unexpected ways. Even at five-and-twenty, he'd been tall and self-assured. His features had been well-carved and unquestionably patrician with a strong, expressive brow and angular jaw. During his absence from England, his frame had since filled out in a pleasingly masculine way and sharpened his features like a whetstone from handsome to devastating. The boy she'd married had been undeniably attractive; the man standing before her was...ravishing. There was no other word for it in her rather extensive vocabulary.

Alaina swallowed hard through her tight throat and prayed he could not detect how unnerved she was.

Especially now that they were finally well and truly alone as the door clicked shut behind the final guest.

It was without a little trepidation that Alaina realized she'd never actually been alone with her husband before...and then how truly absurd it was that she was a married woman of six-and-twenty and that was a pathetic fact of her life.

Sterling took several steps toward her until he was close enough to make her tilt her head back so she might look up into his face. Her memory hadn't failed her in this aspect; despite her best efforts, she'd never forgotten how tall he was and how much she'd had to tip her head to accept his kiss.

Alaina gave herself a rough mental shake, steeling her resolve.

This was the man who had abandoned me, she reminded herself. *Humiliated me.*

Deserted the life we were supposed to create together and left me to pick up the pieces and weather the consequences alone.

She should slap him, kick him in the groin, spit on his boots, but she was far too well-bred for such behavior. That did not stop the malicious thoughts from playing out in her mind to a satisfactory degree.

Sterling's mouth propped up into another half-smile that might have been charming had it reached his eyes.

"What? No welcome-home kiss for your husband?"

Chapter Two

THE WHITE-HOT FLASH in Alaina's remarkable sapphire eyes made Sterling tense as he awaited the stinging slap he undeniably deserved but it never came. Instead, a becoming blush tinged her smooth cheeks, lightly dusted in freckles he didn't recall ever having graced the downy skin. It appeared his wife had on her strolls and excursions foregone her bonnet more often than not, allowing the sun's caress to alter her porcelain features with flecks of pale cinnamon. Despite their antithesis to modern beauty standards, he didn't mind the delicate marks. He found them intriguing as well as enticing because they spoke of a woman who no longer forced herself to adhere to strict standards and who forged her own way. He looked forward to finding out what else about her had changed now that the moment he'd dreamt about for years had finally come.

Alaina retreated a step without removing her stormy gaze from his face, crossing her arms over her bosom once more—a gesture that did not go unappreciated by Sterling. The devil inside him prodded his back with its pitchfork. It stirred to life urges so powerful, his fingers twitched with the need to pull her into his arms despite the evident danger to his person if he committed such an act.

He'd left behind a slightly gangly filly all those years ago, and now a true woman stood before him. Self-assured. Womanly curves in all the right places—all the places he most enjoyed. And the passion, the rage in her eyes…it was enough to set his pulse to simmering.

If he'd known his wife was going to develop into such a stunning beauty, would he have pushed harder to come home? Would he have fought to throw off the weight of his obligations and leave the Continent behind in favor of this woman's arms? His heart knew the truth of it, though: He'd never forgotten her and regretted their separation, and he'd make sure she believed him if it was the last thing he did.

"The chances of being received with a kiss are nonexistent when one's husband abandons her within twelve hours of the vows," Alaina snapped bitingly.

A return trip to the Continent is growing more appealing by the second... Sterling grumbled inwardly.

"It is a pleasure to see you, too, Alaina," he replied, his voice dripping globs of sarcasm.

"May I ask why you've suddenly decided to bless us with your presence, Your Grace?" she returned with equal venom, addressing him with scorn rather than the usual reverence with which he was spoken to. Sterling supposed he did deserve that.

"I thought it was time to return."

"That moment passed years ago," Alaina spat, her eyes consumed with blue flame. "It is long dead and buried."

He realized his once acquiescent wife had developed a flair for the dramatic...though she was probably correct at the heart of it if he viewed their situation objectively.

He'd done innumerable regrettable things these past several years, but none more painful than ducking out of Morton House when he knew she'd been waiting for him in her chambers, likely nervous and shaking in anticipation of their wedding night. Alaina had been a sweet girl and he had genuinely cared for her; she hadn't deserved to be abandoned like that, but it simply could not have been helped. He'd spent year after year considering how he could have handled it all differently—if trying to speak with her before he took his leave might have made a difference—but to gamble with the possibility of her patience and understanding after he'd already convinced her to give him her trust and her future wasn't something he had been prepared to face. For better or for worse, his younger mind had been made up and now it was time to face the consequences of his rashness.

Home once more, Sterling could only hope his decisions hadn't destroyed their marriage beyond repair. Gazing down at Alaina just then made him wonder if that selfish hope wasn't completely in vain.

They were stuck together, after all. He agreed with the belief that marriage wasn't intended to be fickle or temporary, contrary to what his past actions may have indicated. A good place to start would be an apology...so he may as well give it a go.

He'd had weeks to consider what he might say—how this return might be received. Thus far, it had been quite the disaster. Not only had there been an audience to his homecoming, but it was evident that his wife held more rancor in her soul for him than he'd anticipated. He was making quite the hash of things, and, if he had any hope of righting his wrongs, he needed to put in more of an effort.

"Alaina..." He softened his tone and hoped his eyes would convey the sincerity he harbored in his soul; "I realize this is long overdue. And I understand how my unannounced return is likely quite the shock. But please believe me when I say I am sorry for leaving—"

"Abandoning," she corrected him in a clipped tone.

He nodded once in concession.

"For *abandoning* you on our wedding night—"

"And for the eight years following," she interrupted once more.

Sterling had to take a slow, bracing breath through his nose.

"Yes," he ground out. "And the eight years after." His words were genuine, but he wasn't a man used to apologizing...let alone being handheld to it like a child.

"Without an explanation," she added with narrowed eyes.

"Enough!" It was Sterling's turn to snap, and Alaina's lips

formed a tight, unhappy line in response. He heaved a breath and resumed more gently. "I am sincerely sorry, Alaina. What I did was the worst sort of rotten…but did you ever stop to think that I might have had a reason?" This last seemed to set her off anew, the tension snapping through her body and charging the air.

"Did you find me repugnant?" she demanded. "Did the thought of bedding me make you ill?"

Sterling shook his head vehemently, taken aback by her bald words. To say he had always been attracted to his English rose of a wife was an understatement; for her to have assumed otherwise made a place deep within his chest ache.

"Certainly not!" he said, staunchly denying her accusations. If only she knew how he'd felt the first time they'd been introduced, how he'd been taken in by her striking eyes and broad smile, how her sharp wit and easy laughter had captivated him from the very beginning, then she'd not have questioned him. If she knew how often he'd pleasured himself to the memory of her lips and taste, imagining what it might have been like to share more with her, then that certainly would not have been the case.

"Then…were you…unable to perform?" Alaina shot a pointed look to the area below his waistcoat.

If her earlier question had caught him off guard, this one shocked him. His cheeks heated even though he was well past the age of being embarrassed.

And where did his wife get off making such a crude comment?

What sort of company had she been keeping where she was aware of such things?

"Of course not!" he spluttered, unaccustomed to being made to feel even somewhat flustered. By anyone. One of the perks of being a duke, he supposed.

"Then *why*? What could have made you leave me, a scared girl alone, waiting up for hours for her husband to come to her bed for the first time? Not to mention subjecting me to the jeers and whispers I was forced to endure after your abandonment. I was the duchess who couldn't keep her duke…" This was the first time her voice wavered; her eyes left his face to find a point beyond his left shoulder. He watched intently as Alaina's slender throat worked while she fought to maintain her composure. It didn't take her long, and he found he admired her bravery as she met his gaze again. This was no girl staring down her estranged husband and stomping a petulant foot, but a woman of her own mind. She was a lioness with teeth and claws and a spirit honed by years of battle.

Battles, much to his everlasting regret, he'd left her to weather alone.

"FOR OVER A year, not a week went by when my name wasn't bandied about by the tabloids," Alaina forged on, though the admission was mortifyingly painful. Her mind spun with the millions of things she'd wanted to say to him over the years, each warring for supremacy and slowing her tongue. She had to begin somewhere, so why not with the ways in which she'd suffered in his absence? "I was unable to attend any events for the shame of it and, when I finally did, the whispers were unbearable."

Everyone had wondered what was wrong with her or claimed she was a fool for believing a duke that young and well-off would truly be ready to settle down, but Alaina kept that last part to herself. She wasn't convinced the man standing before her wouldn't take perverse pleasure in the fact that many speculated *she* was to blame for his flight from the country. The truth was, she didn't know him; he'd been her husband only in name for nearly a decade, but he was a relative stranger to her. She eyed the changes in his features once again and realized this was truer now than even when they'd first wed. Time changed people.

And the same could be said about her, she supposed. Her husband knew little to nothing about who she was now—about her life and her passions. About how she'd been forced to retreat into herself until she'd uncovered a stronger part of her soul that could withstand the gossip long enough to find true companions amongst the hidden thorns in the garden of the *ton*. That had been one of the greatest catalysts to the creation of her Reading Society.

Over time, Alaina realized that there were other women in her world equally in need of a place where they wouldn't be judged—where no one cared if you were married and to whom. They were like-minded friends who had helped her cultivate a haven in which they might expand their horizons and experience honest companionship; how they could come together to pool their resources and make a difference for whatever cause they felt most necessary—be it charities, schools, feminine rights, or foundlings. As she eyed the man standing before her, she decided that he'd likely never even considered such struggles existed for anyone. If he had, then he wouldn't have left her to fend for herself for so long.

It was entirely possible he'd never thought of anyone beyond himself and any ounce of empathy or kindness she'd witnessed during their courtship was naught more than a carefully calculated facade. It stung to think that he'd plied her with lies and pretty words, and, not for the first time, she berated her younger self for being so foolish.

"Then why?" she demanded evenly. "Pray, what is the real reason you ran away? Surely you should be able to tell me this now though you never deigned to send a single line in a letter explaining yourself?"

Several tense heartbeats passed before her husband finally responded. "Just know that I had to go…and that I hope you will eventually find it within you to forgive me for any pain it may have caused you."

Alaina's mouth gaped in disbelief. Even after all these years, the man couldn't justify his actions. The least he could do was put some effort into his explanation, but it appeared she wasn't worth even that much to him. She scoffed and shook her head disbeliev-ingly, propping her fists on her hips. It wasn't what her hands itched to do, but it was better than swinging from the gallows for mariticide.

She heaved as deep a bracing breath as her stays would allow. "If that is all, please excuse me, Your Grace. I now have a supper to plan in honor of your *glorious* homecoming." She bobbed a sarcastic curtsy and brushed past Sterling, not allowing him to naysay her or further fill her ears with hollow platitudes and embarrassingly meaningless apologies.

She needed space.

She needed to *breathe,* as the world she'd so carefully curated began to crack and crumble around her.

STERLING TURNED TO watch his wife's ramrod-straight spine as she trudged down the hallway with impressive speed and determination. He shook his head and rubbed the back of his neck, suddenly feeling every one of the miles he'd traveled these past several weeks.

Well, that had gone nearly as poorly as possible. The only thing worse might have been physical violence against him.

Sterling swore he wasn't a volatile man—despite the evidence of this first encounter with his wife in nearly a decade. He'd never been a lad who threw punches at school. He'd been known for a temperate disposition at university. However, something about the stress and nervous excitement about finally returning home to England—and to Alaina—had created a roiling tempest of frustration and anxiety the likes of which he'd never experienced. It had made him into a man he didn't like and he already regretted it.

He didn't know what he'd been anticipating upon his return. He wasn't foolish enough to have hoped Alaina would throw her arms around his neck and wrap her grateful body around his. He wasn't a returning hero—to Alaina, he was the villain in her story…and he couldn't blame her for her perspective.

"Your Grace?"

Sterling turned to find his aging butler standing at attention a respectable distance away. Though the man's countenance remained stoic, he didn't doubt that the servant (and likely many others) had overheard their row. Maxwell had known Sterling his entire life, working his way up from footman to under butler and then butler of the London residence. Even if Sterling's marriage had gone up in smoke, something was reassuring about the older man's familiar face there to help him find his footing after he'd been set on his ear.

"Will your luggage be arriving later this evening?"

"Yes, Maxwell. My valet will be arriving from the docks in short order. Please see that Allan is shown around and introduced to the staff." He'd written ahead and had a valet hired from a service as part of his preparations for his return to English soil. He'd briefly met the middle-aged valet upon disembarking and, unable to wait any longer, left Allan to oversee the unloading of his belongings so he might return home and to his wife more quickly. And now Sterling felt as if one of those trunks had been placed squarely on his chest.

He spared a glance down the hallway where his wife had retreated but thought better of his impulse to seek her out and set things on a better path. Tracking her down now would surely only unleash more wrath from the lioness, and he was wise enough now to know that trying to force her acceptance of his return could prove disastrous. Instead, he made his way to the grand curved staircase.

"I've a mind to freshen up. Have a bath drawn if you would." Maybe he'd feel better after washing away the salt air and grime of travel. He'd spent weeks on ships, in carriages, and on horseback traversing the seemingly endless distance between Italy and Spain, weathering both the sweltering sun and bone chilling rain, stopping very little to rest, driven ceaselessly by the image of his wife at the end of his journey. Even if a bath didn't revive him entirely, at the very least he'd be able to refresh himself for another round with Alaina.

"Very good, Your Grace," the butler said with a bow as he quit the room.

Sterling stood in silence for several minutes, simply absorbing the fact that he was *home*. Seeing the English shoreline had released a deep-seated knot in his chest. Riding through the streets had unleashed a wave of nostalgia. But Morton House with its familiar rooms was the place he knew as home.

And he was determined to finally make a future with its mistress.

IT WAS ALL Alaina could do not to slam the heavy door to her bedchamber.

That man.

That infuriating, fickle, boorish, unfairly handsome man!

Alaina had long since come to terms with her sham of a marriage. Oh, to be sure, it had taken many tears and a great deal of time for her to reach a place of acceptance, but that did not mean she would be grateful for the man to return out of the blue—that she would fall to her knees and kiss his dusty boots in gratitude for his presence. She was no fool. She recognized that life as she had known it...as she had *made* it to be...these last eight years was as good as over.

And it was all Sterling's fault.

She didn't doubt that he'd attempt to take her in hand. For all she knew, he'd try to mold her to his needs, stuff her back into the tiny little box he'd supposedly found attractive enough to wed all those years ago. Alaina had fought too hard against her training and society's dictates to allow that to happen...but she had the distinct suspicion Sterling, too, would do everything he could to see his own goals through.

She stomped over to the immaculately made bed and proceeded to unleash her wrath upon an unfortunate pillow. She pummeled it until her hands ached and she collapsed upon it, face-first, to release a muffled wail of frustration.

Why now?

Why did he suddenly have to reappear and throw everything topsy-turvy?

She'd finally found peace and happiness in her own life and, once again, Sterling would toss all her good intentions to the flames of his whims. It wasn't the least bit fair.

Then again, Alaina had learned that fairness wasn't often in the cards.

Not for women.

A fair life would have meant her husband had cared enough not to abandon her to the wolves.

A fair life would have meant her husband would have stayed to protect her and honor their vows.

There was a light scratch at her bedchamber door. She bid the person to enter, but it came out more like, "Mmmurfferr", against the smothering feather pillow.

"Well, aren't you a sight?" came her maid's cheeky tone as she slipped into the room.

Alaina lifted her head; golden ringlets had come loose and cascaded into her field of vision. "Please not now, Penny. I haven't the strength."

Only a few years older than Alaina, her maid, Penelope, had become one of her closest confidants in those early months of her marriage-turned-abandonment. When she'd been too ashamed to leave her home or accept callers, too dejected to eat and too restless to sleep, the maid had stepped in to be sure Alaina took enough sustenance and cheered her with stories of her childhood on her grandparents' farm just south of the city. Penny had faithfully stayed with Alaina during the seclusion of her farce of a honeymoon and comforted her when even Alaina's own family was unsure how to handle the embarrassment of the situation. The Earl and Countess of Brendt were known for their strict adherence to social propriety, but their daughter's situation was unprecedented. What man disappeared on the wedding night without consummation? It was decided—rather, they decided for her—that the date of the duke's departure would remain a closely guarded secret. If anyone asked, Alaina was the true wife of the Duke of Morton.

And they'd promptly treated her as such…leaving Alaina to find her way without the guidance of her husband.

This relative abandonment by her parents also meant young Alaina desperately needed a confidant. A companion.

Enter Penny.

While the line between master and servant remained, it had been blurred enough that Penny felt comfortable enough to poke at Alaina's occasional dramatics. Only, this time, Alaina wasn't so sure her behavior was all that unwarranted.

The maid's sandy brows rose as she bustled through the room, gathering things to prepare Alaina for dinner. "I suppose you'd rather dine alone than with His Grace, then?" Despite her words, she didn't stop her preparations.

Alaina released a definitively unladylike snort. She'd rather chew off her arm than face Sterling again so soon.

But she'd been raised properly, and her good breeding wouldn't allow her to ignore her husband's homecoming…no matter how unwelcome his presence was. Besides, as much as it galled her, this house did belong to him.

"I'd give anything for it to be this morning again," Alaina sighed and righted herself, tucking her wayward curls behind her ears.

"Is everything so different, then?" Penny asked as she re-trieved Alaina's cornflower blue dinner gown and held it aloft for approval. Alaina nodded. The gown was one of her favorites and she knew she'd need every bit of armor she could if she was to survive this meal.

"How could it not be?" Alaina groaned. "We've an intruder in our household. *Everything* is about to change." She pushed herself to her feet and plodded over to her dressing table. Dropping down to the stool with a huff, she proceeded to remove the pins from her hair so Penny could redo her unruly coiffure.

There was no mistaking the maid's jocularity when next she

spoke. "I could be mistaken, but isn't this actually the duke's household?" Leave it to Penny to voice Alaina's earlier thoughts.

Alaina's unamused gaze met her maid's in the mirror as she began to unlace her dress. Doubtless, the servants were atwitter about Sterling's return. They'd all been without a lord for so long, it was natural for this drastic change to cause a stir. In Sterling's absence, Alaina had found her footing in running the household, and she liked to think everyone got along quite well; however, the dynamic would be inevitably different with a lord in residence.

"We've all managed just fine without His Grace. I don't see why a good thing must come to an end," Alaina grumbled, knowing full well how childish the comment sounded, but she was past the point of caring.

The maid tilted her head in understanding, but the wry twist to her lips told Alaina that Penny hadn't been entirely convinced.

Alaina rose and allowed Penny to finish undressing her. As she stood in her shift and drawers, a thud sounded on the other side of the wall. Her head whipped around to the adjoining door to Sterling's suite of rooms and her heart leaped into her throat. She'd never before heard noises from that room and it was more than a little unnerving—as if a spirit was just now making its presence known. In a way, she supposed it had. The discarded bones of her marriage were even now rattling, demanding her attention.

Though she could not hear what was being said, she could make out the low rumble of masculine voices as words were exchanged, likely between Sterling and one of the servants. She supposed she'd have to grow used to sharing space with him, whether she cared to or not. Penny was right. This was technically Sterling's home. Everything within it was his. Even *she* was his, according to the letter of the law. How nauseating that a system could afford a man the right to abandon his wife for years and still be allowed to hold all the power. Her soul railed at the unfairness of it all.

There she went again about fairness…

There was a rustle of silk as Penny held up the gown for her; the sound broke the spell the adjoining door seemed to have upon Alaina's attention. She stepped into the dress and laced her into the garment. Tiny seed pearls and glass beads caught the flickering lamplight in dancing fractals of glitter. She examined her reflection, gradually gaining confidence as her appearance came together.

Her earlier meeting with the housekeeper, Mrs. Frank, and Cook had started poorly. Alaina's temper had been boiling over and, unused to seeing her quite so flustered, her staff hadn't quite known how to handle it. To their credit, despite some fits and starts, they took her churlishness in stride.

Did she want to have a special supper for the duke?

We can't not *have supper. We must eat, regardless.*

Would she prefer it to be served on the fine china?

It seems rather excessive to do so for two people. (Plus she didn't trust herself to not throw a few of the plates and/or utensils at some point during the meal.)

Were there preferences on what should be served?

This inquiry had given her pause. She realized that neither the housekeeper nor the cook had been in residence when Sterling was last in residence at Morton House.

At last. Inspiration struck her.

Peas. Lots of them. Pea soup. Mashed peas. Pea pudding—if there is such a thing.

No one could ever accuse her of knowing *nothing* about her husband.

"Glad to see something has made you smile." Penny grinned as she tucked and pinned the last curl into place and met Alaina's eyes in the mirror.

She hadn't realized her expression had altered as she'd pondered her supper plans. She ignored the comment and, instead, thanked the maid when she brought out Alaina's pearls.

Donning her last bit of armor, Alaina made one final assessment and enjoyed a final cleansing breath.

It was time to face her husband.

And this time she was better prepared.

Chapter Three

STERLING RETURNED ANOTHER book to the shelf in the library after idly leafing through its pages. The collection of rows and rows of books in the room had already been substantial when he'd left, but, over the years, Alaina had made significant contributions of her own. Now, each shelf was stuffed from floor to ceiling with leather-bound tomes in shades of brown, black, blue, green, and even red. Where his materials—his favorite collections of essays and novels—had once been within easy reach, he'd had to search only to discover most of them relegated to the highest and most inconvenient corners of the room. It appeared that his wife had even installed several additional cases in his absence to accommodate the increase in the collection's volume. He felt a grudging amount of admiration as he stood back and surveyed it all. Alaina had found a passion and possessed broad literary tastes… things which had initially drawn him to her and he was reminded of this as he examined the shelves. A quick skim of the titles showed him everything from philosophical works to popular literature commonly sold in smaller install-ments. Alaina had certainly made herself at home in his absence.

There were touches of her in every room he'd explored thus far.

Well…not every room.

The ducal chamber had remained untouched for nearly a decade.

The hearth had been clean but the room was stuffy, and likely hadn't been aired in years, given the stale atmosphere and film of dust coating the sheets draped over the furniture. His old clothes remained in the wardrobe where they'd been left—woefully out of date, slightly moth-eaten, and likely wouldn't have fit him even if they hadn't been. He'd gained at least a stone on his frame; his routine of riding and boxing had kept him in fine physical form. What was intended to be a twelve-month absence had been continually extended and he'd needed a way to keep himself from going mad as he chafed against the role he'd been assigned to play. It was far easier for a debauched duke to flit in and out of the lavish parties and gatherings thrown by Europe's powerful and influential men. He drew less attention when it was believed he was nothing more than a pleasure-seeking rogue with fewer thoughts in his brain than notches on his bedpost. However, because he'd cultivated his actions, behavior, and speech in public, that didn't mean he'd changed who he was in his heart and soul; his greatest task was now getting Alaina to see and believe that. He was still a man who loved to ride and read, who enjoyed spirited verbal discourse and as many sweets as he could stomach.

Despite what anyone now believed, he was still the same man who'd been raised by a loving mother and a father who'd instilled in him a rampant sense of duty to King and country. When he'd inherited his title at only four-and-twenty after both his parents succumbed to separate illnesses within weeks of one another, Sterling had vowed to do whatever he could to uphold his father's noble beliefs. And, when he'd been approached with an opportunity to do so, he'd accepted without a second of hesitation. He'd chastised himself for his rash decision time and time again over the years, but he couldn't have known that he'd meet Alaina mere months after that choice, one that would alter the course of his life.

Now, nearly a decade later, he was both the same man and a different one. He maintained his unwavering loyalty to duty and he'd sheltered what parts of him he could while he molded his exterior to fit what was required. As much as he'd hoped to fall back into the life he'd left behind, it had become immediately apparent to him that it would not be so easy.

Walking into his bedchamber at Morton House felt like stepping into a shrine to his former life—a much simpler time when he had been foolish enough to form hopes and dreams and aspirations. His naiveté was nauseating to him now.

How could he not have predicted the impact his decisions would have on his life?

On Alaina's?

Suddenly, the hair on the back of his neck stood at attention, his instincts tuning into the slight stirring in the air telling him he was no longer alone.

The thrum of his heart slowed, his senses pricking to full attention.

He pivoted on his heel; his muscles tensed in preparation, fists clenched at his sides, mind focusing with lethal intensity. His body reacted on instinct born of years of training and the honing of his senses. It had been impressed upon him early on that danger lurked in even the prettiest of settings.

Instead, he found only Alaina standing in the double doorway of the library...and his body clenched for an entirely different reason.

She dazzled in the golden lamplight of the room. Her blue gown, the color of the hot summer sky in the country, made her skin appear dewy and set her eyes aglow. Her golden hair had been woven into a complicated coiffure of ringlets and plaits, proving an unhindered view of her delicately wrought features. An impossibly long strand of perfect pearls was wound around her swan-like neck several times before it spilled down the delicate flesh of her décolletage framed by the low, scalloped neckline of her gown. His gaze was naturally pulled to follow the alluring trail of glowing, creamy pearls...

Through the years, he had steadfastly guarded and cherished the memory of how beautiful his wife had looked on their wedding day, but the image before him proved his recollection faulty. If he'd thought his wife an angel then, the woman before him was a goddess—regal and composed, self-assured and resplendent.

Realizing perhaps a moment too late that he was staring at his wife like a randy youth eyeing his first glimpse of female flesh, Sterling wrenched his gaze back up to Alaina's face. He had to clear his throat before he could speak.

"You look quite lovely, Alaina," he murmured before approaching her to bring her hand to his lips. The compliment sounded weak and unworthy to even his ears, but words seemed to escape him at that moment when faced with the more mature elegance of the woman who'd waited for him all these years. The knowledge that she'd remained in his house and had continued using his name despite it all was more humbling than he cared to admit, and it was a struggle when he attempted to reclaim his practiced cool composure with a quip. "That is when you're not disheveled from jumping on the furniture like a manic spaniel." The corner of his mouth lifted in an attempt at a flirtatious smile, but the years appeared to have eroded Alaina's appreciation of his humor. Once, she had laughed at his jests; now, she stiffened and wrenched her hand away as if he were a particularly disgusting insect. He strongly suspected she called him several creative unsavory names beneath her breath as she stormed off unescorted toward the dining room.

Sterling shook his head and followed in her simmering wake.

ALAINA WATCHED WITH barely masked amusement while her husband less and less politely rejected dish after dish laid out by the footmen. It was obvious that Sterling's patience had worn thin when yet another course smothered in green appeared on the white linen before them. She could feel his piercing eyes upon her as his suspicions grew, all while she tried not to smile as she took a bite from the mountain of peas on her plate. It was clear he still loathed the innocent little vegetable.

How utterly *tragic*.

Alaina should have been put off by this absurd quantity of legumes in a single meal, but it was more than worth it. In fact, she could see herself developing a passion for them.

Peering at him from the corner of her eye, she saw Sterling gesture for a second glass of wine. He had yet to place a single morsel from his plate into his mouth and, instead, feasted upon the fine vintage from the cellar.

To his credit, he steadfastly made several overtures at conversation throughout the meal. The best Alaina could force herself to do was provide monosyllabic responses. It was all she trusted herself to say without losing control of her emotions. Again. The last thing she wished to do was create a scene directly in front of the staff—her earlier confrontation with her husband had been bad enough.

Two footmen hovered around the periphery and, though she knew the men were longtime, faithful employees, she didn't doubt any confrontation between the duke and duchess would be repeated below stairs as soon as it ended. She'd spent years garnering the loyalty and respect of her carefully selected staff, but she wasn't blinded enough to realize a public spat would incite gossip from even the most loyal servants.

She settled for silent triumph, mentally placing a tally in her column of victories. Her wayward husband had caught her unawares when he'd arrived home so unexpectedly, but she refused to be set on her heel anymore when it came to this man. She was determined never to allow him to slip past the hard-won armor she had compiled piece by piece, tear by tear. She was a duchess now, not a frightened, shy young girl striving to be everything everyone told her she should be.

Not anymore.

"Is your plan to starve me out, then?" Sterling asked suddenly in a low, flat tone as he swallowed another sip from his crystal glass. He eyed Alaina as she savored another bite of beef and creamed peas. His stomach whined in desperation. As much rich food as he'd imbibed in his travels, he'd been looking forward to experiencing an English meal.

This particular menu was not at all what he'd had in mind.

She offered him a noncommittal tilt of her head. "I think Cook has quite outdone herself." It was the longest response he'd managed to wrench from her that evening, but it certainly did not feel like progress to him. The chill in her tone could fairly freeze off a man's bollocks.

His hand clenched with dangerous force around the stem of his goblet.

He'd reached his limit.

Stiffly, he raised his free hand to dismiss the footmen attending them.

They didn't move.

Brows twitching in consternation, he made a more obvious gesture for them to leave…but again, it produced no results.

It wasn't until he fixed deadly, pointed stares at each of the young men in Morton livery that they finally, very slowly retreated from the room.

Alaina sat down her utensils and took an inordinate interest in the yellow bouquet gracing the center of the table, flanked on either side by twisted gleaming silver candelabras.

"I don't appreciate the frigid reception, Alaina," he ground out when they were alone, the frustration coming to a rolling boil within his chest. "The least you can do is try, as I am trying. Do you hate me so intensely that you cannot feign the least bit of civility?" Her gaze remained stubbornly fixed upon the flowers, but the rigidity of her posture told him she was listening. "I gave you a bloody apology."

Alaina threw her linen napkin on the table and finally turned her attention to him. "It is clear you don't appreciate the gravity of your absence if you feel as if you can stride in after all these years and have all be well between us," she snarled. "And if you believe your earlier apology qualified as such, then you must think very little of me, indeed."

Sterling shot to his feet, his chair teetering dangerously on its back legs. "I said I was sorry! I told you there was a reason for my absence." He ran a rough hand through his hair. "Dammit, *I* am your *husband*!"

"I dare you to name one instance from the past eight years when you acted the part," she hissed in response.

His eyes strayed from the rancor in her face and sparks in her eyes to the heaving swells above the neckline of her gown. Despite his anger—despite every rational part of him—he wanted her. He ached for her.

He always had.

He'd never stopped.

The desire had haunted his every moment, conscious or not, suffusing his blood with tendrils of heat that burst into an inferno in Alaina's presence. They sparred like warriors, and he couldn't help but wonder how that might translate to their chemistry in bed.

"Perhaps I should change that, presently." His tone was dangerously deep as he spoke without thinking. The threat rang through the room like cannon fire. It was a grave mistake that slipped from lips plied by the wine boiling in his empty stomach.

Several tense, impossibly heavy moments passed between them before Alaina rose from the table and made to storm from the room.

"Alaina," he growled. She was wise enough to hesitate in her steps. "I would be well within my rights, and you know that." Sterling doubled down on his blunder, unable to stop the words though he knew how awful they sounded.

"I don't know who you are," she whispered harshly before fleeing.

Sterling listened to her retreating steps and dropped back into his chair. He shoved away his glass of wine, spilling ruby drops of the liquid on the pristine tablecloth before he snagged a roll of bread from the platter. It had long since grown cold, but it somehow felt fitting, given the stale, inhospitable state of his marriage.

"THERE," PENNY PATTED Alaina's hair when she finished the long plait and then turned to gather up the discarded items of clothing. As Alaina smoothed her hair over her shoulder and down the front of her cream-colored nightdress, her fingers went suddenly numb. Her mind returned to that night all those years ago when she'd sat in this very room and awaited her husband's first nocturnal visit.

The night she'd been abandoned.

The start of her betrayal.

"Is...is everything alright, Your Grace?" Penny's gentle voice broke through Alaina's reverie.

Alaina attempted a wooden nod, but it didn't fool her maid. Penny's hand gently covered her own, silently forcing Alaina to meet her eye.

"I—I shouldn't say anything, but they're speaking of what happened in the servant's quarters." Lines of worry bracketed the maid's mouth.

Alaina should have known the volume of their voices would have carried further than the dining room. She didn't doubt the footmen, Paul and Andrew, would have stayed close by. even though they'd been told to leave—not primarily to eavesdrop, but in case they were needed. She had noted their hesitancy to exit the room when Sterling tried to dismiss them. It was likely clear to everyone in Morton House that the tension between Alaina and her husband was thick enough that Michelangelo, himself, probably couldn't have chiseled away at it.

"You know," Penny continued, "there are some who've been 'ere for a long time—longer than me. They say the duke ain't a bad man."

Alaina met her maid's eyes. She realized Penny was trying to comfort her, to reassure her that Sterling wasn't cruel....that he would not follow through on his threat to demand his husbandly right when she had made her aversion perfectly clear.

"If they were here before—" *before he abandoned me* "—before...then they knew the boy he once was. The man who returned is no boy. He is not the master they once knew, nor is he the man I agreed to marry. I doubt there is anyone who truly knows him anymore." She squeezed Penny's hand and released her before rising from the stool. "I certainly do not."

The man who had once courted her—that she'd once agreed to marry what felt like a lifetime ago—would have replied to the multitude of letters she'd sent.

This man hadn't bothered responding to a single one of them.

The man she'd married had been infinitely tender and patient in his pursuit of her.

The man who had returned from the Continent was boorish and unnerving.

Following Sterling's abandonment of her on their wedding night, Alaina had collected the shards of her heart and reassembled them in some semblance of normalcy, and then made the decision to hunt down Sterling's solicitor to demand he provide some way for her to contact her wayward spouse. It had taken several weeks of pestering, but she'd finally obtained a forwarding address. She knew it likely only led to a middleman who might deliver the correspondence wherever Sterling had landed that particular week, but it had been more than she'd begun with.

She'd heard enough in the gossip rags to know her husband moved around the Continent quite a bit...and enjoyed a variety of entertainments. He would have been near impossible to track down, even if she had been inclined to attempt a solo journey across the Channel. She'd cursed her limited skills and experience keeping her from anything bolder than putting ink on parchment.

Again and again, she'd written to her husband, persistent in her hope and faithfully sitting down to write to him several times each week and then sending them off to be delivered to the middleman who might then hand them over to her husband.

Regardless, Sterling hadn't once seen fit to reply to any of her notes.

At first, she'd been pathetically hopeful that there was a delay in the post. Then, she told herself that perhaps some of the letters had been lost in transit.

Despite her husband's silence, she'd kept writing.

And writing.

Until Alaina finally forced herself to admit her husband wanted nothing to do with her.

Two could play at that.

Despite her withered spirit, she'd decided to press onward. Her husband may have left, but he hadn't taken all of her life with him. Gradually, Alaina had put herself back together and created an existence all her own. It had been hard-won and not without its mistakes, but she was proud of all she had achieved. Of who she had become. And nothing Sterling did or said could change that. She simply refused to allow it.

"I'm sure it'll work itself out in the end," Penny whispered as she carefully draped the blue gown over her arm. "Perhaps you just need to be reacquainted?"

Alaina wanted to say that she had no interest in knowing the man Sterling had become, but she simply nodded and Penny took her leave.

As soon as she was alone in the silence, Alaina's heart began to pound painfully in her breast. Her limbs grew shaky with anticipation and she was forced to pace in an effort to channel her anxiety and restlessness.

What if Sterling *did* follow through on his thinly veiled threat to finally consummate their marriage?

Technically, there wasn't anything she could do about it...he was correct, it was his right.

She could scream and fight, but he was much larger than she and undoubtedly much stronger. Additionally, no matter how the staff loved her and were loyal to her, they wouldn't dare come to her rescue even if they did hear her pleas and cries. Deep down, she couldn't blame them. How could she expect them to put their lives and positions at stake by defying a duke? They'd be forced to stand idly by as she was degraded in the worst possible way.

Alaina's stomach roiled so terribly that she was forced to press the back of her hand to her lips to keep from being sick.

What was the natural wedding night anxiety eight years earlier had been left to fester with insecurities and anger, and it was now an ugly wound upon her soul. It gnawed at her, needled her in her most vulnerable moments; it cast doubt upon who she was and everything she could be. It had taken years for her to unlearn the meek and subservient ways her mother and the rest of Society had engrained in her before she could carve out the woman who'd lain buried and sleeping deep inside her soul, waiting for the moment to share her voice. It was only after a great deal of reflection and searching for the well of strength in her heart that she became who she was. As a result, she'd learned to project to the *ton* a confident, worldly woman who was a pillar of Society…but she knew a part of the hurt girl she once was would live in her heart forever. And she loathed it.

Her throat grew uncomfortably tight, and her palms became slick.

Her lungs moved in halting fits and bursts.

Her eyes darted back to the door adjoining her room to Sterling's.

She couldn't do this.

Not tonight.

She flew to the door in a whirl of gauzy white nightdress only to realize for the first time there was no lock on her side to bar the duke from entering… The blasted thing had probably been designed by a self-important man.

Frantically, she contemplated shoving something before the door to barricade herself in; however, the only furniture she had a chance of moving was the dressing table, and that delicate piece would provide pathetically little protection against a determined husband.

Her thoughts were cut short as heavy, muffled steps thudded on the other side of that dreaded barrier.

Not knowing what else to do now that her time had run out, Alaina sprang across the room, threw her dressing gown across a chair, and vaulted into the bed. Yanking the coverlet up to her ears, she turned to face the window and curled into what she hoped was a believable sleeping position. She attempted to slow her heavy breaths as her heartbeat throbbed and deafened her.

The slow turn of the knob grated on her frayed nerves.

She tried not to flinch when Sterling's deep voice spoke her name.

She forced her eyes closed as she listened to his feet crossing the plush rug.

Then, he stood over her and every last one of her nerve endings screamed with anxiety.

She could sense his nearness, the heat rolling off his large body; she experienced the firm sweep of his piercing eyes upon her huddled form.

There was a small rustle of fabric as he bent over her, and her breath stalled as she waited for him to violently rip the covers from her body and have his way with her.

Instead, there was a gentle caress of knuckles upon her cheek and his long fingers tucked a loose lock of hair behind her ear. She felt him still as he watched her for several more heartbeats before his footsteps retreated.

The adjoining door closed with a soft click.

Alaina didn't move or open her eyes for a long while, unable to believe he'd left her in peace after his earlier threat. She struggled to reconcile the angry man with the one who'd left her untouched. She hadn't misheard his earlier threat, that was for certain. So why, when he had her alone and at his mercy, had he refrained? For that matter, why had he visited her with something akin to tenderness?

She'd been so solid in her convictions and now…the flutter low in her belly was most unwelcome, as was the cascade of unbidden memories unlocked and freed from the shadowed recesses of her memory. There had been a time when a girl fancied herself falling in love with a man who'd liked to tuck her hair behind her ear and trace the curve of her cheek as if she were the most precious creation.

It was a long while until Alaina's mind slowed enough to allow sleep to finally claim her.

Chapter Four

STERLING AWOKE EARLY the following day and dressed in buff breeches, a dove-gray waistcoat, and a hunter-green coat of the finest tailoring. He'd also insisted his new valet affix his cravat with nothing more than a simple knot—he was so very tired of the fussy fashions of the courts on the Continent, and he relished the simplicity and ease his life in London would now offer. His trunks had arrived from the docks the evening before, and his valet did an impeccable job of unpacking and organizing, following Sterling's strict instructions that anything gaudy and absurd was to be immediately disposed of. He cared not if the items were donated for repurposing or made into rags, as long as he needn't see them ever again. He was finished with dressing to perform.

Pleased, Sterling then sat down to an informal breakfast of eggs and sausage, toast, jam, and tea in the morning room. Not a pea in sight, thank Heaven. After taking a moment to savor the array laid out before him, he paused and then asked the maid who had appeared with another serving spoon, "Is there any coffee?" The poor girl apologized profusely for the deficiency, but Sterling kindly reassured her that they couldn't have known he preferred it in the mornings since he'd developed a taste for it during his travels. Coffee was far more common in the myriad countries he'd visited; few held tea in such high esteem as the Brits. She bobbed a curtsy and rushed from the room with a promise to return as quickly as possible after the beans were procured and brewed. It was likely that they'd dip next door or across the square and beg some off another household to make due until the next time the kitchens could purchase their own store. Either way, Sterling appreciated the efficiency.

Taking a bite of the perfectly cooked eggs, he picked up the ironed paper and found that he was uncommonly pleased with how, for the first time in years, he could behave without censure. He could eat when he wanted, dress how he cared to, and do whatever he wished. He was able to act, speak, and move without dozens of eyes upon him. He no longer had to exist behind a façade. He was once more the master of his own future, his own man. An aura of peace settled around him, making his heart feel lighter. The buzzing in his skull lowered to a gentle hum—more background noise than insistent pressure.

He'd missed the warm closeness of this particular room in Morton House, and its familiar vista outside the window overlooking the park. It was comforting to return to England and see how not everything had been left irreparably damaged by his absence.

The maid eventually returned with coffee in a silver pot and Sterling savored the steaming black brew. It wasn't quite as rich or strong as he was used to, but it was enjoyable, nonetheless. In all, it was a satisfying start to his first full day home.

When he'd eaten his fill, Sterling gathered up the newspaper and folded it beneath his arm, intending to finish reading it at his leisure in the library. He'd once enjoyed the warm morning light in that room regularly and he was determined to savor it once again. The day appeared pleasant, and it would be interesting to watch the characters in the street outside—though it would still be hours yet before the *ton* began making calls.

He wondered how long it would be before word of his return spread. Doubtless, the front table would soon creak beneath the weight of calling cards and invitations from old friends, acquaintances, and curiosity-seekers alike. A plethora of estate business needed attending to as well, but it would keep a few more hours while he continued pondering his day and the wonder of his new freedoms. He thought he deserved this much respite after doing nothing but work and put his neck on the line for eight years.

Until he collided with his wife as he exited the morning room.

Sterling immediately dropped his newspaper and steadied Alaina with his hands wrapped around her slim upper arms. Her wide blue eyes told him she was genuinely surprised by his appearance…as if she'd briefly forgotten his existence and was caught entirely off-guard by him all over again.

For his part, he was set on his heels by her intoxicating scent. Violets. Soap. Warm womanly flesh. It was all he could do not to haul her against him so he could drown in it. The fragrance was, at once, familiar and refreshing.

Instead of following his fanciful urge and bathing in her scent, his eyes swept her up and down, from her jaunty, wide-brimmed black hat pinned to her starkly contrasting golden curls to the long sweep of her gilt lashes, the raspberry sweetness of her wide lips, her lithe frame garbed in a high-waisted gown of plum and simple black beaded accents along the low neckline. She had yet to button her spencer, so he was afforded a delicious glimpse of her smooth, pale décolletage. Being so close to her—only a breath away from the sweet curve of her cheek—enticed him to recall the prior evening.

She'd been so stiff and determined while attempting to feign sleep in her bed; though she was a poor actress, his wife.

He'd never had any intention of following through on his threat…in fact, he'd gone to her hoping to apologize, have a civil discussion, and come to a reconciliation for that evening. When he'd seen the lengths to which she'd gone to ward him off, however, he'd felt nothing but simmering anger…at himself.

It was painfully evident that he'd done a horrific amount of damage to his marriage and—no matter how Alaina infuriated him—the blame was solely his.

She slipped from his grasp and took several steps back down the hallway, turning her attention to the task of tugging her kid gloves onto her graceful fingers. A beaded black reticule dangled from one of her wrists.

"You are going out?" His tone made it more of a statement than an inquiry.

"It would appear so," Alaina murmured as she focused on the satin-covered buttons of her pelisse.

"So early? And without breaking your fast?"

She still refused to meet his eyes and, instead, plucked an invisible piece of lint from her sleeve. "I am a married woman, and I availed myself of my right to break my fast in my rooms."

Sterling barely suppressed a sigh of annoyance at her flat tone. "Did you not think to inform me you would be leaving this morning?" he asked while carefully modulating his voice.

Alaina finally met his eye, the blue fire again springing to life there. "I never required permission before. And you did not seem overly concerned about what I did and when I did it while you were away on the Continent."

Sterling's fists clenched reflexively.

"I understand," he began, schooling himself to tamp down the frustration welling inside his chest, "but now that I am in residence, it would be courteous to at least advise me of your comings and goings." She said nothing, so he plodded on. "Perhaps I would like to join you…" he added more gently than he thought himself capable. "I should like to know you, Alaina."

His wife remained silent, but she caught her lower lip between her teeth. Whether it was because she was considering his words or biting back a scathing retort, he could not be sure. Judging by what he'd experienced thus far, he wondered if it wasn't the latter.

"It is the least we can do to try to be civil." He hazarded a step closer to his wife. "I believe our lives would be better served if we aimed for civility."

OUT OF THE corner of her eye, Alaina saw Sterling's hand begin to lift, but it quickly dropped back to his side.

Her mind spun helplessly with the possibilities. What had he been about to do? Did he desire to take her hand in a show of sincerity? Perhaps tuck another lock of hair behind her ear as he had last night in a confusing display of tenderness?

Alaina silently chided herself.

The last thing she should want is to have him touching her—no matter if she wondered if his hands were as soft as she recalled, or if they, too, had hardened and become calloused by time like the rest of him.

And Penny was far too skilled with hairpins to allow her to leave the house with wayward curls in need of tucking, so his touching her could only be born of something inexplicable—something she did not have the patience or stomach to analyze right then.

Alaina's lips tightened into a fine line a moment before she finally spoke. "I plan to call upon a friend," she offered.

One of his brows rose. "At this time of the morning? Unless the habits of the *ton* have changed drastically in my absence, there are hours yet until customary calling time."

"She is a habitually early riser," Alaina sighed impatiently; "and it is easier to meet uninterrupted before most others are out and about."

Sterling's lips tilted into a charming half smile and the clouds lifted from his hazel eyes.

Alaina's traitorous heart stuttered.

It was disconcerting for her to witness these small glimpses of the young man she'd once known—the man who'd spent hours discussing literature with her, taking her on her favorite walks, endlessly wandering through the exhibits at the British Museum and lingering as long as she liked. His handsomeness had been a single facet of what had drawn her to him, the least of which being his title. She'd once genuinely believed him to be a man whom she could love with every part of her. It was far easier to hate Sterling when he was out of her sight and when he acted like the relative stranger he was. It was unfair how, with one glance, one tilt of his head, she was transported eight years in the past and he could make her blood hum.

"There now…" His deep voice vibrated the air between them. "That wasn't so difficult, was it?"

The momentary spell was shattered with those few words; Alaina rolled her eyes and stepped back further from his reach. She heard him mutter a curse beneath his breath as if berating himself for severing whatever thread of tenuous peace that had begun to form.

Good.

It would be satisfying to be the one to walk out on him for a change.

Before she could leave, however, he spoke once more.

"Upon which friend are you calling?"

"One you don't know," Alaina practically snapped. Why couldn't he understand that she had created a life outside of this sham of a marriage? Why couldn't he accept that she'd managed well enough on her own in his absence? She wasn't about to report to him every one of her comings and goings. For one, he had no right to them; for another, she had her own duties and obligations to uphold. There were people who counted on her and she would rather die than let them down. Not everything in her life revolved around this man, and that was his own doing. She'd have given him everything if only he'd seen fit to stay by her side.

Sterling heaved a sigh and ran a hand through his hair, tousling the once-tidy chestnut locks. Alaina hated that it only made him more attractive. "Fine," he growled. "Just go."

He snatched up the sheaves of newspaper from the floor and the heels of his polished hessians clipped across the entryway toward the library as he held his broad shoulders uncomfortably stiff within his rich green coat.

A niggling grain of guilt rubbed at Alaina's conscience. Even she couldn't lie to herself and call that exchange entirely "civil."

It had been years since she'd had to answer to anyone. Having someone ask such questions of her—let alone the man whom she'd cursed for so long—felt like a scrape upon an old wound to her personality and sense of self.

Anyone could see that she'd managed well enough alone. She prided herself on the fact that she had found occupations of her own, remained free from scandal for the most part (above and beyond that which Sterling had caused), and had never been a woman who lived above her means (not that she could have spent her full pin money each month had she tried). And now to have Sterling question her—after all he'd put her through!—was beyond unfair and nauseatingly galling. He'd never had to answer for his actions, so why should she?

She shook off any hint of guilt and left the house, descending the front steps to the Morton carriage awaiting her.

"YOU MUST ADMIT, Alaina, the duke *is* uncommonly handsome."

Alaina did a poor job of masking a cough as she set down her cup of tea. Juliette had been counted among her friends for years and she liked to think they could speak plainly, but it seemed marriage had loosened her friend's tongue and given her a new boldness.

For things like commenting on the attractiveness of one's spouse, it appeared.

"From a purely objective standpoint, of course," Juliette added, though Alaina never had any cause to doubt Juliette's loyalty to her beloved husband.

Alaina dabbed at her lips with an embroidered napkin before setting it beside the tea service. The china and settings were finer than one would expect in a physician's home; however, Dr. Ian McCullom was no ordinary physician, and his spouse was no ordinary physician's wife.

Alaina and Juliette sat in the newly refinished parlor of the three-story townhouse the McCulloms had purchased shortly after their recent marriage. Juliette was the twin sister to the Earl of Hopesend and her marriage to a man who worked for a living—even one as respected and honored as Dr. McCullom—had caused quite the uproar. Nearly everyone in the *ton* had abandoned Juliette, looking down their patrician noses at the love match, but Alaina remained steadfastly true to her longtime friend.

Eventually, some of Society did follow Alaina's example, setting aside their inane delicate sensibilities and, once more, calling upon and extending invitations to Juliette and her husband. It wasn't a perfect recovery, but it was a far better result than it could have been. Alaina supposed this was an advantage to being a duchess—if one couldn't use her position to help others, what was the point?

Juliette and her husband had recently moved from the rooms above his medical practice and handed over the space to Ian's new protégé—a young Italian who had proven to be quick-minded and vastly talented. And now Juliette had her own space where she and Alaina could meet outside the uncomfortable shadow of Alaina's awkward marriage.

Juliette tilted her dark head, letting Alaina know she was still awaiting a response. Alaina tried to look anywhere—the walls repapered in tasteful shades of blue stripes, the fresh ivory curtains, the well-made reclining sofa and spindle-legged table inlaid with alternating patterns of cherry and mahogany, a loose black glass bead dangling from the design on the skirt of her dress—anything to delay providing an answer to the question.

She sighed in resignation.

Sterling's face materialized in her mind. He'd always been undeniably attractive to her—that and his kind personality had been the reasons she'd accepted his courtship in the first place. Her mother could overlook all of those for the dukedom, but even back then, Alaina had silently hoped for more…and she had thought she'd found it in the young Duke of Morton.

Fool child that she had been.

As handsome as Sterling once was, time had found a way to mature him into something more. His hazel eyes smoldered when he was upset, his straight, well-formed nose suited his strong features and the expressive set of his mouth possessed the possibility to be charming…when he wasn't frustrated with her, of course. When he had steadied her that morning after their minor collision, his solid strength called to an afore-unknown primal part of her (much as she tried to deny it). Her better judgment chimed in to remind her that this was the man who had abandoned her…left her to shed her tears in lonely silence. She'd once cared for him, but his abrupt flight from their home following the marriage ceremony was surely proof that he hadn't taken their contract and his responsibilities too seriously. It mattered not that she (still) found him objectively attractive—there were any number of attractive men of the *ton*, many of whom vied for her attention when she attended events—he was unequivocally a cad of the highest order.

Her friend, however, had seen Sterling at the prior day's disastrous Reading Society meeting; Juliette would see right through any petty denial Alaina might attempt. Juliette was no fool. They'd known one another for many years at that point, had seen each other at least once each week, and worked together to organize various events and fundraising. If anyone was going to be able to sense Alaina was lying, Juliette was one of those people. It would only be fair, though, because Alaina had certainly done her fair share of meddling in Juliette's love life. Normally, she quite liked the thought that Ian and Juliette might never have been able to find one another were it not for Alaina's bold assistance, but she didn't particularly care for the roles to be reversed. Perhaps she should have considered that earlier…

"I suppose," Alaina began cautiously before gaining more speed; "when he isn't doing his best to drive my sanity into the ground."

Juliette chuckled. "It isn't the least bit…*enjoyable* having him home?" Her dark brows rose suggestively.

Alaina wasn't dim; she could see where this conversation was headed, and she hadn't the slightest desire to discuss that aspect. She was too determined to continue clutching her animosity like a shield to examine Sterling's shocking tenderness the night before.

And whether or not she'd welcome it again.

"The man has been on English soil less than twenty-four hours, and he's already interrupted a meeting of my Reading Society, ran me out of supper, and interrogated me before allowing me to leave the house this morning. If this is any indication of things to come, then my life has been forever changed and I care not for it one bit." What Alaina wouldn't give for something stronger than tea… How unfair that men should be allowed to imbibe spirits from well-appointed sideboards while women were relegated to nothing stronger than watered-down wine on rare occasions. Woe be to the woman who took alcohol as a man would, regardless of the circumstances.

And Alaina felt rather strongly that these were, indeed, mitigating circumstances.

"What harm could there be in giving him another chance?" Juliette tilted her head and held her hands up in supplication. "You are still married, regardless."

"As he gave our marriage a chance when he fled like a man outrunning his execution?" Alaina scoffed despite Juliette's perfectly rational comment. "Right. I'll begin the reconciliation immediately…" She narrowed her eyes, adding, "And whose side are you on?"

Juliette smiled and shook her head. "You have been my friend for more than a decade, Alaina; there is no side other than yours, as far as I am concerned. I'm simply…playing advocate to the devil. Trying could make your marriage more palatable. You're living together and forced into each other's presence, after all."

"You sound like the duke," Alaina groaned with a roll of her eyes, though more good-naturedly than not. "How can we possibly expect to get along when he has yet to explain why he left?"

Juliette's shoulders lifted in a gentle shrug. "Part of marriage is working through those difficult questions; learning about one another. To practice being honest and open."

Alaina heaved a heavy sigh. Juliette had been married for such a short while and she already knew vastly more about the matrimonial state than Alaina…who had been married for eight years… Undoubtedly, it came both from being confident in one's state and—perhaps more so—actually living closely enough with one's spouse to know him.

"I am not a woman who can simply forget the fact that he abandoned me and partook in any number of debauched activities on the Continent." Alaina's cheeks warmed and she averted her eyes from Juliette's sympathetic gaze. They'd both read the same tabloids, heard the same rumors. If the *ton* enjoyed anything, it was a naughty scandal. Tales of the Runaway Duke who'd fled his new bride to live a life of freedom and vices fit that bill to perfection; and each time a rumor was presented to her with exaggerated sympathy, it pierced Alaina's heart like a pin in a cushion.

Every member of the *ton* and their servants were privy to the rumors of the decadent, lush lifestyle Sterling had enjoyed while on the Continent; the salacious whispers of his many torrid love affairs with exotic, beautiful women. Alaina had always refused to discuss those rumors with anyone—or even acknowledge them openly until that very moment alone with Juliette. Now that Sterling was home, she was forced to face the embarrassment of the gossip and come to terms with the fact that, while he hadn't seen fit to share her bed, he had so obviously found solace and satisfaction in the arms of many other women. It was beyond mortifying.

"I am not built that way," she finally added.

"Do not feel sorry for yourself," Juliette demanded as she rose and moved around the table to sit beside Alaina and take her hand. "This isn't the hellion I know." In spite of herself, Alaina cracked a smile at the moniker she'd been given by one of the popular tabloids following a scene at a ball wherein she'd publicly and bluntly chastised the hostess after the woman had slapped a maid for dropping a glass. Alaina had been accused of "inciting a scandal" when no less than two dozen guests had followed her example and immediately quit the event. She didn't think "hellion" was necessarily an apt title for her, but she'd come to enjoy ruffling feathers and shows of social justice, and if that was how she was viewed, then so be it. "If you won't forgive him, and you're so determined not to allow him to live this down, what will you do about it?"

Alaina's despondent mind perked at that.

What *would* she do about it?

Her mind instantly reeled with the possibilities. There were few things sweeter to her than someone receiving their comeuppance, and all the ways this might be served to her husband nearly made her giddy. She'd been made to weather embarrassment alone for all these years and she felt it was well past time Sterling had a taste of it.

She wouldn't attempt to divorce him (for a multitude of reasons she'd already spun round and round in her skull many times over the years) and she refused to be the one to tuck tail and run to live elsewhere now that he'd once more taken up residence in Morton House. It was her home.

Sure, he'd been the one to grow up there, but it had been the only home she'd ever known as a married woman. She'd traveled outside of London several times for respites in their country seat at the end of the Season, but, as far as Alaina was concerned, Morton House was the touchstone of her life as she knew it. To leave it was unthinkable, even if so many other married couples of the *ton* led relatively separate lives...sometimes in entirely different spaces.

No.

Alaina knew she could do better than that.

She would get even.

She didn't think she'd be able to make her husband's life eight years' worth of hell, but she could certainly do her damnedest. If Sterling was going to try to tame her to fit into this vision of his life he suddenly decided to live and impress upon her, then she vowed to make it as difficult and miserable as possible for him.

The Supper of Peas the previous evening was a start…

But she had a glimmer of inspiration that would be even better.

She squeezed Juliette's fingers with her own, a mischievous smile curling her lips. "We have a trip to make to the bookseller; there are manuscripts to purchase."

Just then, Juliette's husband had the misfortune of walking into the room. The tall, broad Highlander was built more for battle than healing, so one might be forgiven for initially doubting his profession as one of London's most sought-after physicians. Alaina quite liked the man's dry sense of humor and their shared desire to help those less fortunate; she positively adored him for the way he cherished Juliette and treated her like the blessing she was. Dr. McCullom inclined his auburn head in a friendly, deferential greeting to Alaina but froze when he witnessed the glint in her eye.

"Why do I have the distinct impression I've walked in on something terrible?" His rich green eyes made his discomfort evident. The poor man obviously regretted his interruption, and he'd known Alaina long enough to realize the gravity of any mischief she might be plotting.

"Do not fret, my love," Juliette said, attempting to reassure her husband. "You are not the aim of the duchess's scheming this time."

Chapter Five

S EVERAL HOURS LATER, Alaina returned to Morton House with a footman trailing in her formidable footsteps. He carried a large parcel neatly wrapped in brown paper and tied with a cobalt blue ribbon, as was the custom of her preferred bookseller in London, Thorpe & Son. The remainder of her order would arrive in the next day or so.

She handed her reticule and pelisse to Maxwell and was gazing into an ornately gilded mirror near the door, attempting to remove her hat pin, when she caught sight of Sterling as he emerged from the library. She ignored him and pretended not to notice the flipping of her stomach while she continued her task for as long as she could do so believably.

"Please deliver that to my private sitting room, Andrew; thank you."

The footman nodded and left to do as he was told.

By the time Alaina turned around, Sterling had propped his tall body against the doorframe, his strong arms crossed over his broad chest as he eyed her. His inscrutable expression made her unsure of her reception, especially after their encounter earlier that morning. Those fascinating eyes of his were shuttered against her, refusing to reveal any hint of what simmered in that maddening mind.

Not only was his stare unnerving, but she was yet unused to having anyone else in the house with her, aside from the servants. Part of her wondered how long it might be before she grew used to his presence; the other part reminded her that, if she achieved her aim, he would not be around long enough for that to happen.

If she had her way, he'd leave her in peace to continue her life as she pleased.

"Your Grace," she greeted him coolly. Even she wasn't rude enough to brush past her husband without acknowledging him.

She began plucking her gloves from her fingers and, absently, she conceded how right Juliette had been about Sterling's looks. He was undeniably attractive in a magnetic way. Were he any man other than her wayward husband, then she might have admitted to the way her feet tried to pull her in his direction. She refused to be swayed as she reminded herself of all the ways he'd put those looks to good use during his time on the Continent.

"Alaina," he greeted her with only a touch more warmth than she'd shown him. "I see you managed to accomplish some shopping as well."

"It is for my Reading Society. Surely you can find no fault in that pursuit."

"Actually," he began and pushed himself to his full imposing height; "I have been intending to speak with you about your 'reading society.'"

Alaina's stomach plummeted and her hackles raised with startling suddenness, her every sense immediately preparing for a battle.

Oblivious to the ire he'd raised in his wife, Sterling signaled to the butler and requested tea and something to eat before he bade Alaina join him in the library. She hesitated only a moment before rolling back her shoulders and following him into the room, mentally preparing herself for yet another argument.

WITH A MOTION, Sterling made an invitation for his wife to sit upon the overstuffed sofa upholstered in a comfortable red fabric. He recognized the ornately carved furniture frame from his youth, but Alaina had had it reupholstered for a more modern look. He appreciated her taste and her economy. As he'd meandered through the house in her absence that day, he'd discovered little changes like this throughout, and he'd been unable to find fault with any of them.

It had been simultaneously admirable and irksome, his wife's eye for design and avoidance of over-spending. She had brilliant taste, a blend of classic and contemporary. The petty part of him tired of being prodded like a bear in a cage wished to find faults with any of her choices or her spending, but there were none.

Alaina seemed to be judging his motives for several heartbeats before begrudgingly assuming her perch, spreading the layers of her plum-colored skirt around her with all the grace and elegance of years of practice. Her poise was remarkable. It always had been. She'd been bred and raised to be the wife of a prominent lord, and, in that regard, Sterling had always known she'd been the right choice for his duchess.

Rather than crowd her, he took up a nearby seat in a brown leather armchair, crossing his outstretched legs at the ankle. He'd much rather have been nearer to her, to have caught a whiff of her intoxicating scent again, but it was probably safer for his well-being that he be just out of arm's reach.

Alaina looked about as eager as a child about to be on the receiving end of a lecture.

She didn't like it.

At all.

And her expression did a poor job of hiding it.

He might have found her inability to shutter her emotions more amusing, were he not so certain that he was in for another spat. He could already see her mentally preparing herself for it.

"What fault can you find with my Reading Society, Your Grace?" she asked stiffly.

He tilted his head and gazed at her.

Then surprised her when the corner of his mouth tipped up into a disarming smile.

"I wish you would dispense with the formality and call me by my given name." It was something Sterling had thought about an inordinate amount of time since his return. He practically ached to hear his name on her tongue, to watch her mouth as she formed the word, to hear his name in her voice. He'd never heard her address him as such, and, more than longing for the sound of it, he wanted the comfort with a fierce desperation. After so many years of holding everyone at arm's length, he longed for the closeness and intimacy it would provide. And he felt almost certain that her doing so would make him more human—less easily dismissed.

Her eyes widened. She clearly hadn't been prepared for such a request and Sterling took pleasure in the parting of her luscious lips.

"I—I WOULD RATHER not. The familiarity is discomfiting."

He rewarded Alaina with a scoff as he steepled his long, elegant fingers together. "Forgive me if I find that difficult to believe." He paused and searched her face—for what, she was unsure. "Then at least call me Morton. No more 'Your Grace'…especially when we are in private."

Alaina hesitated but found it impossible to completely deny him. A part of her she'd believed long dead and crumbled to dust began to rise and prod her conscience. A part that had once desired to please this man above all else…to be the object of his desire and his pride. She eventually nodded in acquiescence.

Just then, two maids arrived with the tea service and a small variety of finger sandwiches prepared with cucumbers and some cold cuts. After they took their leave, Alaina's schooling overrode her desire to stay as far away as possible from Sterling. She leaned forward and began to pour the steaming brew from the pot decorated in a delicate pattern of Grecian scrollwork, preparing his tea with several spoons of sugar and a wafer-thin slice of lemon. When she was done, she held out the dainty bone china cup to Sterling, only looking up when he didn't accept the saucer from her fingers. He stared at her offering as if he expected it to contain an elixir of death.

"You watched me prepare it; I hardly had an opportunity to slip poison into the tea," Alaina said acerbically.

This seemed to snap Sterling from whatever oddity had occupied his mind. He accepted the drink and it took everything in her power not to snatch her hand back as the tip of his middle finger grazed hers. Instead, she averted her eyes and busied herself preparing her own drink as she waited for him to resume whatever he'd been about to say.

There was a gentle click of china as he took a sip and set down the saucer.

"I have heard about your reading society, Alaina," he began slowly—more calmly than cautiously. "You have created quite the stir."

Alaina took a bracing sip of her tea, wishing all the while it was something stronger. "And how, pray tell, would you know that? I wouldn't expect the news of our humble meetings to survive the distance to whatever Continental city in which you found yourself." Her tone was bitter, but not venomous. She decided to hold that in check until she heard what he had to say.

As it was, however, she didn't think this was headed anywhere she wished to go.

"I may have been out of the country, but do not believe I ever for a single moment forgot I had a wife here in England."

Alaina released a most unladylike snort of disbelief, and she was shocked to find she felt not the least bit of remorse or embarrassment over it.

"I always watched over you as much as I could," Sterling continued as if he hadn't heard her. "I made sure you never wanted for funds to be used as you saw fit, the staff's wages have always been timely, and I helped ensure a replacement with immaculate references arrived whenever a new addition was required."

Alaina couldn't argue those points. On those things, Sterling had remained...well...sterling. The issue was that he'd failed to consider her emotional needs.

And, perhaps, some physical ones…

"But what I have learned of your society leaves something to be desired."

Alaina carefully set down her saucer, believing it to be safer than continuing to hold the steaming cup, and modulated her tone with cautious intensity. "And what, may I ask, have you heard which has given you such an opinion? I find it difficult to believe anything you might have learned could have been so catastrophic as to precipitate your return to English soil." He cocked a chastising brow, but she continued. "Why don't you tell me what you believe you know, and I shall tell you if there is any merit?"

Sterling leaned forward to speak, pulling a folded bit of parchment from an inside pocket of his coat. "You have become rather notorious for hosting meetings where women of rank are encouraged to read incendiary literature." He opened the letter and read what was written there. "'Works touting extreme social reform, lurid romances, explicit and violent plays—'"

"Things which might cause some women to question their world and their place within it—might make them think with their God-given brains and intelligence? Why, that does sound terribly *dangerous*," she mocked, crossing her arms beneath her bosom, incensed that anyone would be so bold as to write to her husband to complain of her activities. This earned her a stern glower from her husband, making him look remarkably similar to the great-grandfather whose portrait she steadfastly avoided in the upstairs gallery. Sterling's ducal bearing and authority were undeniable and intimidating—even to Alaina—but she refused to be cowed on this.

"I should hope you know that I, of all men, do not condemn reading for knowledge and the joy of it," he said, referencing the fact that they'd once bonded over a shared passion for the written word.

"I do not think I know you at all, Morton."

THE WORDS HIT Sterling with the burning suddenness of a bee sting. This was now the second time Alaina had told him she didn't know him, and the unwelcome truth of it was discomfiting.

He'd once known her.

And well enough to believe he wanted to marry her, to have her as the mother to his children, to grow old with her.

But now they'd been made strangers by time and distance, and the animosity boiling between them was thicker than treacle.

"I only mean that the act of encouraging other women—wives and daughters and sisters of fellow peers—is problematic. The reputation that comes with some of this behavior is unflattering for a duchess. I didn't expect such descriptions to reach me when I'd married a quiet, proper, demure young woman."

The effect his words had on Alaina was instantaneous. The elegant rises of her lightly freckled cheekbones bloomed crimson, and her fists wound around the plum fabric of her skirts so tightly that it was a wonder it didn't shred in her grasp.

"A great deal can change in a few years when people are left to their own devices...to find their own place in the world," Alaina hissed dangerously, sapphire flames sparking in her eyes. She tilted her chin to the parchment he still held. "And it is so nice to know some letters made their way to you. I wonder if that one was important enough to warrant a response."

The jab struck as intended, but if only she knew how he'd longed to reply to her letters, how he'd yearned to let her know she was not as alone as she felt. Sterling opened his mouth to reply but was interrupted when a maid arrived, flanked by one of the footmen.

"Beggin' your pardon, Your Graces," the blond girl chirped, bobbing an apologetic curtsy as she flicked her eyes between her employers. "Mrs. Frank and Cook asked me to see if you'd like to discuss the rest of the week's menus now." The query was directed at Alaina, but the young woman's wide, pale eyes darted to Sterling. She seemed to assess the tenseness of his posture, his impatience that he be left alone with his wife to continue the conversation, his frustration as he drummed his fingers on the arm of his chair.

"Her Grace will be available shortly," he finally answered for Alaina.

The maid and footman did not move.

Sterling turned to face them fully.

"That will be all," he added in no uncertain terms.

They remained unmoving like bloody gargoyles.

Until they looked at Alaina.

Sterling followed their gazes quickly enough to catch the subtle nod from Alaina, to which the servants bowed and curtseyed before taking their leave.

First, the footmen at dinner the previous eve, and now the servants today?

Something inside of Sterling shattered.

"Why in bloody hell does it take everyone multiple commands before they obey an order?" he demanded, not caring who overheard. Perhaps it might even be good for the servants to witness this. "This is my home, and I am lord and master here!"

"You may be their lord, but these people have become near to friends to me these last eight years!" Alaina punctuated her words with a closed fist upon the embroidered cushion beside her.

"What?" he asked, taken aback by the waver in her voice.

"You may pay their wages, but you've been naught but a faceless name to everyone for so long—some of the staff had never even laid eyes upon you until the last twenty-four hours. I am the one who has been here. They—" Her voice broke and she averted her eyes for a moment before regaining her composure and meeting his gaze once more. "These people were my only company in the early days of my tenure as your wife when I was little more than a girl, unsure where to go or how to navigate the incomprehensible hand I'd been dealt."

Too ashamed to show her face after the scandal of his flight.

The ensuing silence rang with emotion as if following the last tone of an enormous brass bell.

The words had been said, the message had been laid across the table between them.

Sterling's fingers maintained their steady tap-tapping against the arm of his chair, disguising the thick, tar-like discomfort welling up from somewhere deep and long-suppressed within his gut.

Alaina's words struck him more deeply than he'd expected. He hadn't been blind to the fact that her life would be drastically changed by his absence; he'd just been too young and naïve to believe it wouldn't alter her in some irrevocable way—that she'd have felt so alone in the early weeks and months of their marriage that her only companions would have been his staff.

His fingers stilled and then moved to rub at an uncomfortable knot in the back of his neck.

He had tried apologizing to her. His regrets were sincere, whether or not she accepted that fact. Did she expect him to apologize for the rest of his days? He was beginning to suspect his rash decision in his youth would forever color their marriage and his life.

His fingers worked around to press against his eyes and the bridge of his nose to quell a burgeoning pounding in his skull.

She'd never accept the truth behind his absence—not that he'd ever once felt that a full explanation could truly compensate for their lost time…however, he must have been an unmitigated fool to believe she'd accept him back with any warmth or gratitude.

And her revelation confirmed it with sickening permanence. The guilt roiling inside of him threatened to consume him. He'd grappled with it almost incessantly since he'd left England, so it was far from a new sensation, but that didn't lessen its impact.

Alaina had been forced to move on and create her space in the world. She'd had to for the sake of their marriage's appearance.

And for her own life.

Though, if they continued thusly, snarling at one another like caged lions, he just might strangle her…

He cleared the stickiness from his throat and diverted their conversation to its original topic. It was far too dangerous to continue down the vein upon which they had touched.

"Now that I have returned, I'll be expected to exert some influence upon the materials in your society. I do not intend to forbid your meetings, only strongly suggest that you choose more suitable options. Your choices reflect upon us both, as well as the St. John name and Morton Duchy." Sterling chose to ignore her insolent brow. "I will also be expected to place a bit of a leash upon your antics—your furniture jumping, for example—and to encourage you to take up your proper role. Divert your consider-able energy into other—"

"So the prodigal husband returns, and the Duchess of Morton turns her life around to become a less scandalous Society matron?" she scoffed. "No doubt the *ton* will assume you've deigned to give up your life of pleasure to rein me in. And where is the fairness in that?" she demanded, flinging her arms out wide as if to demonstrate the breadth of the affront. "No one attempt-ed to chastise you when you did whatever wished in the last eight years…but Heaven forbid I do something I enjoy in your absence—something which truly harms no one, mind you—and I am judged harshly for it. I do not see why I shouldn't be allowed to continue my life as it was. I certainly managed well enough without you—"

"Because it is well past time both of us grew up and assumed our proper roles!" he roared, pounding a tight fist against the arm of his chair as an outlet for the tension thrumming throughout his body. "I, as Duke of Morton and in my proper place in the House of Lords; and you, Alaina, as my wife and the mother of my heir."

The last caused an icy veil to fall over her face, and he berated himself all over again. What was it about her that made him say things he instantly regretted? He immediately cursed his unthinking words. The last thing he wanted her to believe was that he'd returned solely to turn her into his broodmare. He normally prided himself on his ability to craft cogent arguments and use words to his advantage. All that went out the window when it came to his wife. The color drained from her cheeks and the fire in her eyes fell painfully frigid and steely. She uttered nothing, but the accusation in her silence rang more loudly than words ever could have.

While the thought of finally consummating their marriage was a boon he had anticipated with more than a little eagerness, it was far from the only reason he'd finally come home. To make it seem as such was a grave injustice to the wounded woman before him.

Sterling sighed heavily, imagining his anger being released in a cloud between them before it thinned and dissipated in the air.

"I realize this will take a great deal of adjustment for us both, but we can accomplish it if we make the effort. Are you willing to give this a go with me, Alaina? As I requested this morning, can we try our hands at even the barest civility?"

Her silent response was unnerving. His only reassurance in this disaster of a marriage was that she'd have filed for an annulment long ago had she truly wished to be rid of him. It would have been within her right and there would have been embarrassingly little he could do about it. An unconsummated wedding would have been grounds enough, along with his abandonment. He assumed either her family had talked her out of it, or she'd seen that the advantages to being a duchess far outweighed the freedom from the marriage.

Whatever the reason, they remained married against all odds...and Sterling had held onto that knowledge throughout his time away. And, now that they were finally face-to-face again, he'd be damned if he lost everything he'd held dear all these years.

Finally, Alaina graced him with a curt nod.

Sterling couldn't prevent the hopeful tilt of his mouth as he retrieved his tea and sat back in his chair. It was a victory…a small one, but a victory, nonetheless. He'd take it for what it was and relish the accomplishment.

"Now that we have dispensed with that unpleasantness, what do you plan next for your reading society—since I take it you'll not be abandoning it altogether?" He took a sip of his tea and watched as she hesitated for a moment before picking up her own cup.

"Oh, only Shakespeare."

Sterling nodded in approving reply before setting his tea aside and taking up the small plate Alaina had fixed for him with a selection of dainty sandwiches. He said a silent prayer in thanks that peas were blessedly absent.

How out of hand could Shakespeare possibly be in a room full of Society women? He quite enjoyed The Bard himself.

The cat in the cream grin spreading Alaina's full lips should have warned him of the impending danger…

Chapter Six

AFTER THEIR CONVERSATION in the parlor, it was clear to Alaina that it would be far safer to have the next few Reading Society meetings outside of her home and out from under Sterling's censorious gaze. She'd scrawled a quick note to her friend, Meredith Stratford, Viscountess Sommerfeld, about hosting the event at her Mayfair Townhouse. The request was accepted with aplomb and, three days later, Alaina and the rest of the Society members were comfortably ensconced in a lovely mint-colored parlor. Lady Sommerfeld had been looking for an informal way to entertain for the first time since she'd given birth to her twin daughters, so she eagerly accepted the opportunity to host.

The viscountess was of Scottish ancestry on her mother's side, and it was displayed in her fair complexion, luminous indigo eyes, and rich red curls. She'd been a young widow when she met her current husband, and watching the two of them together left no doubt that they'd been a love match—especially when the viscountess had been enceinte. The viscount and heir to the Aldborough Earldom was nothing shy of golden. He was a stunningly handsome lion of a man whom Alaina had first met years earlier during her one and only Season as an unmarried young woman. Sommerfeld had already garnered quite the reputation for youthful carousing, so her mother had warned her off him immediately following her first dance with him. Apparently, a future earldom was not quite enough for her mother to overlook the depth of his wild ways...but a dukedom was somehow forgivable for anything.

Sommerfeld's sardonic, singular brand of sarcastic humor was a consistent source of amusement. Pairing him up with his fiery wife—one of the only people who seemed relatively impervious to his effortless charm and guile—produced entertaining banter whenever Alaina came to call. The two of them were supremely well-matched and a joy to be around.

It had taken several years for the marriage to produce offspring and the wait had taken both a mental and physical toll. The pregnancy hadn't been easy on Lady Sommerfeld, either, and Alaina had moved several of their meetings to accommodate Meredith's physical limitations. Carrying twins had been a trial, but matters had been helped greatly by the skill and knowledge of Juliette's husband, Dr. McCullom. Alaina had been present when there was a slight scare early in Meredith's pregnancy, and, eventually, the babes had come a few weeks earlier than anticipated, but McCullom's expertise and reputation for immaculate cleanliness helped both mother and infants survive and thrive without illness or childbed fever.

Though the delicate skin beneath Meredith's eyes was slightly bruised from sleeplessness, there was no mistaking that her friend was infinitely happy with her life in the way women were only when they felt entirely fulfilled. Meredith's normally slim figure was still slightly plump from pregnancy, but it seemed not to bother her. She was confident in her place and fairly glowed with love and contentment.

That day, Alaina arrived at the Sommerfeld Townhouse an hour early for their planned Society meeting purely for the joy of holding and cooing over the perfect, petite infants uninterrupted.

"You are going to be a true beauty, little Catherine," Alaina whispered as the tiny strawberry-blond babe in her arms pursed her lips in sleep and nuzzled more closely.

"My poor husband will be a mess during their first Season," Lady Sommerfeld chuckled as she tucked the swaddling more tightly around the other infant nestled within the crook of her arm. Elizabeth was identical to Catherine in every way from the dimples on her fingers to her round little nose. Alaina was unable to tell them apart, but Meredith was possessed of a keen mother's eye and never lost track of who was who.

Alaina pictured the tall, green-eyed Sommerfeld viciously glowering at every man who dared so much as look at his daughters. "Those unfortunate lads," Alaina replied with a rueful shake of her head.

"Poor lads?" Lady Sommerfeld laughed softly. "I say, my poor girls! Any suitors will be scared off without a chance. They'll be lucky if they're allowed to leave our sides for a single dance."

Alaina leaned in to inhale the downy scent of Catherine's hair and whispered, "Do not fret. Men aren't as wonderful as they'd have you believe, anyway." In response, the babe turned her plump cheek and began rooting against Alaina's bodice. Each little nudge was accompanied by a small coo which tugged at a thread deep within the core of Alaina's being. She'd been raised to be the wife of a peer and mother to his heirs—a very small world when one considered it. And, while it was easy to place that abstract notion aside when one's husband was absent, the reality of it all sat heavy in her breast now that Sterling had returned.

If Alaina was honest with herself, it wasn't only the idea of being a mother…it was the idea of being the mother of Sterling's children. Her heart skipped, and not for the first time. There had been several instances where he'd alluded to consummating their union and doing their procreative duties. It was his right, as well as his responsibility. Society marriages were all about alliances and bloodlines, creating financial and familial bonds where the title would be strengthened for future generations. Alaina had always known her role in this game, but the idea of motherhood had been forced to the back of her mind out of necessity—what good did it do to pine after cherubic infants with their round bellies and dimpled hands when one's husband was nowhere to be found? It had morphed from a duty to an abstract, faraway notion…only to come full circle with Sterling's return from the Continent.

The thought of holding a babe of her own to her breast gave her a thrill. She had always adored children and the cause of their care and wellbeing was something she held close to her heart. The impossibility of having children of her own with her husband so far away made it necessary to set aside the dream of raising her own child. Now, it was sinking in that the possibility of rocking her son or daughter wasn't as far off as it might once have been.

Imagining the prologue to that scene created a whole different sort of fluttering within her.

The infant's coos became more frustrated when she realized there was no food to be had. The nursemaid who had been standing off in the corner moved to retrieve the child for a feeding. Alaina was loath to release the soft, warm little bundle, but she couldn't very well give the baby what she desired. Alaina's arms felt suddenly, woefully empty, but it was for the best since one glance at the clock on the mantle told them the rest of the Society would arrive in short order. Lady Sommerfeld handed off her other daughter as well.

"I am so grateful that you agreed to host today's meeting." Alaina squeezed her friend's hand in gratitude. "I hope it wasn't an imposition." Though Lady Sommerfeld was not privy to *all* the strife and clashes occurring between Alaina and Sterling, her friend had been entirely accommodating without a moment's hesitation. Alaina was infinitely grateful to have women such as her in her life. Juliette and Lady Sommerfeld had proven time and again to Alaina that there were good, kind-hearted people in Society.

"Think nothing of it!" the viscountess replied with a grin. "Sommerfeld is out for the afternoon anyway; we shan't be interrupted by any intrusive husbands." She gave her a cheeky wink, earning a lighthearted chuckle from Alaina. It felt so good to be uncensored, unabashedly herself once again. "Though I must insist that you and the duke join us for supper one evening.

I would like very much to meet him and see if he is as you and Juliette have described."

"Of course!" Alaina replied a tad more cheerfully than she felt. "Send 'round a note whenever it is most convenient." So far, she'd managed to convince Maxwell to pass along all cards and invitations directly to her, thereby subverting her husband. It was easy for her to pick through them and send regrets on both their behalf to people for whom she cared little; it was far more complicated when the invitation came from someone she genuinely adored. No matter. Alaina would deal with that when the time came.

The other women arrived promptly, even if some were mildly disappointed that there wouldn't be another encounter with the duke. They said nothing about it to Alaina, but they were easy to read with their glancing about as if wondering from which corner the next excitement would erupt.

Juliette arrived and claimed the seat beside Lady Sommerfeld and her sister-in-law, Mrs. Simon Stratford—a petite blonde with enviable curves.

Juliette and Alaina shared a fleeting knowing smile over their friend's head.

Alaina savored a bracing breath and stood; the buzz from the dozen other women slowly drifted into an expectant hush. She took a moment to smooth the skirts of her azure-striped morning gown before addressing the group.

"Welcome, ladies. And thank you to Lady Sommerfeld for so generously offering her home as today's meeting place. I feel an apology is in order for the way in which our last meeting was so rudely and unexpectedly interrupted." Several ladies exchanged glances, clearly eager to hear more, but Alaina moved on. A mischievous smile unfurled upon her lips. "Since then, it has been brought to my attention that our meetings have become somewhat notorious." This was met with more than a few amused titters. "As such, I have been asked to select more palatable reading materials—to temper them slightly, if you will."

A murmured mixture of concern and confusion bubbled and rose around her, and she witnessed several shocked brows head toward hairlines. Alaina knew well what unsettled them.

For many, her Reading Society was the only place they could be themselves—the sole space where they would not be criticized or judged for their thoughts and feelings and opinions. They could speak their mind and have new experiences over which they might bond.

Places such as this were few and far between for women, let alone women of their class who spent their entire lives beneath the constant scrutiny of Society's dictates. To allow such censorship to influence their Reading Society could spell the end of their little sliver of freedom; a terrifying prospect, indeed.

For another thing, Alaina bending to this request went against everything they knew of her temperament. The Duchess of Morton was not known for being easily cowed or weak-willed. The situation must be dire if she was becoming acquiescent.

Alaina held up a hand and patiently awaited silence before she spoke again. "This is why, with the help of Lady Juliette, I have decided upon this for our next reading choice." She retrieved a bound sheaf of papers from the neat tower on the table before her. "It seemed rather appropriate and kept to our current theme of plays."

Stack after stack was passed out to those in attendance. The title initiated a new round of confused disbelieving titters.

"*The Taming of the Shrew?*" questioned Mrs. Stratford. It was widely known that her mother was an actress and that Odette had been raised in the theater—who better to know plays than she? "Reading and discussing a play about a man controlling a woman is not something I'd have believed to be a part of our usual repertoire."

A few other coiffured heads nodded in agreement and turned to Alaina for an explanation.

Alaina hugged her own manuscript to her chest, barely able to contain her eagerness. "You have never experienced this play through the lens I intend to apply," she replied with a wicked smile.

If her husband wanted her to read "more suitable" material, then they would do so.

He'd simply failed to specify *how* they should read it.

Chapter Seven

STERLING SPENT THE following week developing a routine for his new, old life. It took some time, but he quickly remembered the unbridled joy of being one's own master without a schedule.

He awoke on his own early each morning, enjoyed a light breakfast with the blackest coffee possible (after the cook finally managed to procure proper coffee beans and practice the best brewing methods), and read in the library until he heard the patter of his wife's slippers on the stairs. Without fail, he'd step away from his reading to greet her.

It seemed the proper thing for a husband to do.

If he were honest with himself, however, the action was more to satisfy his curiosity about this woman than a social nicety. It needled him more and more frequently that he'd married her years earlier and yet did not fully know her.

He had already learned one thing since his return: Alaina had taken the last eight years to become gloriously uncensored. If she ever attempted to hide her moods, then she did a hideous job of it. He also learned that he could tell how the rest of the day would go within those first ten seconds of seeing her each morning.

Some days he'd catch her smiling to herself, humming a jaunty tune as she bounced down the last few steps. Sterling enjoyed those days and took extreme pleasure in the softness of her graceful features...even if her smile would disappear the very moment she saw him. The wall she hid behind would be erected once more; however, at least she'd mumble a curt reply to his "good morning" on those days.

There were times he could tell she hadn't slept well; pale bruises dared to mar the delicate skin beneath her eyes. He wondered if his presence in her life once more had concerned her greatly enough to cause sleeplessness and a pang of guilt prodded at the edge of his conscience. Regardless of what Alaina believed, he took no pleasure in her discomfort.

Other days, she'd stomp down the stairs and, without preamble, berate him for moving something in the library the prior evening or for making the mistake of requesting one of *his servants* perform some task. Those mornings—even if she didn't bite his head off like a bloodthirsty mantis—he swore the temperature in the room plummeted well below freezing.

To call her moods toward him mercurial would be unfair to her because, for the most part, once she picked one, she stuck to a mood for at least that day. She hated him on bad days and tolerated him on good ones. She glared at him as if trying to decide which poison would best do him in, or she was an ice queen who kept herself at a safe distance from his sullying presence. He might have been more concerned that she'd actually attempt to do him harm were she a woman with less forethought and reason, but she'd always been intelligent, his wife. She'd realize it did not behoove her to do away with him, but that didn't mean she couldn't try to make his existence uncomfortable.

Despite his resolve, the impression that he seemed to be the only one on the receiving end of Alaina's frigidity and scorn began to erode him like acid from the inside out.

Sterling had witnessed firsthand several times how the flip in her personality occurred when she interacted with someone else after being in his presence. As cool as she'd acted toward him, the newcomer would be greeted with the sweetest of smiles on those full lips of hers and the most pleasant tone in her voice.

It grated upon his every frayed nerve.

What in God's name did he have to do to earn even an ounce of that sweetness?

He'd buy her half of London if he thought it would make a difference, but his wife had made it abundantly clear that she wanted nothing to do with him...and, for the most part, he obliged...no matter how little he liked it. They kept to their separate endeavors and areas of the massive home, encountering one another with relative infrequency.

It was hardly the marriage Sterling had imagined when he'd requested Alaina's hand nearly a decade prior.

Nothing about this life was what he'd once imagined for them.

Lately, the only extended amount of time she spent in his presence was at supper. Together, they would eat in near complete silence, despite Sterling's determined inquiries. Most often, regardless of his inquest's nature, his efforts were met with cool civility. She could be downright frosty. They'd continue on until Sterling's efforts died a slow death, strangled by Alaina's unwillingness to cooperate.

Their lack of pleasant conversation, however, was not the only thing bothering him.

Despite the persistent ache in his loins plaguing him since well before he'd set foot upon English soil, Sterling hadn't returned to Alaina's chambers since that first night...a fact that she seemed more than pleased to accept.

This, perhaps, irked him most of all.

It wasn't as if he was conceited (above and beyond the expected self-assurance a man possessed when he was born into more than passable attractiveness on top of a dukedom), but he would be lying if he claimed he was used to a woman's rebuff. Females, young and old, had always been drawn to him. Whether his looks or his wealth or his title or his charm were the draw, he'd never lacked companionship.

He was pursued by women he didn't want, didn't desire,

didn't set his blood aflame, yet the only woman he longed for couldn't stand to be in the same room as he. He'd have gladly given all those hollow, unwanted attentions and advances away a thousand times over if Alaina would only look at him like she used to. It would certainly be a cruel twist of fate that he'd be married to the one woman who wasn't attracted to him.

The real shame was that he wanted *her*, even with her decidedly frigid treatment of him.

And he was damned if he knew why.

Perhaps some twisted part of him was drawn to the challenge.

Or the torture.

Alaina was a beautiful woman; she always had been. But maturity had granted her grace, and experience had lent her tongue a biting wit for which—though its daggers were frequently aimed at him—he couldn't help but afford her begrudging admiration.

That, or he was simply losing all his mental faculties and required institutionalization.

A very small, very quiet part of him refused to be cowed. *She remembered how he took his tea.* He had to believe some minute part of her still cared, whether it wanted to or not. It had been years since she'd prepared him a cup of tea, but she'd performed the task with flawless efficiency, and she'd done it to perfection. Despite her reticence to accept him back into her life, the seemingly innocuous act gave him a ray of hope warm and bright enough to bolster his resolve. He'd been so taken aback by the gesture that he hadn't been able to react at first. He recognized it was a silly thing—tea was tea—but it had told him in no uncertain terms that she hadn't forgotten him…not completely.

On one of the "bad days," Sterling found Alaina reclining on a chaise longue in a warm patch of sun in the library. With bated breath, he watched her in the unguarded seconds before she noticed his arrival.

She caught the manicured nail of her thumb between her

pearly teeth as she buried her nose in a cloth-covered manuscript. The golden light lent her a shimmering halo and kissed the gentle curve of her cheek in such a way that it made him ache. A heat more palpable than the very sunlight streaming into the room blossomed from deep in his chest, sinking lower and lower until he was half-hard so quickly it was painful.

He wanted to pluck the papers from her hands and toss them aside. To press her back until she was prone and pliant beneath him. To bathe in her scent. To fit his thigh between hers as he melded the curves and hollows of their bodies and tasted every inch of her silken flesh, every curve, every crevice. To finally, irrevocably claim her as his.

Though he was loath to break the spell, Sterling cleared his throat and Alaina stiffened. A new pain prodded his innards, dousing his ardor with a healthy dose of reality. He was about as close to his wife allowing him any liberties as a fish was to sprouting wings and flying.

Alaina did not look up from her reading, but he could tell from the tilt of her head that she was listening. "I'm off to my solicitor's office," he announced. She raised her hand in haughty dismissal and hunkered down more deeply into the chaise. He suppressed a sigh as he backed out of the room and retrieved his hat from Maxwell.

In truth, his meeting wasn't for another three hours. He just desperately needed some space to breathe and think…and defrost his bollocks.

AFTER A BIT of wandering, regaining his bearings along the streets of London, savoring the familiar—if sometimes unpleasant—smells and sights of home, Sterling found himself on St. James's Street at the foot of the steps leading White's. As one of the most coveted memberships for men of the *ton*, the prestigious gentlemen's club was one of his former haunts. Morton association dated back to the club's formation more than a century earlier. His membership had been a foregone conclusion as soon as he'd come of age. Staring up at the familiar Greek columns propping up the building's stately facade, he wondered if that membership remained valid after an eight-year hiatus.

He climbed the steps and was somewhat amused when he had only to mention his name to the doorman before he was admitted with a buzz of barely contained excitement. The Morton name still created a stir, it seemed. In no time, his hat and gloves were whisked away by silent, efficient hands, and he was escorted into the hallowed hall of masculinity.

Engulfed in the warm, musky scent of cheroot and oiled leather, parchment and spirits, Sterling felt more at ease than he had since he had returned to England. No furious wives were lurking around the corner, driving him mad with their barbed tongues and sinfully gorgeous bodies.

He selected an upholstered armchair in the corner and took his seat. Its position afforded him both a clear view of the rest of the room and its inhabitants, as well as an interesting vista outside the tall windows swathed in heavy velvet draperies. He settled in and awaited the drink he'd requested, but his senses remained keenly aware of the interest his arrival had stirred. This was his first real outing since his return to England, so it was unsurprising that his presence garnered such a reaction.

Sterling slowly scanned the room through the light haze of smoke billowing from a portly lord flipping through a newspaper. He marked each man present, where he stood, with whom he spoke, and how often his eyes flicked in Sterling's direction. He recognized several familiar faces, though they were older or softened by years of overindulgence. Curiosity flared in their eyes; several men bent their heads together as if discussing whether Sterling was, in fact, the Duke of Morton returned…and whether or not he could be approached without offense.

He'd known even before he set foot outside of Morton House that his presence would attract some interest—in fact, he was surprised that word hadn't gotten out before then—but it was a far cry from the greeting in his own home. It was refreshing to be around people who, even if they weren't his closest friends, didn't try to commit his murder with their eyes... It was a welcome difference from the climate at home, and that realization was at once sobering and depressing.

His warmed brandy was delivered by a silent servant, and it was as if a bell had been rung at the starting gates. Several lords took that as their invitation to approach Sterling and renew his acquaintance.

He spent the next hour being greeted by a variety of White's members. Men who had known his father and wished Sterling well; former classmates at university were eager to reminisce and be counted once more amongst his comrades. Others simply wanted to be able to say they'd conversed with the notorious Duke of Morton.

He received several verbal invitations to balls and gatherings from husbands who claimed their wives would never forgive them if they didn't present the opportunity to the newly returned duke. He shared drinks and answered questions about his time on the Continent; artfully dodging the inquiries he wished to avoid answering and, instead, responding with a practiced tepid smile and falling back on his rank and his right to dismiss anyone without a word of explanation. This especially came in handy when a couple of comments edged toward rude with references to stories of some of his more debauched activities. Those were the ones that earned the full force of his icy glare and most withering rebuff.

When those topics were exhausted, conversation naturally shifted toward more serious subjects. He was asked by those who were more politically minded when he might finally assume his seat in the House of Lords. It wasn't a lie when he reassured them that he looked forward to educating himself on the issues coming up for vote. He hadn't lied to Alaina earlier; he knew it was long past time he made a difference at home. His influence was more than substantial, and it had cost him no small amount of guilt that it was yet another thing he'd abandoned for the "debauched life of excess" everyone believed he'd led on the Continent. It was one more deep-rooted regret he doubted he'd ever reconcile. All he could do was move forward. Turn a new leaf. Whatever bloody aphorisms one used when he was trying to make himself feel better about turning his back on the life he'd once had.

Sterling signaled for another drink and it appeared with all the speed and efficiency for which White's was known. He deftly steered the conversation to places he wished to go; he presented the proper ducal facade and, with each man who eventually returned to his day or excused himself from their group, Sterling knew all of London would be abuzz with news of his return well before he set foot outside of those walls.

In all, he was able to forget himself for a while and settle back into the role to which he'd been born. While not free of artifice, it was a different sort than that which he'd become so adept at practicing over the years. To him, this was child's play.

Another brandy and several conversations later, Sterling enjoyed a brief period of peace before he was approached by a tall, immaculately turned-out man with a pronounced limp and a silver-tipped cane. He appeared to be around Sterling's age, perhaps a year or two older. Sterling scoured his keen memory.

The cane.

The shockingly green eyes and golden hair.

"Sommerfeld," Sterling greeted the man and received a warm grin in response.

"Morton. I'd been unsure if you'd remember me—we were a few years apart at university, after all."

"How could I forget?" Sterling gestured to the vacant seat beside him, and the viscount nodded in thanks. He sat with only a little awkwardness before propping his cane against the small cherrywood table between them. The last time Sterling had seen the man, he hadn't required the cane's assistance. He wasn't privy to the exact nature of the injury, but he'd heard of the near-death incident even while on the Continent. Anytime something happened to a handsome, wealthy, well-connected man, news traveled remarkably fast. Though the viscount's physical limitations were clear, he seemed otherwise healthy. "You managed to create quite the reputation."

Sommerfeld waved away the comment on his rakehell youth. "I thought I would take the opportunity to welcome you home. Are you here to stay, then? Will we be seeing more of you in Town?"

"I suppose so," Sterling replied as he settled more deeply into the comfortable chair. A carriage rumbled by outside in the street and he watched as the gray and green conveyance disappeared from view. "It was long past time to return home," he added somewhat wistfully as Alaina's face materialized in a dreamy haze against the glass. She was a specter, forever taunting him with her nearness, yet always out of his reach…determined to hold his sins against him like a sword above his neck.

"Then I suspect we shall be seeing a great deal of one another." Sterling could hear the wry grin in the viscount's voice and he turned to face him. "Our wives are rather close," Sommerfeld added by way of explanation.

"Of course." Sterling nodded to mask his discomfort over the fact that he knew so little about Alaina when it came to who she had become. She was close friends with a future countess who had married into a family known for their more liberal political leanings…and he knew nothing about it. He'd have to remedy his lack of knowledge about his wife's companions, if only to ensure her wellbeing. He'd failed in many of his obligations, but this was one thing he hoped he might correct. Alaina had gone so long without someone to directly look after her, and he fully intended on doing so.

It was also disheartening how the list of things he didn't know about Alaina was steadily growing far larger than the ones he did. Yet another of his shortcomings.

He set those thoughts aside for the time being and simply allowed himself to be in the moment—something he hadn't done in what felt like a lifetime.

He and Sommerfeld wound up passing another hour in companionable conversation. They took a light lunch while Sterling enjoyed another brandy, and the viscount sipped overly-sweetened tea. Though he and Sommerfeld had never been great friends prior to his trip to the Continent, Sterling found the man to be immensely likable and easy to talk to. This—coupled with the several drinks in him—allowed Sterling to drop his guard more than he had in recent memory. Despite common belief, he had avoided strong spirits as much as possible these past eight years. Lowered inhibitions were not something to be taken lightly.

While Sterling recounted a couple of amusing anecdotes from his travels—one of which involved a particularly aggressive donkey and a German prince—Sommerfeld returned the favor by catching Sterling up on the latest news in Town. There was some interesting legislature being prepared for voting in the House of Lords; a few old disputes between ancient families continued to boil. Though Englishmen were not known for being overly demonstrative, the viscount did explain a little of how he'd met his wife. The viscountess was immediately endeared to Sterling when her husband warned him off of ever playing cards with her because she couldn't be beaten.

At one point, Sterling accidentally knocked his foot into Sommerfeld's cane and sent it clattering to the ground. He quickly apologized and moved to retrieve it, recognizing the distinctive snarling sterling silver lion with glowing garnet eyes from university. The young viscount had used it in a prop during a prank on one of the crueler professors and quickly adopted it as a signature accessory. Now, it was clear the cane was much more utilitarian.

Sterling handed it back to Sommerfeld and, though he said nothing, he must have read the curiosity in Sterling's eyes.

What had happened to bring down a man so young and full of life?

The viscount averted his gaze and propped the cane against the table once more. "I am sure you've received any number of invitations since your return," Sommerfeld said, smoothly transitioning the conversation. "Forgive me for adding one more to your plate, but I'm certain my wife would enjoy having you and Lady Morton join us for supper one evening soon. She is only just reentering society after confinement," he added the last for clarification.

"Confinement? Well, then congratulations are in order. My apologies for the delay; I hadn't realized." Sterling held out his hand to Sommerfeld and the other man took it gratefully.

"Thank you," Sommerfeld replied, beaming with undeniable pride. His entire countenance glowed with it and his grin was remarkably wide. "My wife and the girls are all doing well. I fear a house full of women is my penance for the sins of my youth," he chuckled and sat back.

"Girls? You've twins then?"

Sommerfeld nodded. "Both are already as fiery as their mother, and all three of them know exactly the ways in which to try my patience and obtain everything they want."

Sterling emitted a small smile at the picture his companion painted. It was clear to even those far less observant than he that Sommerfeld adored his wife and wasn't the least bit disappointed that she'd given him daughters instead of an heir. To say Sterling found the situation enviable was an understatement.

How pleasant it must be to have a wife who could stand your presence.

"It can't be that miserable, can it?" Sommerfeld asked with an exaggerated grimace. Sterling was appalled to realize he'd grumbled aloud, but the viscount didn't appear to be taken aback by his informal bluntness. "See here," Sommerfeld began as he sat forward with his elbows on his knees; "If I may speak candidly—and do know that I genuinely like her quite a bit and that I say this with the utmost respect—Lady Morton is a handful. Of course, I've only ever seen her in public settings and as a guest in her home, but I can only imagine what she must put you through in private. A more determined, outspoken woman I've never met, though she is also undeniably, unapologetically herself."

Sterling's mouth twisted into a wry grin. Far from being offended, he actually appreciated the assessment of his wife and found it aligned with what he'd come to know of her these past several days. There was something oddly reassuring about it...like he'd finally learned a fact about this new Alaina.

"I cannot claim my memory to be impeccable, though I will say she has always been a true friend to my wife even if she may not be the same girl I remember from her debut. In fact, I am unaware of any woman who would dare call her a false or fickle friend. She is kind to a fault, if meddlesome; she is a woman driven by her moral compass." Sommerfeld inclined his head. "And I'm sure you are aware just how rare that is in our circles. Women are more likely to throw a dagger as soon as your back is turned as they are to smile sweetly to your face."

"I do respect your estimation, Sommerfeld," Sterling said honestly as he polished off the last of his drink and set aside the cut crystal glass. "Tell me, what is your opinion of this Reading Society? You mentioned your wife was a member and I would like an honest reply. Everyone is either trying to ingratiate themselves to me or they beg me to intervene to make their own lives more tolerable." It was instantly clear that Sterling didn't need to elaborate further. Sommerfeld shrugged and sat back to rub a knuckle into the muscle of his thigh; the movement appeared to be more a subconscious action than anything.

"I admit, it is nice to see Lady Sommerfeld reading things other than her medical treatises and journals. She never had a Season in Town and knew precious few people at the time of our marriage, so the Society has afforded her a way to meet and make friends and connections within the *ton*. I know some question the ideas they discuss and the materials they read, but I gather quite a few of those people are simply jealous they've not received an invitation to attend, or they are husbands irked by their wives discovering their own passions." Sommerfeld chuckled. "For her part, my wife doesn't seem much worse for the wear, even if she does return home with the occasional radical idea. In fact—" He lowered his voice to a conspiratorial whisper so it wouldn't carry further than their corner of the room. "I quite appreciate it whenever they read the naughtier books because she will come home feeling particularly adventurous."

Sommerfeld winked.

Sterling choked and wished he had a drink to blame it upon.

Naughty books?

Where in God's name had Alaina found those…and why had he not yet reaped the benefits?

Who was he fooling?

He knew exactly why he hadn't.

His wife loathed him. Couldn't stand the sight of him. Likely fantasized about the myriad ways she might rid herself of him.

The last thing on her mind would be ways she might implement things from her illicit stories…even if *he* couldn't stop pondering all the ways he'd like to give *her* pleasure.

Sterling signaled for another drink and decided he'd have to delay his meeting with his solicitor another day. This conversation was far too riveting, and he'd already imbibed two drinks too many. He couldn't be trusted to perform business of any worth.

He, like most men, preferred to believe he could hold his liquor well…but he'd admitted to himself long ago that drinking was not his game of choice—especially when he needed to keep his head about him. It was precisely why he'd avoided anything more than a few nips here or there for appearances. However, there, in White's with a man whom he'd very much like to eventually call one of the first true friends he'd ever had, Sterling felt at ease. He could step away from the angst within his home, he could breathe a little easier now that he was in a familiar place, but he would never be able to fully release the habit of scanning the room and anticipating the motives of everyone within. It was nice to pretend, though, and to allow himself to be a little less cautious with his actions and his words.

If only he could do the same with Alaina.

"Ah," Sommerfeld began thoughtfully, reading volumes in Sterling's silence. "Your homecoming has not been what you expected, then?" It was more a statement than a question.

Sterling laughed sardonically, his words ringing with harsh candor, "I received exactly the reception I expected…I simply did not anticipate it being this protracted." He hadn't believed Alaina would welcome him with open arms and drag him into her bed, but he'd hoped by this point that he at least would have earned a modicum of warmth. Perhaps consummated their union, if he was lucky. But he was quickly coming to realize that he'd vastly underestimated the female ability to hold a grudge.

"If I may?" Sommerfeld held up his palms but didn't wait for a reply. "If marriage to my own spitfire has taught me one thing, it's that a little groveling can go a long way."

"I'm a duke. Dukes grovel to no one and for nothing," he replied flatly.

"Now *that*—" Sommerfeld pointed a finger in Sterling's direction. "—is precisely the attitude that will keep your bed cold. To the world, we are wealthy, powerful, titled men. At home, in private, our wives rule." Sterling cocked a skeptical brow. "Oh, we like to think we are in control," Sommerfeld added quickly; "but we aren't. They hold our hearts and our bollocks in their pretty little beaded reticules. *We* are the ones at their mercy, whether we wish to admit it or not. When we do wrong, no simple apology will suffice."

"You and I suffer from a similar affliction," Sommerfeld added gravely, but paused as Sterling's next drink was delivered. The employee retreated silently to a faraway corner to await his next task and the viscount continued. "We, both of us, are possessed by women who know their worth and they'll be damned before they allow anyone—even us—to treat them as anything less."

Sterling took a sip of his fresh brandy and pondered Sommerfeld's words while the sweet heat slid down his throat and curled through his veins. He decided he was simultaneously appreciative of the other man's bluntness and irked that everyone seemed to know more about his wife and his marriage than he did.

"It sounds to me as if a little *wooing* is in order," Sommerfeld added with a sympathetic smile.

"Wooing?" Sterling scoffed. "We're already married and well past that."

"Wrong, again," Sommerfeld said, cutting him off, then leveled another finger at him. "For a man married as long as you have been, you still have a great deal to learn."

Sterling's mouth adopted a displeased twist. He sat back and took another drink as the wheels in his mind began to turn.

Woo his wife? Could that really be the solution to his ills?

Normally he wouldn't place this much stock in another's opinion, but he liked Sommerfeld. He respected his candor and there was undeniable logic there when one considered how everything else Sterling had tried thus far had all but exploded in his face.

Perhaps the viscount was correct and another tactic was in order...

Chapter Eight

THE NEXT MORNING, Alaina woke as usual. She dressed in her favorite mint green morning dress trimmed in delicate white lace and Penny twisted her hair into a serviceable chignon. After donning her slippers, she descended the staircase to the front hall.

By all accounts, the sunshine streaming through her bedroom window foretold a glorious day; the perfect sort of day to enjoy the sliver of nature London afforded. She was contemplating a walk in the park to take some air before she ran her errands when she reached the ground floor.

And she froze.

Something was different, but she couldn't immediately place her finger on what it was.

No furniture had been moved. The voluminous arrangement of hydrangea and tulips she'd composed the prior day still sat atop the round table near the front door. The black-and-white marble floor was polished to a glorious shine; the banister was freshly waxed and glowed warm in the morning light. It was quiet. A confused frown furrowed her brow as she turned in a slow circle, trying to discern what had thrown her off. Finally, her eyes settled on the doorway to the library.

It was empty.

Her head tilted in confusion as she wandered over to the portal. She peered inside to find the room abandoned. Everything was as it should be. The hearth had been cleaned and laid. The furniture was arranged as she preferred it. No books lay strewn about. No newspaper was draped over the arm of the leather chair nearest the wall of windows.

Sterling was not there.

He was what had been missing.

How strange that—despite her reticence—she had already begun to develop a subconscious routine with him. She would deny it even upon pain of death, but the sight of him waiting for her at the bottom of the stairs, his arms crossed over his broad chest as he propped up the doorframe, never failed to make her stomach flip-flop. Even when she showed him her worst, he never failed to greet her with a charming smile and a pleasant word.

The man was maddeningly incessant.

And there was something rather intoxicating about his persistence.

To suddenly not have him in his usual spot was surprisingly...disappointing. But Alaina gave herself a literal shake and reminded her wayward thoughts that this was what she had wanted.

She desired to be left alone.

She was better off without him.

She turned on her heel and made her way down and across the hall to the morning room. Though she rose much earlier than typical town standards, Sterling still tended to rise and break his fast before her. The staff had grown accustomed to two separate breakfast settings on the days she did not eat in her rooms, and she looked forward to her usual peaceful repast.

She pressed open the door and was instantly assailed by the heady perfume of dozens upon dozens of arrangements of roses in every shape and shade imaginable. Vases covered every inch of the available surfaces from the table to the banquet, even lining the floor and filling all four corners of the room. Standing in the center of it all was Sterling.

He wore his most charming of smiles—one she hadn't seen in all its glory since he'd asked for her hand all those years ago—and it made him appear more boyish, more approachable. He wore a smart dove-gray coat with a charcoal waistcoat and breeches, making the green in his hazel eyes stand out as an arresting hint of color. The intensity she witnessed there made her heart stutter.

Alaina's eyes began to sting and water.

And she began an uncontrollable fit of sneezing which forestalled any words she might have squeaked out of her congested throat.

When he realized she wasn't stopping, Sterling moved from offering her his handkerchief to ushering her from the room with a hand on her lower back. Alaina coughed and snatched the bit of fabric he still clutched in his hand. She gestured in a furious indication to shut the doors as she removed herself several steps further to wipe at her streaming eyes and blow her hopeless nose with a great, unladylike honk.

"My God, are you alright?" Sterling asked as he turned back to her after slamming the double doors. The expression on his face was one great swimming blob in her watery vision, but she recognized concern and confusion in his tone.

"Are you trying to kill me?" she demanded with a cough.

"Kill you?" his voice rose. "I always brought roses whenever I called upon you."

"Well, I am horribly allergic." She sniffed and wiped ineffectually at her eyes. "Clearly. But Mother insisted it would be rude to refuse them and forbade me to tell you of my condition. And, besides, I don't even care for roses."

STERLING LOOKED HEAVENWARD for strength. God save all well-intentioned men from the subterfuge of marriage-minded mamas.

He ran an exasperated hand through his once-tidy hair and looked back at his wife. It was clear this was no act; her reaction had been so violent and instantaneous. Her eyes were puffy and her elegant nose was red; her voice had adopted a ragged quality as she struggled to be understood around coughs and sneezes. He felt tremendously guilty for having put her through this—and that he didn't have the pockets for ten more handkerchiefs—but he couldn't have known. She said so herself. Here, he'd been trying to do something kind with a grand gesture...to *woo* his wife...and it had ended disastrously.

How appropriate.

"Then what flowers *do* you like?" he asked gently as he stepped closer and used the pad of his thumb to brush a tear from her cheek. This was the closest they'd been in days. He shouldn't have enjoyed her nearness when she was in such a pathetic state, but he couldn't help it. The heat from her body called to him in a primal way. "Ones that won't cause another crisis, that is," he added, his voice barely over a gravelly whisper.

Alaina looked up at him and did her best to approximate an eye roll. "I believe the more appropriate question is why you're only just *now* asking." She took several steps backward and dabbed at the cheek he'd touched as if trying to scrub him away. "If you'll excuse me, I need to splash water on my face." She turned in a flurry of mint-colored skirts and headed back toward the staircase. Sterling watched her until she disappeared before turning back to the morning room.

After releasing a frustrated growl, Sterling wrenched open the doors. What an unmitigated disaster. He yanked on the bellpull and surveyed the scene, trying not to consider how much money had gone into this farce.

Shortly, several maids poked their heads in through the servants' doorway, careful not to knock over any of the floral arrangements.

"See that all of this is cleaned up."

"Yes, Your Grace," the first one bobbed a curtsy. "Where would you like us to take them?"

"I care not," he snapped, and the little maid jumped. He breathed in air thick with roses before continuing in a more tempered tone. He was frustrated with his failure and ignorance and shouldn't take it out on others. "Throw them out. Give them to sweethearts or family. Donate them somewhere. Just don't allow a single rose to remain in this household."

He didn't think he was mistaken when he thought he glimpsed both maids attempting to hide knowing smiles behind deferential dipped heads.

Of course, Sterling thought morosely while the roses were slowly whisked away by the armful. The staff would know of his wife's allergy and her aversion to roses. They were probably having a great laugh below stairs at his expense.

Round one had been a complete and utter failure.

Now, how to move forward and try to win round two?

IT WAS NEARLY half an hour before Alaina recovered enough to request that Penny bring some food to her rooms. She had absolutely no desire to face Sterling anytime soon after the flower debacle.

Her head felt stuffed with lead; her eyes still itched and her nose was clogged, but at least she'd stopped her coughing, sneezing, and wheezing. Any dignity she'd had in her appearance earlier that morning had been destroyed by the incident downstairs. The neckline of her dress was damp from the water she'd splashed on her face and used to rinse her eyes. Her once neat hair had begun to slip from its pins. And she refused to gaze in the looking glass because she knew she'd find a splotchy red complexion with hopelessly swollen eyes. How utterly unattractive. Not only that, but now she'd have to rearrange her schedule and she hated doing that.

She sighed and leaned her head back against the wall of the window seat in her suite. Closing her eyes did nothing to relieve the sensation of abrading sand, so she gave up and pulled her knees to her chest beneath her crossed arms, resting her chin atop them.

She considered the room crammed full of flowers downstairs; the number of bouquets would likely have paid any London florist's rent for the next several months.

It was all rather ridiculous, really.

And excessive.

And immensely charming, were she to analyze it from an objective standpoint.

If Alaina set aside her feelings, she might be able to admit that Sterling's gesture had been sweet and entirely unexpected, especially given the frigidity that often filled the space between them since his return. When he'd stood there surrounded by those noxious bushels of roses…

He'd looked so handsome and hopeful. The glint in his eyes would likely have taken her breath away had she not been choked with pollen.

Standing before her had been more than a hint of the man she'd known in her youth. She'd been a girl again, hopelessly close to falling in love with the charming, thoughtful young duke.

Even if his gesture had created such a mess, Alaina had her suspicions about his motivations…and the realization unnerved her. He was making an effort with gestures, trying a new tactic to ingratiate himself.

She sat up and began pulling the remaining pins from her head. She'd likely have to change anyway thanks to the water spotting the front of her gown, so she might as well give Penny a head start with her hair.

She'd just dropped the last pin beside her book on the nearby table when there was a single knock on her door.

"Enter," she called absently as she ran her fingers through her waist-length locks and shook them free.

She looked up to find Sterling standing in the doorway, watching her with an unwavering intensity in his piercing eyes. Unfortunately, it would seem that Alaina's peace was to be short-lived.

She was immediately self-conscious, and she dropped her hands from her head and slid her feet to the floor, hastily tugging at her skirts when they got caught beneath her hip. She didn't miss how her husband's eyes darted to the length of the stocking-clad calf that had been exposed, if ever so briefly. Her lips pressed into a firm line, hoping he wouldn't notice the warmth spreading to her cheeks.

"Forgive me," he murmured, and his eyes met hers once more. "Both for the interruption and for—for the roses." He rubbed the back of his neck in a charmingly contrite gesture.

She didn't want to feel a pang of sympathy for him. She really didn't. But her heart had other ideas when faced with the sincerity in those eyes of his, the endearing tilt to his head that made one chestnut lock fall across his temple. Her fingers itched to brush it back and know if it was as soft as it looked.

Stop it! she chastised herself. What a silly thing to consider. Who cared if the man had hair softer than goose down? She should be the last woman who wanted to touch him.

"Why would you do such a thing?" she asked, pleasantly surprised when her voice wasn't as hoarse as it had been earlier.

"Isn't it obvious?" His voice was very near as close to a purr as a man could make. Her toes curled inside of her slippers. "I am wooing you."

Alaina swore her heart tripped and momentarily forgot its job. So had her tongue. It was several moments before she could even think of speaking.

Sterling explained further, saving her from having to form words of her own. "I intend to woo you, win you over, and make a true wife of you yet, Alaina. Just know that I'll never force you, but I will wait with bated breath until you decide you are ready to finally be my wife in every sense."

Alaina's lips parted as she hung onto his words.

Was it her imagination or did the corner of his mouth twitch as if attempting to smile?

"I think you will find I am an uncommonly determined man,

wife." Sterling's voice was so low that it made her toes curl. "And I'm not easily scared off. When I set my mind to something, I do not stop until I obtain it. And you, Alaina, are what I want. I want you as my wife. I want you in my bed. I want you beneath me, on top of me, and every other way a man can have a woman." His words sent an unexpected shaft of heat straight to her core and fairly made her quiver. She had to press her thighs together to ease the throb there. "I want you screaming my name in gratitude instead of anger. I want you as my partner in all things. And I will have it."

If she'd been stunned before, now she was struck dumb.

Without waiting for a reply, Sterling executed a smart bow and quit the room, leaving Alaina gaping in his wake.

She was still staring when Penny appeared in the open doorway toting the tray with Alaina's breakfast.

"Is everything alright?" the maid asked with a frown as she set the tray on the table.

"Yes," Alaina croaked and stood from her window seat. As she spread some blackberry preserves on a slice of toast, she decided that she would not allow Sterling to win. His selfish actions had caused her years of pain, and she refused to allow him to claim a victory so easily.

She had to remind herself to harden her heart against whatever he might throw at her. This was all too little, too late. If he'd ever truly cared, then this belated wooing would never have been necessary.

It mattered not how charming or endearing his efforts were.

Alaina couldn't allow herself to yield.

Chapter Nine

STERLING TRIED SEVERAL times over the ensuing days to make progress in the "wooing" of his wife, but he found the process much more frustrating and exhausting than he remembered.

That, or his wife was now just more difficult.

Each of his overtures was met with one complaint or another, threatening to drive his sanity into the ground. He strongly suspected Alaina was doing so intentionally, and that bolstered his resolve regardless of his apparent lack of progress.

Alaina didn't care for rubies—she claimed they "washed her out," whatever that meant. He'd simply seen a lovely piece of jewelry crafted by a very exclusive jeweler and he had purchased it for her.

When he gifted her with an obscenely expensive perfume, she behaved as if the gesture insinuated he did not care for her scent. Quite the contrary, actually. He hadn't been able to stop thinking about the delicate hint of floral aroma he'd caught when he'd stood close to her following what he would forever remember as The Rose Incident. He couldn't place the exact fragrance, but he'd tried, only to have it turn out horribly.

He had hired the most exclusive modiste in London to come to their home and fit her for some new gowns in anticipation of the invitations that would undoubtedly come now that he was showing his face around town. That had gone about as well as the perfume had. Alaina testily reminded him that it was technically inappropriate to gift clothing to a woman whom one was courting.

Sterling was at an utter and complete loss. His wife seemed determined to resist him and any efforts he might put into reconciliation; however, rather than defeat him, he became all the more steadfast in his aim.

Trying to woo his wife became an obsession. He'd lie awake at night, alone in his cold bed, frustrated, trying to concoct ways to make the infuriating woman sleeping just on the other side of the wall happy.

Thus far, it seemed like the only thing that worked was his leaving her alone.

That, however, was most certainly not an option.

She drove him mad with everything she did, and it only spurred him on.

He'd never failed at anything before in his life, and he wasn't about to allow that to happen now. Not when the stakes were so high. He knew he had to find just one chink in her armor, one crack in her facade, and he'd win.

He was sure of it.

One night, unable to sleep and too restless with nerves, he decided to do some research into his wife. Perhaps he might locate some clues into her mind—something that might help him finally make a slight bit of headway toward his goal.

Sterling slipped silently from the ducal chamber and made his way down the hall on practiced silent feet. No sound came from Alaina's bedchamber as he passed by and turned, instead, for the adjoining room. The duchess's private sitting room abutted her bedchamber and was connected by her dressing room. It was designed to allow the lady of the house to move with ease between her private rooms without having to fully dress if she did not wish to.

Pushing the dangerous thought of his half-naked wife aside, Sterling tried the polished brass knob to Alaina's sitting room, but it was locked. No matter. He'd anticipated as much from the woman who wished to shut him out of her life.

He slipped a small leather case from his pocket and selected the proper silver tools before he crouched and went to work. It would have been far easier to use the key, but the only two copies remained in possession of Alaina and the housekeeper. It took him less than one minute to gain access to the room and slip inside. The skill he'd learned nearly a decade prior had come in handy on numerous occasions, but he'd never thought to employ his lockpicking skills in his own home.

He held still as a cat and allowed his eyes to adjust to the silver moonlight. He could make out the shapes of several tables and chairs, the bulbous, irregular forms of several vases filled with flowers—none of them roses, judging by the scent. The far corner held what he desired.

The delicate escritoire contained neat stacks of clean parchment, bottles of ink in several colors, a candle, and the implements necessary for her to seal her correspondence. He examined her neat, confident handwriting on what appeared to be a draft menu for when she would next host her Reading Society. A list of odd items filled another page: yards of fabric in plain colors, ink, chalk, parchment, and a variety of books ranging from didactic literature to fairytales. He saw no immediate value in the list, so he set it aside.

Another piece of parchment held a few lines of text to her mother, but it was riddled with lines and corrections before it was ultimately abandoned. He knew Alaina and the countess had never been close—had never shared the warm, comfortable relationship one might hope for between mother and child—and it appeared that hadn't changed much in his absence. His heart lurched at the realization. A part of him had maintained hope that her family would rally around her after he left for the Continent, but this only confirmed his suspicions that that had not been the case. Likely, Brendt and his wife had been more concerned about saving face than comforting their daughter in her time of need. He cursed both them and himself for the selfish actions which had impacted Alaina so.

Setting the page aside, Sterling moved on to quietly opening and closing each of the dainty drawers in turn. Most of it was unremarkable and unhelpful…until he came to the largest drawer in the middle. The lock was engaged, but he made short work of it to discover it held a significant stack of envelopes. Careful to remain as silent as possible, he began flipping through them, peering inside at their contents whenever he was particularly intrigued. Titles, names, and dates flashed before his eyes.

And his jaw clenched so tightly it was a miracle he didn't crack a tooth.

EACH MORNING, ALAINA woke with dread, wondering what surprise Sterling had in store for her that day. Up to that point, he'd been horribly off the mark, but he'd somehow managed to remain determinedly charming in his disappointment.

And, each day, Alaina was afraid that he might finally get something right and she'd be forced to admit as much. She could admit to herself that it was a ridiculous thing to be concerned about—having one's husband make too sweet or thoughtful a gesture—but this was how things stood.

There was always such a hopeful gleam in his arresting eyes the moment before she crushed him, but he was persistent. She had to concede that point.

Each time she felt the slightest wavering of her resolve when faced with his handsome features and charm, she had to remind herself that this was still the same man who'd abandoned her and lived the extravagant life of an attractive, wealthy, titled bachelor on the Continent while she languished in loneliness in London. And then she'd set her jaw and pick up her manuscript to read through her parts to prepare for the next Reading Society gathering.

That morning, Alaina crept from her chambers, hoping to avoid an ambush of thoughtfulness while still bracing herself to find yet another surprise awaiting her. Instead, she found only Sterling seated at the table in the morning room, apparently waiting for her. He stood as soon as he heard her enter, but his determined joviality seemed to have dissipated. Where he'd developed a habit of greeting her with a heart-melting smile each morning, his face remained a cool, unreadable mask. The fact that he sat beside her in silence while her tea was poured and she settled in to break her fast was more than a little unnerving, even to a woman used to dining quietly.

She eyed him over the rim of her teacup, attempting to read his stony features to discern what had changed. Unfortunately, she was no longer as familiar with his expressions and moods as she'd once been, and the man he'd become was far more difficult to read than the newspaper he held before him.

She nearly jumped when those intense eyes of his found her watching him over the corner of his paper. Her heart raced unexpectedly, and she quickly snapped her gaze back to her plate. The last thing she wanted was for him to know how drawn she was to him.

Sterling folded and flicked the newspaper to the table. "What are your plans for today, wife?" he asked in a suspiciously even tone.

Feeling oddly cornered, Alaina was careful to present the same emotionless voice in her response. "Perhaps some shopping; I require a new pair of gloves. And the ladies of the Reading Society are coming over tomorrow afternoon for our gathering, so I will be meeting with Cook to plan some refreshments. We shouldn't be more than a couple of hours in the front sitting room beginning at half-three."

Sterling eyed her carefully, causing Alaina's breath to catch in her throat. She had the distinct feeling she was being hunted, and she'd never felt more helpless.

"Perhaps," he began in a low, dangerous tone; "you may wish to carve some time out today to handle your correspondence."

She sat back in her chair. Now that was one of the least likely things she thought she would hear from his well-formed lips. "Whatever do you—"

Alaina's mouth snapped shut when he pulled a large stack of

bound envelopes in various shades of cream and white from between the pages of his newspaper and dropped them with a resounding thud on the table between them. She tried not to flinch.

Blast.

Schooling her features and her voice to remain as calm as possible, she asked, "Why would you riffle through my desk?"

"Why would you ignore or decline *all* of these invitations, Alaina?" he demanded, mocking her inquiry. "Every single one of these possesses a date since my return to London. Why would you hide these from me?" Was it her imagination, or was there a flicker of hurt in the mossy depths of his eyes? Could he possibly have been injured by her omission of these invitations? "If we are going to coexist in this marriage, then I need to know about these things." The rough tone of his voice told him she hadn't imagined it.

Her mind raced, but Alaina knew there was no way to lie herself out of this situation—no way to spin it to mask the embarrassing truth of it.

"What would you like me to say?" she snapped in an effort to disguise her own pain, her heart thrashing like a caged wild bird. "That I did not wish to face all the questions and leers?" While her husband's eyes remained steadfastly locked on hers, there was a methodical flex of a muscle in his chiseled jaw that told her he was listening and not liking what he heard. "Some of those invitations may be genuine—old friends desiring to welcome you home—but I know these people well enough to say with confidence that many are simply morbidly curious about your return...about the state of our marriage." Her fists clenched around the cloth napkin in her lap, twisting it over and over again as she was transformed back into the abandoned girl, so lost and hopelessly alone. "'Why did Morton return *now*? Did the duchess finally grow enough of a backbone to yank his leash and drag him home?'" she mocked in a nasty approximation of only a small fraction of the gossip she'd endured over the years. Her cheeks warmed painfully, and the backs of her eyes began to sting. She cursed inwardly; she'd believed herself to be past allowing such thoughts and words to harm her, but it was clear their venom still festered deep inside her soul.

Sterling suddenly stood and moved to her side. Taken aback by the gesture, she forgot to fight when he removed the wrinkled napkin from between her fingers and pulled her to her feet, gently tugging her into his arms. There was only a heartbeat between when Alaina froze in shock, and when she was overcome by how Sterling overwhelmed nearly every one of her senses.

He smelled just like she remembered—clean, leather and sandalwood. His arms were so sturdy around her, making her feel so small and protected. The hard length of his body was firm against every inch of her, and yet, it was comfortable and comforting in the most unexpected way. She fit there…just there with her head tucked beneath his chin and her cheek pressed against the thrumming heart beneath his breast. It was foreign to her to be cradled in his strong arms, held against the solid wall of his chest, cocooned in his masculine scent, but it was more shocking to her to realize that it wasn't as unwelcome as she'd believed it might be.

All the frustration Sterling had displayed seemed to have dissipated and, in its place, was this unexpected tenderness.

Though Alaina had initially stiffened against the unfamiliar contact, she gradually melted into the embrace. Hesitantly (and against her better judgment), her arms wound 'round Sterling's narrow waist; this only prompted him to hold her closer, tighter, and rest his chin atop her hair. Her eyes slid closed and, though her conscience railed against it, she allowed herself to be carried away by it all.

How long had it been since she'd been held like this?

For that matter, had she *ever* been held quite like this?

The gesture spoke to a secret part of her soul she'd kept locked away for fear that its release would break her…a part that desired this closeness with another person…had always craved this tenderness and understanding from *him,* above all others.

She counted the steady thrum of his heart.

One…two…three…four…five…

And then Sterling loosened his hold on her just enough to allow her to take half a step back while keeping her within his arms. Alaina looked up to find his hazel eyes staring down at her intently.

"It is unfair," he began gently, his voice reverberating in the space between them, entering her chest like tendrils of intoxicating smoke; "that you must concern yourself with such things. And I don't believe I will ever successfully express how sorry I am for it." His thumb began to stroke her back from side to side, and it was difficult for her to concentrate. "But wouldn't it be wonderful to accept some of these invitations and present a united front? We are, after all, a duke and a duchess…we cannot hide from social obligations forever."

Alaina's lips parted when she saw his eyes dart to her mouth. Her lungs released a shaky sigh of their own volition.

His arms tensed around her.

The dark pools of his pupils dilated.

"A—Are you going to kiss me?" she asked in a voice more breathless than she would have liked.

"Do you wish for me to kiss you, Alaina?"

It was Alaina's turn to lower her gaze to his lips. He'd kissed her before and, though it was many years ago now, this felt entirely different.

This was more powerful.

More dangerous.

His mouth held her mesmerized; even more so when it tilted into a smile.

Sterling's voice lowered further when he said, "It's more than alright if you do. It is your right as a wife to demand kisses, a right I will always wholly support and even encourage."

Alaina swallowed involuntarily. The tip of her tongue darted out and wet her lower lip.

Unable to resist, Sterling lowered his head in slow increments. He afforded Alaina every chance to pull free while mentally preparing himself for a stinging slap to his cheek, but some unseen force kept her captive in his arms, in his eyes.

His lips stopped a breath away from hers.

Waiting.

Alaina's eyes slid closed and, though he knew it likely grated against her better judgment, she tilted her head a fraction of an inch to touch her lips to his.

Sterling emitted an involuntary groan at the tender contact. She was sweeter and gentler than his wildest imaginings. It was a tragedy above all else that he'd forgotten how petal-soft her lips were…how very sweet she tasted.

Through no small feat of strength, held himself in check, kissing her back with similar tentative gentleness as they learned one another again.

Chills danced across every one of his nerves when she ran her hands along his side to splay against his chest and the pounding heart it barely contained.

His body hardened with painful swiftness at her hesitant touch, the blood fleeing his brain so quickly that it nearly made him blackout. Instead, he clutched his wife more tightly, using her as his anchor in a world that had suddenly been thrown on its side. Every part of him screamed out to have her hands on his bare flesh. He was desperate for her to touch him, to touch her in return.

It had been far, far too long…

Sterling couldn't resist a gentle pass of his tongue against the seam of her velvet lips. She responded with a sigh, parting them for his exploration. He drank of her deeply—like a man gasping for air after being submerged in stormy waters for far too long—and held the full length of her body tightly to his own. Silently, he marveled at the way they fit when he pressed himself more closely to feel every one of her curves. What he wouldn't give to have the barrier of their clothing removed so he could finally show her just how much he had thought about her all this time… His body yearned to demonstrate all the ways he'd longed for her, to prove to her, as his words could not, how deeply he had always desired her.

Abruptly, Alaina levered all her weight against Sterling's chest and shoved him away. He released her without resistance and she stumbled a few dazed steps backward, leaving him standing there bereft and painfully aroused, his chest heaving.

It was a study in futility for Alaina to attempt to slow her pounding heart.

Sterling had kissed her a few times in the past, but those had always been very chaste affairs. What had just transpired had been different.

Very different.

Very exciting…

This particular kiss had involved touching with other parts of their anatomy, teeth, and tongues. This sort of kiss had always seemed decidedly messy and unappetizing in theory; in practice, however, Alaina was shocked to discover how weak her knees had become and how hot her body had grown. It was as if Sterling had fanned banked coals beneath her skin and she was helpless against the rising sparks as they raced through her veins.

Alaina felt as if she was being lured out onto a dangerous precipice and the sensation caused her breath to stall in an approximation of terror. She'd very nearly drowned in Sterling's heady scent and taste, his overwhelming assault upon her senses…but she'd been saved when her last shred of sanity reminded her that this was the man whose intimate exploits were the juices of the *ton*'s gossip and had been for many years now. His lush behavior and association with some of the most beautiful women the Continent had to offer had consistently poured salt in her wounds, leaving her an oxymoronic virgin wife while he sought solace everywhere but in her arms.

Sterling's sudden, slow smile only caused Alaina's ire to rise further. "I doubt," she practically panted as she snapped, "we will ever be able to present a convincing performance of unity; not when I and the rest of Society know how you've spent the last eight years. It was made clear many times over with whom you chose to spend your time, and it certainly was not me."

"What are you—" her husband began and then his mouth snapped shut when he recognized what she was insinuating. He ran a rough, frustrated hand over his face and back through his burnished chestnut hair. "Surely you cannot be serious?"

Alaina's jaw clenched as tightly as her fists. It was clear Sterling would not be accepting accountability for anything, and she refused to allow herself to fall victim to his disarmingly handsome face, unjustly kind words, and distracting kisses. She moved to brush past him and storm from the room, but his hand shot out and grabbed her upper arm. His grip was strong but not bruising; he exerted just enough pressure to keep her from leaving.

"It is not what you believe."

"Then what is it?" she demanded brokenly, certain that he could read the pain in her eyes. "Was the number just an exaggeration? Are a dozen lovers a more realistic figure? What should I believe when so many sources reported nothing but your immoral behavior and your infidelity as you made a mockery of me and of our farce of a marriage?"

Sterling pleaded with his eyes, doing his best to silently convey his sincerity. His inability to disclose the details of his absence to Alaina was torture. Scouted in his youth for his charm, intelligence, and eventual dukedom, he'd been deemed an asset beneficial to England's aims on the Continent. He'd proven too useful, and what should only have been twelve months turned into two years, then three, then eight. He ached to tell her so much of what she'd heard had been a lie—carefully planted stories and clever acting to make him seem no more a threat than a dandified womanizer. Somehow, he needed her to understand this without betraying his mission or placing her in unnecessary danger by giving her classified information. Though it had caused him no small amount of guilt, he'd worked endlessly to separate himself from his wife and make her seem less important to him than she was—all to keep her safe. If he'd been discovered, it was not outside the realm of possibility that Alaina might have become a target if it was discovered just how much she mattered to him. He wouldn't undo all of that now.

It pained him beyond reason that she believed in the rumors of his extensive promiscuity—that she felt he might have wanted those women more than her—but it wouldn't do much to argue with her other than stoke the flames of her anger. He'd learned as much about his wife in the weeks since his return.

He was more than frustrated by the situation, disgusted with his helplessness to undo the damage his choices and his behavior had caused. He took a deep breath, but it did almost nothing to calm his roiling emotions. The lust he'd experienced with her body pressed against his was quickly being smothered by annoyance at himself—at the situation they were in and the state of their marriage—because of an obligation he'd taken on many years prior, and regret over having caused Alaina such pain.

"It is not what you think because it didn't happen." His voice was a low rumble.

Alaina scoffed in reply, but he refused to release her when she tried to leave once more. He held her arm and her gaze for one, two, three heartbeats and then stepped back, freeing her.

"Fine," Sterling bit off. "If you would rather believe the drivel in *The Prattler* over your husband, then so be it. Why trust me over the hundreds of wagging tongues who've nothing better to do than prey upon and exploit the weaknesses of others." He had a feeling he'd come to regret his next statement, but all rationality had fled him at that point, drained from him by the gaping wound in his heart: "No wonder you don't wish to accept any of these invitations when you care more for what others believe than my word."

Alaina said nothing.

Instead, she spun and fled the room.

Chapter Ten

KNOWING WELL HE would tear the place to shambles if he stayed in the house, Sterling tore from the room and bellowed for his valet. He needed to get out of these clothes. He needed to burn off this energy before he did something he regretted…above and beyond the horrendous mistakes he'd already made.

Less than an hour later, Sterling slipped through the back streets of Mayfair with one thing on his mind, and after night fell in full force, he found himself in a dingy Covent Garden alley. His entire day had built up to that moment, every frustration and emotion slathering layer upon layer to his foul mood.

Ignoring the scrabble of fleeing vermin and the stench of the overflowing gutters, he closed his eyes and listened. Creaking doors. Vulgar catcalls. A screaming child. A shattering glass in the nearby public house. A peal of overzealous female laughter followed by a slurred masculine tone. He leaned back against the damp brick wall, allowing the shadows to absorb him and his rough, unremarkable dark clothing, as the doxy and her client sauntered toward him. He was so well hidden that they didn't see him until they'd nearly collided.

"Oy!" snarled the man.

"Looks like this spot is taken," said the woman, her eyes narrowing at Sterling. "A few pennies'll earn you the right to watch." She leaned toward him, her unlaced bodice dipping low enough to display a dusky nipple and several bruises shaped like fingers and teeth. Her hair hung in lank strings from a simple bun at the nape of her neck and her dark eyes were glassy with, Sterling suspected, cheap gin. "A couple more 'n' I'm yours for a suck or a tup." Her sizable male companion grabbed her upper arm hard enough to make her wince and yanked her away.

"I already paid me money 'n' I don't take no one's leavin's." He jerked the doxy deeper into the alley and began untying his loose trousers. "Now is you going to give me me money's worth or's I goin' ta have ta get rough?" His trousers dipped to his thick, hairy thighs and he began to push the girl to her knees but froze when he noticed Sterling hadn't moved. "You dumb 'r stupid?" He spat a thick wad of saliva near Sterling's boot. "This is me alley now. Fuck off!"

A low chuckle rose from deep within Sterling's chest. It was almost a relief when his muscles tensed with the familiar rage, his senses heightening to near-preternatural degrees.

"Somefink funny?"

"Besides your small, pathetically limp cock?" Sterling pushed off the wall and tsked. "Oh, Angus. The fact that you believed you could continue harming women, and that no one would care."

"How d'you know me name?" he demanded suspiciously, thankfully hiking up his trousers.

"Why is it always the idiots who think they're the masterminds?" Sterling asked while looking at the wide-eyed doxy, not expecting an answer. He returned his frigid gaze to Angus. "You're clumsy, Angus. I will say, it was a nice touch growing a beard to hide your birthmark, but not good enough."

"I ain't done nofink."

Sterling raised a finger at him. "That is where I beg to differ, old fellow. And I'm sure the six women you assaulted and maimed would agree."

"What? You a bobby?"

"Oh, Angus…" Sterling sighed regretfully. "You only wish I were one. Unfortunately for you, their rules do not apply to me."

"Them's just whores!" he bellowed and took a threatening step forward, seeming to forget his earlier denial thanks to the icy bite in Sterling's words.

"And you are just a cowardly slug who takes his sexual incapabilities out on those who cannot defend themselves."

The other man's lip curled to reveal a yellowed, gap-toothed mouth. "You won't live to regret that..." The man whipped a small blade from the pocket of his brown homespun coat and lunged for Sterling's gut, but Sterling was faster.

The doxy shrieked as Sterling side-stepped the clumsy blow, pushed the other man's arm down, and elbowed him in the side of the head. Angus bellowed a curse and stumbled, barely catching himself before he careened into a very questionable pile on the alley floor.

Spittle flying from his loose lips, Angus charged him again and again, the blade glinting in the dim light. Muscle memory from years of training and practice guided his movements. He hadn't been sent to the Continent until it was determined he could fend for himself in all manners of combat. Close-range was, by far, his preferred method. Far more skilled than this rough brute, Sterling could have disarmed him immediately, but he needed this. He needed the exertion. He needed the fight. He needed to sweat.

Most of all, he needed to punish someone who truly deserved it.

Realizing he wasn't going to win that way, Angus sought an easier target. His bloodshot eyes flicked over to the doxy, who'd made the mistake of sliding in the direction of the alley's mouth to attempt an escape.

Sterling swore under his breath as Angus charged her. A perfectly timed kick to the man's wrist sent the blade flying. Angus screamed, clutching his wrist to his chest, doubling over and giving Sterling the perfect angle to ram his knee into his snub nose. A spurt of crimson flew, preceding a garbled scream, and the man fell backward into a filthy puddle. He pressed the heel of his boot into the other man's doughy gut.

"Are we finished, Angus?" he asked condescendingly as he leaned over the man.

The man whipped another small blade from an inner pocket of his coat.

Apparently not.

In one fluid move, Sterling swiped the blade from the other man's meaty, bloody hand and rammed it through the fleshy part of his bicep. He gave it a little twist for good measure. Angus's scream echoed through the alley before it was swallowed up in the cacophony of London's nocturnal activities.

"Give me a reason to end it," Sterling snarled, overflowing with feral violence. "I just need a reason." He recognized in the curl of Angus's lip that the man was preparing to spit. Sterling deftly avoided the bloody spray by sliding the toe of his boot up and averting the man's face so it splattered ineffectually against the wall of the nearby building.

Sterling righted himself and found the doxy huddled against the wall, her arms over her head to shield her. He crouched down and held out his hand to the woman. She shied away, tears streaming down her face, and he noticed just how young she actually was. He would have been shocked to discover she was even as old as Alaina had been when they'd married. His chest clenched at the thought.

She flinched when he reached into his pocket, but her eyes perked at the glint of coins. "Have a meal and find a safe place to sleep tonight." Her eyes darted from his face to his offering only a second before she snatched them, muttered her gratitude, and fled. He hoped she'd do just that, but there was a good chance the coins would be spent on enough cheap gin that she wouldn't care where she slept.

Sterling cast a glance at the prone, bleeding, cursing man on the ground before he released a loud whistle through his teeth. Five men dashed forward toward Angus and Sterling slipped from the alley into the night.

He made it only a quarter of a block before a shadow peeled itself away from the darkness and matched his stride.

"Isn't this rather beneath you?" the shadow murmured drolly, its voice as silken and deadly low as if Satan, himself, had deigned to walk amongst the mortals.

"I count locking up a rapist and abuser in Newgate a worthy cause beneath no one," Sterling replied without turning his head. "Though London would likely have been better served if he'd been killed."

"You know what I mean." Sterling only grunted in response to that. "Imagine my surprise when I was informed you'd stopped by the offices requesting an assignment—any assignment as long as it was quick. The last time we spoke, you informed me in no uncertain terms that you were finally returning to your wife and that I should put my head in a rather creative place."

Sterling's fists clenched so tightly that his knuckles blanched. He didn't need a reminder of how hopeful, how pathetically optimistic he'd been when his years-long assignment had been completed. He'd naively believed there had been something to come home to.

But he saw now that the tabloids and the persona he'd been forced to adopt had deprived him of any chance at genuine reconciliation with Alaina. He'd spent years as an agent infiltrating foreign circles, and he'd put his life on the line for king and country for nearly a decade, but he understood now that none of it meant a damn if he couldn't have the one thing—the one woman—he desired above all else.

Especially not if she hated him because of it.

He learned too late that all the achievements and accolades meant nothing if she was not there to share his peace.

"Someone else could have handled it, you know," added Adrian Ramsay, Sterling's one-time boss, and leader of the secret spy society to which he'd once dedicated his life. The man was terrifying in every sense of the word. Bred and born to the underworld, he'd clawed his way out through sheer cunning and a penchant for violence to be drafted by an intelligence agency so secretive that it acted as its own entity and operated without any oversight outside of its self-contained hierarchy.

"They were dragging their feet," Sterling growled. "You shouldn't have left unseasoned agents to track down a man like this. He continued to hurt women while they spun in circles." Potential recruits to the society were often given lesser assignments to hone their skills; these tasks were ones Scotland Yard and the local police force were unable to resolve on their own for one reason or another. The file Sterling had procured focused on a slew of violent attacks on prostitutes. Those survivors who weren't downright hostile to police involvement described their attacker as rough, brown-haired, somewhat heavy-set with beady black eyes, and a reddish pear-shaped birthmark running from his left ear to curve under his non-existent jawline. The offender paid the women upfront for their services but quickly became enraged when all their…professional efforts produced no results from his limp and ineffectual body. He'd beaten them to within an inch of their life, done unspeakable things to their bodies, and then left them for dead after retrieving his money from their pockets.

The attacks had taken place over the past five weeks, but it had taken Sterling no more than an hour to map and triangulate the attacks, uncover a pattern, and narrow his options down to three public rooms where he believed he'd be most likely to find the villain. Sure enough, at the second, he'd spotted a hulking man bending an elbow at the far end of a poorly lit bar. Sterling supposed the atmosphere was for the best because he'd rather not have seen what caused the soles of his boots to stick to the floor.

Claiming a seat in the opposite corner, Sterling smoothly assumed a rough accent, ordered ale he had no intention of drinking, and ingratiated himself with a boisterous group of drunken men…one of whom he'd seen speaking with the suspect when he'd walked in.

Some time into a game of cards, Sterling had tipped his chin toward the man at the bar, feigning inebriation with a slight slur to his speech. "That man's name John?" *Always use a common name; it would either be correct or it would not draw attention to the inquiry.*

The grizzled, gray-haired man beside Sterling looked where he was gesturing and shook his head. "Nay," he hiccupped. "That be Angus Smith. Why? Ye lookin' fer a John?"

"Aye. A John that owes me coin for a job. Same build as that'un."

"Well I pity John," the man had chuckled drunkenly and clapped Sterling on the shoulder. "Ye got the Devil in yer eye."

That he did.

Shortly thereafter, Sterling watched from the corner of his eye as the man he now knew as Angus Smith snatched one of the milling doxies and hauled her into his lap. This particular establishment allowed prostitutes to procure business within its walls for a fee.

Sterling's keen eyes were just able to make out a port wine birthmark beneath the shadows of the man's patchy beard...and Sterling knew Angus was his man. He held himself still as Angus settled his tab and all but dragged the girl toward the exit.

Sterling counted to five before tossing a few coins on the table and excusing himself for a piss. Once outside, he doubled back to head Angus and the doxy off before they could reach the closest alleyway first, and...it did not end well for Mr. Smith.

"That is regrettable." Ramsay's voice was flat regarding his failed trainees. "And they'll be handled appropriately."

Sterling nodded. Not every man had the skills or training to become a member of Ramsay's spy society. It took considerable abilities to be considered, and even those select few would fail further testing. Whoever had been assigned to this case would be dropped from Ramsay's list of potentials, but they'd likely continue on with their lives and careers none the wiser that they'd once been in the running to be a part of the most exclusive, highly trained secret society beneath the Crown.

When he was younger, Sterling had liked to think he'd been selected because of his wit, knack for languages, and uncanny physical stamina. In truth, his title and innate charm had been the biggest draw. Few members of the spy society were peers, and none so high-ranked as he. A duke with blood as blue as Sterling's could enter even the most impenetrable social circles without suspicion.

"Am I to take tonight's adventure as a sign that you are ready to return to the fold? Is domestic life not suiting your tastes? Too tame?"

"No," snapped Sterling, finality deadening the single harsh word.

Ramsay's shrug was nonchalant.

"I will watch for any interesting developments I believe might suit you and keep you apprised."

"Don't bother. I'm finished with that."

"Ah, but we are not necessarily finished with a man of your talents. And tonight's performance indicates you may not be done either."

Sterling's jaw clenched; his fists itched to deal more blows. Ramsay was a master manipulator and the best interrogator the society had ever seen. He'd also been watching Sterling for more than a decade at that point; he was keenly familiar with Sterling's ingrained sense of duty to one's country. This was precisely how Sterling had become wrapped up in the society in the first place, and Ramsay knew tugging at that string would give him pause. What Ramsay didn't count on was the intensity of Sterling's desire to begin a life with Alaina—most likely because Ramsay did not possess a heart of his own. That argument had kept Sterling in the society far, far longer than his initial agreement had stipulated, but no more.

Hadn't he given enough of himself already? Hadn't he sacrificed enough?

"Sod off."

Ramsay's chuckle was cool and mirthless. "I'll be in touch."

The footsteps beside Sterling stopped, and he needn't look around to confirm his former boss was nowhere to be found, vaporized into the nighttime fog like the specter he was.

Chapter Eleven

ALAINA MANAGED TO avoid her husband for the remainder of that day, leaving her to spend several hours making her planned calls without hindrance, take the rest of her meals in peace, and see to the tasks she needed to accomplish without further intrusion. As she helped Alaina fix the damage the damp wind had done to her hair, Penny had offhandedly mentioned that the duke had gone out to see to some business. Alaina couldn't have cared less where he went…as long as he stayed out of her way. Her mind and her heart could not handle Sterling's polarizing effect. One minute, she wished he'd never stop kissing and touching her, the next, her heart cracked all over again when she thought about all the ways he'd betrayed their marriage. Space was good; space could allow her to breathe and sort through the emotions he unleashed within her. She had plenty of other things requiring her attention.

Her Reading Society gathered the following afternoon in the blue drawing room at Morton House once more. Ladies were scattered about, sharing sofas and perched upon dainty chairs, flounced down on ottomans. Tea and delicate iced cakes had been laid out beside a selection of buttery shortbread and gingersnaps. The room was filled with the pleasant clink of china, bubbly laughter, and excited conversation. Alaina surveyed the group with a sense of comfort. These were her people. Unlike her husband, they didn't make her uneasy or set her world on its ear. She prided herself on the fact that she'd cultivated an environment where these women could be comfortable and that they all trusted one another. There was no artifice or peacocking here, only genuine companionship and striving toward common goals. Not only were they friends who shared an enjoyment of literature, but they pooled their resources together and championed worthy causes. Over time, they'd discovered that they might be ineffective separately, but, together, they could be a force for good. And Alaina would do everything in her power to guard this sanctuary.

After it was clear that most women had caught up with one another and enjoyed their refreshments, Alaina stood and called their meeting to order. The women quickly settled in and expectantly held their manuscripts in their laps. Some were marked with thin strips of colorful ribbons; others had folded corners of the parchment over to save their places. Each face looked to her with eager anticipation.

The discussion began.

As she'd anticipated, several of the first women to speak admitted to their skepticism as to the play's true nature.

"A man essentially breaking a woman like a horse and creating a biddable wife is not normally within our purview," said Mrs. Stratford, the actress's daughter. "I don't quite see how it fits the spirit of this Society," she added not unkindly. Several heads bobbed in agreement.

"I'm having trouble understanding how Kate began so strong only to be cowed into becoming the woman Petruchio wanted her to be," admitted Miss Jocelyn Finchley—a quiet young woman who usually remained on the outskirts of their conversations.

"Shouldn't we be reading something more, I don't know, empowering?" chimed in Lady Sommerfeld with a little Gallic lift of one shoulder.

"You didn't see it as empowering?" Alaina asked, affecting a tone of deep concern. It was everything she could do not to smile when she met Juliette's eye. Her friend had been integral in choosing the piece and working with Alaina to craft this plan. "How did you view Kate?" she asked the assembly.

"Tamed," said one voice.

"Browbeaten," chimed in another.

"Forced to fulfill a role she didn't want by a society that viewed her only as a pawn," said Miss Finchley. Several wide eyes swiveled to the young lady. This seemed to strike a nerve as several more members spoke up in agreement.

Alaina waited patiently for the murmurs and side conversations to die down before she spoke again. "I interpreted Kate as supremely powerful and infinitely more cunning than Petruchio." Several women sat back in disbelief. "I am a firm believer that Mr. Shakespeare was crafting one of the first truly powerful female leads of the stage when he wrote Kate. Here, allow me to demonstrate…"

STERLING WAS SEATED at the desk in his study, innocently reading through some correspondence, when the most unholy shrieking reached his ears.

Body still tainted with wisps of the bloodlust unleashed the night before, he was quicker to act than he was to think.

Alaina was in trouble, and blood would spill.

Heart pounding, he threw down his papers and sprang from the chair fast enough to send it banging to the floor. He sped out into the hall just as another screech shattered the peace of the house. Sprinting toward the sound, his mind frantically raced with possibilities, his muscles tensing for battle, as he burst through the door to the blue drawing room near the front of the house.

And into a space brimming with Society women.

Some were standing, others were sitting, but all of them had the same manuscript open in their hands or draped across their laps. And, to a one, they stared at him with the same astonished expression.

In the center of it all was his wife.

Alaina smiled sweetly at his harried, hurried appearance. She cared not one whit that his heart was beating out of his chest, that he'd feared her in mortal danger and desired nothing more than to charge headlong into the fray to give his life for hers.

That should have been Sterling's first clue that this situation did not bode well for him.

"Hello, Morton," Alaina greeted him in an unfamiliar chirping tone. "Your timing is impeccable as we find ourselves in need of a convincing Petruchio."

He released his body's tension in a low, deep exhalation and straightened his posture. A couple of women tittered from behind their papers. It was now the second time he'd barged in on one of these meetings and he'd certainly made enough of a memorable impression at this point. He had to save face however he could if he was to retain any dignity.

Alaina accepted the manuscript offered to her by a fair, raven-haired woman before crossing the room and holding it out to him. It had already been marked to a specific page with a strip of ivory cloth.

His second clue, that minx. She had prepared for him—this was no whim.

He held up his hands in defense. "I fear I am no actor. There must certainly be a better option here among these lovely ladies." He finished off with a flash of his most charming smile. The determined gleam in Alaina's sapphire eyes was unnerving in its intensity.

"Please, Your Grace," said the raven-haired woman. "You couldn't possibly be a more miserable Petruchio than I."

"Truly," piped in the stunning red-haired woman beside her. As the only woman in attendance with such a shocking shade of hair, Sterling assumed she must be Sommerfeld's wife. "Nothing can be worse than Lady Juliette."

"I beg your pardon?" the woman Sterling now knew to be his wife's other close friend exclaimed with mock indignation.

"Are you familiar with *The Taming of the Shrew*?" Alaina asked, cutting off the banter between the other women. More than a dozen pairs of expectant eyes awaited his answer.

"I have seen it performed once," Sterling admitted as he accepted the manuscript from his wife.

"Good." She flashed him a smile that made his knees feel slightly weak. How long had he waited to have her look at him like that again? Faced with it, his brain went slightly mushy, and he'd later blame that for his caving into her request. "We're going to try the scene where Kate and Petruchio first meet."

Despite his reservations, Sterling quickly found himself enthralled with his wife and her passionate rendition. He was in awe of the way her eyes flashed and how her color rose to wash out her delicate freckles. She practically danced around him, prowling like a lioness as she spoke. The rest of the room fell away, and he forgot all about their audience of interested guests. He struggled to reconcile this intoxicating woman with the prim and proper rose he'd wed, but that wasn't necessarily a bad thing. She may have been acting—performing words written centuries prior— but there was no mistaking the spark was all hers...and it was arousing beyond measure.

At the scene's conclusion, the room materialized around them once more as the ladies erupted into enthusiastic applause. Alaina broke character and turned away from him, back to their guests.

"Now," she addressed her Reading Society; "let us compare that to Kate's behavior in the final scene of the play." She motioned for Sterling to flip through the pages of his manuscript and locate the other marked section. Meanwhile, she rapidly assigned a few roles to some of the other ladies. He skimmed the scene to refresh his memory, and a part of him wondered how well Alaina would play the part of obedient wife. He tried not to smile at the image. Perhaps he'd give her another kiss as a reward.

The scene began with other voices chiming in; their tones ranged from confident and loud, to peppered with nervous laughter and self-conscious glances in his direction. One girl who was so shy her voice could barely be heard from where he stood. Her cheeks flushed when Sterling gave her what he hoped was a non-threatening, reassuring smile. He noticed Alaina nodding her head encouragingly to the young woman as well.

Finally, "Kate" returned to the scene…and Sterling was taken aback by Alaina's performance.

Her haughty look and defiant stance starkly belied her words. Her flashing blue eyes never left his.

Clue three: She'd learned her part well enough to set aside her manuscript entirely.

He all but stammered his way through the lines, so set back on his heels that he was unable to match his wife's defiant fire.

Sterling felt the sudden snap of the trap as the scene concluded, and Petruchio—*he*—was summarily chastened. The quirk of one of her well-shaped brows underscored her point, and she turned back to her congregation.

"Do you see how Kate manipulated the situation, as well as Petruchio? And how Petruchio is foolish and gullible enough to believe he could quash Kate? He believes in his innate superiority as the surety of his success—not to mention that it excuses his *childish* behavior."

All at once, Sterling realized just why she'd drawn him into this situation… Alaina wanted to teach him a lesson. She wanted to shame him. Publicly.

His fists clenched suddenly and violently, crumpling the manuscript in his grip as his wife continued to speak. She was so obviously pleased with herself, and making a spectacle of their marriage in front of her friends was her modicum of revenge upon him.

A grudging part of him admired her creativity—he'd clearly underestimated her torture tactics—and her keen understanding and analysis of the text.

The other part of him (the ducal part) didn't appreciate the undermining behavior.

Not one bit.

"Leave us," he barked to the room, interrupting Alaina's oration.

She frowned and turned back to him. "I hardly think it is polite to demand our guests leave. Again. What about—"

"Manners be damned," he snapped, cutting her off once more. Several of the women gave little jumps. He'd likely be on an apology tour the next day for this, but he cared less than the weight of a feather about it at that moment. He needed to get Alaina alone. "Out." The last word was uttered in such a low, dangerous tone that there wasn't a moment's hesitation before the women gathered their things and all but fled. They rushed past Sterling without making eye contact and Alaina followed their progress until she met him near the drawing room door. Neither said a word until the last woman had gathered her pelisse and rushed from Morton House.

Alaina scowled and opened her mouth—no doubt to utter a scathing set down—but Sterling immediately pressed her bodily against the door frame, every inch of him meeting her unapologetically. His mouth found hers and kissed her deeply, possessively. His tongue forced its way past her lips, stroking her mouth and tangling with hers. He lapped up her squeak of indignant surprise and swallowed it whole like a draught, struggling not to smile when he felt her falter. At first, she stiffened against him and fisted her hands in the sleeves of his coat, but she did not shove him away this time. Whether shock or desire held her in place, it mattered not to Sterling. He could only think about this moment, tasting her, feeling her, devouring her fire, breathing her in to keep her with him forever.

He wanted to grind his pelvis into hers until she was as weak-kneed with raging desire as he. He longed to strip the layers from between them—the tangible and the imagined—until they both were laid bare. No secrets. No clothing. Just this clash of passion that made them both gasp and ache and, at long last, scream in relief.

She spun him to distraction, and he needed her with everything inside of him. Alaina drove him mad with her words, but even more so with the heat she drew from his loins. His every nerve roared to possess her wholly, body, soul, and even indomitable spirit. It would be a challenge to even attempt to harness this wild woman of his, but Sterling was up to the task.

He hadn't fought tooth and nail for the last eight years to not finally, truthfully, be able to call her his.

He ripped his lips from hers, his chest heaving with a myriad of emotions. "Do you realize how maddening it is to not know whether I'd prefer to punish you or fuck you senseless? You infuriate me beyond measure; you enthrall me beyond reason. You are Kate incarnate, my little hellion, and I cannot stop thinking about you," he growled as if the admission were painful. "You make me want to throttle you as much as you make me want to take you to my bed and make love to you until we're both too spent to move." He found the catch in her breathing to be unbelievably erotic. His eyes flew unbidden to the rise and fall of her swelling décolletage.

And then she tensed against him.

"I—I cannot," Alaina eked out. "I am not a woman who will turn a blind eye to her husband's countless indiscretions."

It was in that instant that Sterling knew their life would go nowhere with only secrets and half-truths between them. The time had come for him to decide between his duty and his marriage, and he knew what he must do.

He gentled his hold on her, sliding his hands up her sides and gently cupping her face between his palms. He needed her to hear him.

His very life depended upon her believing him.

"There never was anyone else," he whispered.

She tried to shake her head against his hands. "Impossible."

"But it is the truth," he insisted, hoping the gentleness of his tone would find her where volume hadn't.

"You expect me to believe that a man like you has…remained celibate for eight years."

"I expect you to believe it because it is the truth."

"But how?"

He couldn't help but release a helpless half-hearted chuckle. "Regardless of what you may think, I do have some self-control. I don't need to mount everything in a skirt."

"But everyone said—"

"I don't give a single damn what the *ton* and their rumors say…and you shouldn't either, Alaina. I am telling you the truth," he reiterated. "I remained true to you and our marriage despite what you may have believed or been told. Even if you haven't done the same, I cannot blame you…" The last slipped past his lips without thinking.

Sterling had heard his share of rumors while he'd been abroad. They had been how he'd learned about Alaina's Reading Society and the stir it was creating. Much as it pained him, he'd also heard about Alaina's retinue of admirers eager to take his place in Alaina's life and her bed. How could he blame her for accepting any one of them when he knew she'd believed he wanted no part of their marriage—that he'd done ten times worse?

The truth was, nearly a decade earlier, he'd been looking forward to marrying and getting to know his pretty, witty young wife; of starting a family with her.

But everything had happened so fast.

He'd graduated from university, mourned the loss of his parents, come into his majority, and taken on the full responsibilities of his title so quickly. He'd met Alaina and fallen for her. He'd never counted on being sent to the Continent with clear instructions for dangerous espionage and what would turn out to be a nebulous return date. Despite the crass recommendation from his superiors in the ranks of the Spy Society, he hadn't been able to bring himself to risk impregnating Alaina on their wedding night and then leaving—not when he didn't know when or if he'd be returning. He had been a selfish bastard to marry her even knowing he would have to abandon her, but he hadn't been able to stomach the thought of her with anyone else. The excuse was shaky at best, but in his youthful ignorance, he'd told himself it would all work out for the best for both of them in the end. However, the threads of regret that would come to color his life began to form the moment he decided to propose and marry Alaina despite his orders to travel to the Continent, though the deepest part of him had always taken comfort in knowing she awaited his return. That, of course, did not absolve him of his actions, but it was the truth. He'd been young, headstrong, brimming with unearned confidence, and ready to face the world; it would torture him to the end of his days how that had so negatively impacted Alaina's life.

Many lonely nights of travel and soul-searching over the years afforded him sufficient time to stew in this regret, eventually coming to terms with the very real possibility that his actions may have driven his wife to seek solace elsewhere. He'd also had enough time to realize it would be unfair of him to expect his wife to take on the same celibacy he had…not when she didn't know the truth: he'd been faithful to their vows.

Alaina flushed at his words.

Was she embarrassed about discussing her lovers? Or that he had admitted that he knew the probability of her having sought comfort in the arms of another?

A surge of jealousy crashed over him, but he clenched his jaw against it.

"I forgive you," he said as softly as he was able, though the words were like razors in his throat. He had expected her to understand his absence with no explanation; likewise, he needed to accept that his wife may have taken certain opportunities out of spite or loneliness or desire. "I—" He was cut off when Alaina wrapped her hands around his wrists and shook her head more forcefully.

"There has been no one else," she whispered.

Sterling's heart stuttered in his chest. He could hardly believe her words. "What?"

"There has been no one else," Alaina repeated meekly, a blush deepening along her elegant cheekbones.

"Why?" It was an inane question, but he had to know. Could he dare to hope that she'd longed to turn back the clock and had held onto their marriage as he had? He tried to ignore the elation in his chest, but it was nearly impossible.

"When you left a girl of eighteen on her wedding night, you left her feeling like the only possibility was that her husband found her to be the least desirable woman in the world." She averted her eyes in mortification as she spoke the most brutally, painfully honest words Sterling had ever heard. "Why else wouldn't you have come to my bed? For that matter, what other man would have wanted me if my own husband did not?"

Sterling cursed beneath his breath, damning himself and the damage he'd wrought. "I've always found you desirable," he swore. "Inexplicably, even more so when your eyes spark and you spit your eloquently venomous darts." He was heartened by the flicker of a smile on her lips. "I happen to find you beautiful and infinitely attractive." That smile disappeared and her eyes searched his. He knew she still didn't believe him, so he set about remedying that. "I find your strength and wit attractive and your body…" He inhaled deeply. "Your body is enough to drive me mad." Her eyes widened and he could tell she was listening intently. "A weaker man would have walked away from the hell you put me through, but I know—I have always known—you to be worth any battle. Continue your plotting. Throw your barbs. Plan other ways to embarrass me before a crowd. I will be here. I will always be here, Alaina. There is very little you can say or do that would make me do otherwise."

Her lips parted as if she wished to contradict him, but no sound came.

Instead, Sterling claimed her mouth again.

Wrecked her.

Slid his hands down to cup and knead the taut, round globes of her bottom as he insinuated one hard thigh between her legs to press against her mound, reveling in the mingling heat of their bodies.

Let her feel how hard he was for her despite her needling; despite her careful plan to humiliate him.

He needed her to know that he would never stop aching for her; that every nerve in his body screamed for her when she was near, when he so much as caught a whiff of her scent.

"Whatever you do, I'll not back down. I want you. I need you," he growled against her neck, savoring how she shifted against his thigh to alleviate the ache he'd ignited within her. She glared like an ice queen, but she was all fire beneath the surface, just like he knew she would be. Likewise, she set him aflame, and together, they would be consumed by it…if she could relinquish some of the animosity she was so determined to harbor toward him. If they could lay down their weapons long enough to allow this connection to take root, then Sterling was confident they would be the excellent match he'd always known they could be.

"Hold me at arm's length, push me away, do nothing but scowl at me, but I am not leaving you. Ever. Again. And I strongly suggest you warm to the idea of sharing this space with me because I want only you." He used his hands on her rear to rock her lower body against his for good measure. "Only you."

Alaina emitted a shuddering breath as he nipped the delicate line of her bare collarbone. Chills danced across his flesh when her hands ran up his arms and clasped the back of his neck. He wished she'd tangle her fingers there, tug at it, use it as a handle to push him to his knees so he could lift her skirts and taste her most secret of places and service her until she was wracked with pleasure.

"As disastrous as my prior attempts have been," he continued; "know that I will wear down your resistance. I'm determined to share our life and begin it in earnest. I'll wait another eight years if that's what it takes, but I won't stop until you believe in my devotion and accept that I do, indeed, find you to be the most arousing woman I've ever met. And, no matter what you throw at me, I will continue to wait for you. I lie awake each night thinking of all the things I could do to you, of all the things I could make you feel… All you need to do is ask, and I will gladly oblige."

She whimpered and clutched him more tightly. Unable to resist, Sterling kissed Alaina's parted lips soundly before suddenly releasing her, somewhat thrilled to note that she had to grip the doorframe behind her to remain steady and standing. His every nerve screaming in protest, he took his leave before his wife could find her voice…before he could go back on his word and lay her down on the carpet and lift her skirts right there.

He needed to cool his blood, but all he wanted to do was wrap his fist around his cock and pump it until he was spent—no matter how unsatisfying it would be. Nothing short of having Alaina could ever be enough for him, and he would not rest until he'd finally accomplished his aim.

OH MY…

That had backfired spectacularly.

Alaina replayed her conversation with Sterling again and again in rapid succession as she remained frozen in the doorway of the drawing room on her jelly-like legs. Even recalling the intensity in his eyes released another pool of heat between her legs where she ached and throbbed, her body begging for relief she could not name.

Alaina felt chilly and bereft when Sterling had retreated. Every part of her trembled, but not from fear.

But from what?

Desire?

She had to wrap her fingers in her skirts to prevent their shaking.

If she hadn't known better, she might have believed Sterling to be sincere.

But…a man couldn't remain celibate for that long, could he?

Certainly not from what little her mother had told her on her wedding night all those years ago. She'd informed Alaina that a man's baser urges regularly overtook him, and, when that happened, he could act without thinking, his only aim to satisfy those needs. It was to be Alaina's responsibility as the duke's wife to lie back and allow him that relief.

Still…

Her husband had been home for several weeks at that point and not once had he forced her into his bed. They'd kissed, but he'd shown more control and restraint than she'd been led to believe the male sex possessed. And she found herself wondering what would happen when that control finally snapped.

It was surprising to her when she experienced a great deal more breathless excitement over that notion than fear or apprehension. Her traitorous body craved in the most primal of ways what he had offered to her, and she feared her resolve was weakening. Not only did his body call to her, but the strength of his determination in the face of her defiance was unexpectedly magnetic.

Alaina didn't know how much longer she could deny how breathless her husband made her. His strength, his power, his words all worked together to chip away at the armor she'd forged and fortified. Soon, she would be laid bare and raw.

She only hoped she'd survive it.

THE FIRST ROSY tendrils of dawn were edging into the sky when Sterling finally gave up trying to sleep. He had been restless and wound as taut as a clock's cogs ever since he'd left Alaina standing glassy-eyed in the drawing room.

How was a man expected to maintain his sanity when a woman such as she resided on the other side of an unlocked door?

She was within his reach, and—no matter how much his body begged for it—he refused to act upon his desire to break down that flimsy barrier to claim her delicious lips again, to finally explore her glorious body. Instead, he suffered in solitary silence.

He held his breath to listen to the tone and cadence of her voice as she spoke to her maid. He focused on the sounds of her undressing and then re-dressing for bed, the slight creak of ropes as she settled herself in bed. Watched the death of the slim strip of golden light at the door's seam when she extinguished the candle for sleep.

Hours of tossing and turning rewarded him with nothing but a crick in his shoulder and an ache in his skull. He was painfully aroused—had been since the moment he heard Alaina enter her bedchamber and knew she was about to undress. What he wouldn't have given just to watch. The speed with which he vacillated from frustration with her to wanting her so badly that nothing else would suffice was mind-boggling.

And now, his powerful cockstand was creating a tent with the bedding, mocking him for being a coward.

He should have taken what he wanted by now…but he knew he couldn't. He wouldn't. He wasn't a man to do something like that to any woman—let alone his wife. And, if he wanted any chance at a future with Alaina, then there could be no further mistakes moving forward. He knew in his soul that she'd cared for him and desired him when they were younger, and he was now convinced that the ticket to their future lay in capitalizing on those feelings. He could taste on her tongue how badly she wished to give in. She'd once welcomed his chaste touches and tame kisses; no matter how she tried to fight it, her responsiveness made it clear to him that she enjoyed this more mature attraction between them. Whatever she threw at him, he'd continue his mission to woo his wife undeterred. He tried not to consider how long that might take.

Instead, Sterling slid his hand down his abdomen, wrapping his fingers around the thick length of his member. His breath hissed through his teeth and his eyes slid closed at the contact. A testing pump made his hips jerk with need. He couldn't remember the last time he'd had a release, and the swirling ache in his balls was a painful reminder.

Immediately, his mind conjured an image of Alaina as she'd been when she read her lines before the Reading Society, glorious and brilliant…and all his. He could still feel her fingers clutching at him while he plundered her mouth and now imagined them on his cock instead of his own. Would she be cautious and delicate or confident? Deciding on the latter, his fantasy began to gain speed.

Changing his grip, Sterling ran his palm up and down the sensitive shaft, rubbing his thumb along the slit in the head and dragging down the beads of moisture already accumulating there, wishing it was Alaina's mouth or her cunny making him slick instead. God, if she would part those plump raspberry-red lips for him, he might just expire right then and there. What wouldn't he give to have her whip-sharp tongue licking him from root to tip? Nothing. He'd give everything to have it.

Sterling's strokes increased in speed and strength, chest heaving, his breath catching on gasps and curses.

He wanted to pound into her from every position imaginable and create a few fantasies of their own. He wanted to hear her scream his name and sob from pleasure. He wanted to spill deep inside of her, to fill her womb with his seed. He wanted her. He wanted Alaina.

One. Two. Three more hard pumps and Sterling lost control. The tingling in the base of his spine snapped and his body clenched, releasing his pleasure in wave after wave of ecstasy as he spilled himself in a white-hot orgasm that left him weak and practically blind with relief.

Floating down from his release, Sterling was overcome by a rush of disappointment because, of course, there was no Alaina beside him. She wasn't smiling up at him in unabashed enjoyment of the pleasure only she could give to him.

He was alone in his oversized bed, his spend growing cold on his stomach.

How long could he go on like this...pining after a woman who was *his wife* and slept not fifteen feet away?

Chapter Twelve

S TERLING PICKED AT his usual early breakfast in the morning room, lost in his musings over the previous day's interactions with his wife. Perhaps he'd said too much.

No.

He *knew* he'd said too much. And, yet, he couldn't relinquish the vision of her face held between his hands, the skin of her cheeks impossibly soft and her golden hair softer than silk against his fingertips. How he could have sunk into her eyes and gotten lost forever.

He didn't know what he'd expected, but he hadn't seen her again after he'd escaped from the drawing room, his sanity barely intact. When she didn't join him for supper, he was informed by a footman that Her Grace had requested a plate be sent to her rooms that evening. No further explanation had been offered.

Following the evening of silence, it had taken every ounce of willpower not to open their adjoining bedchamber door that morning and speak to her. See her. He heard not a sound from the other side of that door as his valet helped him dress. He heard not so much as a sigh as he stood within an inch of the barrier, holding his breath and willing Alaina to hear him and invite him in so they might speak. Every last one of his nerves screamed for him to lift his hand and turn the knob. It was agony to have admitted what he had, to have made such confessions and declarations, and not be at all certain how she felt about it. Still, Sterling was determined to stay true to his word and give her time. He refused to believe the Alaina he'd married wasn't buried somewhere within this woman, and that his diligent efforts wouldn't pay off. He'd seen the spark in her eyes, heard the catch in her breath. His nearness had moved her, and he dared to hope that maybe some of his words had seeped through her defenses.

He was lost in such thoughts and pouring himself another cup of strong, dark coffee when his ears caught an almost inaudible sound from the doorway near his left shoulder. The whisper-light scuff of a shoe on the marble floor.

Slowly, he wrapped his fingers around the handle of the heavy silver knife beside his plate, careful to keep the rest of his body immobile to mask any hint that he'd heard something.

He tensed from his neck to his feet, each of his muscles acting solely on memory.

And Alaina slid into the room, garbed in a cerulean morning gown cut to accentuate her trim frame and bosom to perfection. She wore her golden hair pulled back into a neat, simple chignon and tied with a matching ribbon. Sweet. Enticingly, deceptively demure.

The sight made his breeches far too tight for comfort.

Sterling's throat went dry.

When his mind worked again, he wondered how lost he must have gotten within his own mind. It was rare that he was still at the table by the time Alaina rose and descended the stairs to break her fast.

He quickly rose and smoothly replaced the knife beside his plate, hoping she wouldn't notice.

A footman pulled out her chair and she joined him at the table.

Her plate was filled, and her tea was poured while Sterling tried to gauge which approach would be best. She had yet to meet his eyes, so it was difficult for him to read any of her thoughts or emotions. Then, she saved him from having to guess when she spoke without looking up from stirring her tea.

"I have accepted an invitation to the Finchley ball this coming Friday."

Sterling was so taken aback by her revelation that he had to pause for several long seconds before formulating a response. "Wonderful." He could have kicked himself for the blandness of his response, but it pleased him beyond reason that it seemed to satisfy her, regardless. Alaina inclined her head and began preparing her toast.

Perhaps this was a peace offering in place of an outright acceptance of his apologies and explanations. It would do. He could work with this. This gave him *hope*.

The meal continued in the most companionable silence the Morton House had seen since Sterling's return.

ALAINA BARELY RESISTED pinching herself the evening of the Finchley soiree. Removed from the battleground of Morton House, she and Sterling both seemed to fall into natural public roles. Much to her surprise, there was a comfortability between them that went above and beyond social niceties. Sterling did more than simply escort her; he smoothly guided her with a proprietary hand on her back. He inclined his head in her direction when she spoke. He smiled and spoke at all the right times, seeming genuinely interested in all she said and did. He was nothing short of an attentive husband. In all, that evening's outing—technically their first function as a married couple—was going even better than she'd ever imagined it might. It was certainly the last thing she'd expected following their volatile interaction in the drawing room.

Her mind had been nothing short of scrambled after Sterling's kisses, his touches…his words. She'd anticipated tenacity, but this went beyond that.

I lie awake each night thinking of all the things I could do to you, of all the things I could make you feel…

It had been her turn to toss and turn that night, her imagination running rampant but continually encountering holes in both her knowledge and her imagination. Not for the first time, she felt like the least-educated married woman in the world.

What could he make her feel?

Even days later, the words caused her cheeks to burn, caused her thighs to squeeze together to staunch the liquid ache that was growing more and more difficult to ignore. She squirmed and rolled in her bed, unable to find relief even in sleep; her dreams were filled with Sterling's determined voice, his forceful touch, his admission that all the rumors had been lies and he'd never slept with another woman. The admission that all the rumors had been false and he'd never desired anyone else…that he'd wanted only Alaina all this time was heady, indeed. Her initial reaction had been disbelief, but there had been something in his eyes that brought her back to their courtship—an honest vulnerability she hadn't expected. And she'd believed him.

It left her shaking in both body and soul; he set everything she'd believed on its ear and she was left confused and unsure how to proceed, uneasy about everything that had transpired between them, and on her back foot when it came to how she might handle future interactions with her husband. Since returning home, he'd been nothing she thought he might be, and she wasn't quite sure how she felt about that. Of course, his touch was tantalizing, his kisses were drugging, and his words excited her, but could she set aside the animosity she'd held so closely for so long?

Many hours of deliberation and one very long, very blunt conversation with Juliette eventually led her to the decision to accept the invitation to Mr. and Mrs. Finchley's ball that week. Her friend's words had spun round and round in her brain as she'd prepared for the evening's event. Having been present at the last Society meeting, Juliette had witnessed firsthand Sterling's rage and, what she described, as his poorly-masked yearning for his wife.

"You do know how badly he wants you, do you not?" Juliette had asked with an arched brow as if it were entirely obvious to everyone except Alaina.

"Physical desire is something men cannot help," Alaina had

replied, parroting something her mother had once told her.

"This is different," Juliette had insisted with a vehement shake of her head. "You were too busy with your lines to see the way he watched you."

"Because he wished to throttle me," Alaina snorted.

"But has he ever laid a hand upon you?"

"Well. No." He'd done a lot of things to her after the women had left, but laying a violent hand upon her hadn't been one of them. As a matter of fact, she'd never once feared for her physical wellbeing with him. It was more than many women could say of their husbands—especially after intentionally (and repeatedly) antagonizing them.

"Then I ask you to trust me that that man wants nothing more than to hold you. You may strum his every nerve, but he can't help but need you. For all his faults, I firmly believe he would do anything for you. We all agree."

Juliette's words had made Alaina's pulse quicken. "So now you are all having meetings without me to discuss the state of my marriage. Some friends you are…"

Juliette had taken her hand in her own and squeezed it. "Do not be cross with us; we are simply trying to look out for you. And we all feel as if this marriage may just be salvageable. I, for one, am brave enough to overstep and ask that you consider giving your situation a real chance. You *are* already married. You've given him many an opportunity to quit since his return from the Continent—and I am guilty of helping to facilitate—but the duke has weathered them all. Why not make a proper go of it?"

Sterling had made it crystal clear to her that he would not be scared off. She'd unveiled her plan to cow him, but it had only ended with her weak in his arms, breathless as he kissed her and admitted to the most wicked desires. And, if he wouldn't leave, they would need a way to coexist. She supposed, either way, this ball would be a turning point for them. They'd either go down in glorious flames in a public fashion, or…

The "or" terrified Alaina.

Before leaving Morton House, Alaina had felt foolish when her hands trembled at the sound of a single knock on the main door of her bedchamber. Her nerves had flooded her from the top of her head to the tips of her toes in alternating waves of ice and fire. She'd made one last perusal in her full-length looking glass, examining the daring neckline of her gold-and-ivory gown, the gauze-like overlay, and the subtle, brilliant glitter of metallic threads. She'd straightened her matching elbow-length ivory gloves with their little pearl buttons at her wrists, adjusted the dangle of her diamond-and-pearl earrings as well as the matching pendant at her throat, and exhaled slowly before bidding the knocker to enter.

Just as she'd suspected, Sterling had been on the other side. He was nothing short of breathtaking in his impeccably tailored black formalwear and intricate white cravat with its diamond stickpin. The healthy color of his face stood in attractive contrast to the stark purity of the fabric at his throat, but it seemed to make his hazel eyes all the more striking and captivating. His chestnut hair had been combed back from his face with a bit of pomade, making him even more devastatingly handsome.

Setting aside all of the years of pain and loneliness, Alaina couldn't believe he was hers. She was a girl again. The confident duchess was reduced to nothing more than a young woman forced to rethink everything she thought she knew about him.

Her uncertainty fled, however, when Sterling's own insecurities about his reception by her became apparent. His shy smile had been almost boyish, reminding her every bit of the young man who'd courted her. While he'd always been confident in himself as only young men born to hold a lofty title can be, even eight years later, he was still learning his place with her, desperately wanting to make the best impression.

It made her stomach flip with just how endearing it was. Her heart thawed a considerable amount more when he spoke.

"You look...my...I mean..." He'd heaved a sigh and wound

up settling for, "You are beautiful, Alaina." The sound of her name on his tongue was nothing short of delicious. Her lips had parted in surprise when he'd entered the room and quickly took her gloved hand in his. He brought it to his lips to press a long, lingering, searing kiss there, his eyes never leaving hers. She'd momentarily forgotten how to breathe and had to mentally shake herself to regain her composure.

She needed to remember that just because she'd made this concession to attend a social event with him, that didn't mean she'd forgiven him entirely. It wasn't an open invitation to allow him back into her life.

Alaina did her best to remain cool and aloof—to treat this like just another evening out—but it was proving to be a nearly impossible task. How could she, when he overwhelmed her senses with his nearness? She felt a shock each time he touched her. His clean scent intoxicated her like fine spirits. His voice was low and intimate, caressing nerves she hadn't known she possessed.

Sterling was steadfastly charming and regal all evening. As strange as it initially felt to her to arrive on his arm, all Alaina's nerves eventually melted away, and she found it rather enjoyable. It helped that he was consistently attentive and warm in every interaction with her.

And, when they danced, it was like falling into a familiar pattern. Held there in the strong circle of his arms, she remembered what a brilliant dancer she'd found him to be back when he'd courted her. Few things had been more thrilling to eighteen-year-old Alaina than twirling around the floor for all to see as she was held securely by the most eligible young man the *ton* had seen in decades. It was oddly reassuring that her memories weren't entirely blinded by girlish infatuation. The man moved with grace and confidence, imbibing her with the same.

As he guided her through the steps of a waltz—their second dance of the evening—Alaina was flooded with memories she'd buried long ago as a way to protect her wounded heart...and all of it helped her remember why she'd accepted Sterling's offer of marriage in the first place.

He was blindingly handsome, he had a lively sense of humor, and he was thoughtful. He was also intriguingly complex, seemingly two men in one—one with her and one with the outside world. He could lean in close to whisper an amusing observation that nearly set her to giggling like a girl one minute, then someone would approach them, and he'd slide a mask over his face, stepping easily into the role of one of the most powerful and influential men of the realm. It was fascinating to watch. To the world, he was the Duke of Morton; to her, he was Sterling. It mattered not that she had yet to take him up on his request to use his given name, she'd addressed him informally in her head for a long while. Now, however, she was presented with the man in the flesh and not some abstract idea to which she'd applied all her frustrations and pain.

Despite her best efforts, Alaina experienced a thrill whenever he took her hand and threaded her arm through his, demonstrating his earnest, gentle possessiveness whenever another man spoke to her or asked her to dance. More than once, she caught him watching her with such intensity that it made her shiver. It served to stir up those confusing, exciting flutters in the pit of her stomach, making her knees weaken and a rush of unexpected dampness between her thighs. When he looked at her like that, she could almost believe what he'd said the day before...he certainly looked as if he was starving and only she could slake his hunger.

How many years had she dreamt of being on Sterling's arm, cutting a swath through Society and sparking envy throughout the *ton?*

How many nights had she woken alone in the dark, tears clogging her throat even before she was fully awake because she knew such dreams were futile?

Now that he'd told her he'd never been unfaithful and even gone so far as to offer her forgiveness if she couldn't say the same, could she set aside her years of pain and anger to take the offer of peace Sterling offered? To possibly have a future with him?

"Lady Morton!"

Alaina turned from where she stood with a group of other society matrons to find Miss Jocelyn Finchley, the daughter of their hosts, approaching quickly. Her friend's presence was one of the reasons Alaina had chosen to accept the invitation. If things had gone poorly, then she wanted to be sure she'd have at least one person on her side. They squeezed one another's hands in a warm greeting. Miss Finchley's warm chocolate eyes practically danced with excitement.

"Mother was quite overtaken with joy when you indicated the duke would be coming as well. I tried to temper her anticipation without giving away what happened at the last meeting, but the fact that you both came and chose her ball as your first event together nearly required smelling salts!"

Alaina couldn't help but smile. Mrs. Finchley was known for her dramatic behaviors (so in contrast to her daughter's reserved nature) but Alaina didn't doubt her friend's report. She risked a glance over her shoulder and found Sterling watching her over the crowd. Again.

"So happy to be of service," Alaina replied.

"I must admit that I was rather shocked when she said she'd received your reply, especially after what happened." The last was said in a concerned whisper.

Alaina couldn't blame Miss Finchley for angling for more information—Alaina would likely have done the same thing were the roles reversed. The last time Miss Finchley had seen Sterling, he'd commanded all the Reading Society guests to vacate his home post-haste, and Alaina didn't doubt that some of them would be relieved to know murder hadn't taken place. If they only knew…

What had happened instead made Alaina's heart race just thinking about it.

"So," Miss Finchley's voice dipped lower as they removed

themselves from the other guests; "I take it things are better after the reading? His Grace didn't seem all that pleased…"

"We've come to an agreement," Alaina replied. "A tentative truce. A temporary cease-fire."

She'd replayed his confession in her mind over and over again, held it between her mind's hands and turned it this way and that, examined it from various angles. She'd concluded that Sterling swearing fidelity to their vows was unnecessary to his cause. In their society, it mattered not that a man remained true to his wife as long as he did his duty to his title and those who depended upon him, and he could demand his right to her bed regardless of what she believed or how she felt. The more she'd pondered it, the more the fact that it was important to him that she knew the rumors of his behavior to be false made her believe strongly that he'd been truthful. And, if he could be honest about that, then didn't she have the obligation to give this life a chance?

She had yet to frighten him off, he'd remained true to his word, and he'd remained determined in his aim to woo her. If he wasn't going anywhere, then the least Alaina could do was use his presence to her advantage and finally snap shut the mouths who whispered so cruelly about her marriage—as if they had any more insight into her life than she.

Alaina had already caught a few whispered words poorly disguised by fluttering fans or behind her shoulder when they'd believed she and Sterling had meandered far enough away. As anticipated, Sterling's return to society had created quite an uproar. And, as Alaina had predicted, some wondered just what she'd done to make him come back to England.

Wouldn't they be shocked to find out the truth?

"Well, I certainly am glad for it!" Miss Finchley offered her a brilliant smile. It really was a shame the girl didn't smile more, it made her already pretty features quite stunning. Of course, with a blustering grouch of a father and an overly dramatic, demanding mother, Alaina couldn't really blame her. A very sheltered young woman of spinster age with no prospects and little freedom did not necessarily have much about which to smile. "At least we know there will be no bloodshed tonight," she added sotto-voce.

Alaina couldn't help but laugh, despite how true the statement was. "You'll have to pass along my regrets to your mother; I could find nowhere to hide my dagger in this gown."

Chapter Thirteen

T HE LADIES' UNABASHED laughter reached Sterling nearly across the ballroom. Every fiber of his being was attuned to his wife's location, her every movement. Though he tried to concentrate on the polite conversation around him, it proved a futile exercise. Ever since he first saw her in that gown, a resplendent golden goddess, he could think of nothing other than bringing Alaina home and tasting every inch of her flesh, finally learning once and for all if her nipples were ripe like raspberries, dusky and sensuous, or the pale, innocent pink of a rosebud. More than once, he'd had to turn his mind to tamer paths in order to avoid embarrassing himself in the middle of a ballroom on his first evening back in Society.

It was nearly impossible for him to focus on anything else, though, because every last one of his senses was finely attuned to Alaina. He knew precisely how far away she stood; he was keenly aware of who watched her, who spoke to her, and who asked her to dance. He far preferred having her on his arm, but he couldn't very well force her to remain there all evening. Things had been going unexpectedly well and it wouldn't do to mess it all up with a bit of over-possessive behavior.

So, Sterling had to settle for feigning interest in the conversation he'd been dragged into despite his best evasive efforts. All the while, he kept his ears perked for Alaina's laughter, his nose searched for her intoxicating floral scent, and his arms itched to hold her once more.

"Your father purchased those mines, did he not?" inquired one of the older lords surrounding him.

"He did," Sterling replied with a nod. "I believe it was shortly after I was born." The Cornish mines were a fruitful investment sprouting from a gamble the old duke had made. The land had proven dreadfully difficult to mine and had been producing little to no income. After consulting with a few men who knew the area best, his father had decided to purchase the land for a pittance, hired a new foreman who changed the direction of the tunneling, and it was then that the Morton coffers went from full to obscenely overflowing.

"And how are the workers?" asked a second, deeply nasal voice.

"By all accounts, they are content. I am planning to visit my holdings over the next several months to confirm, but I've made sure the wages are fair and I've employed physicians in the town who see to their wellbeing and that of their families—"

"No, no," the man said, waving. "I mean how *are* they? The men in my operation are showing a maddening proclivity toward entitlement."

"Entitlement?" Sterling's eyes whipped up to meet the other man's eyes for the first time. Lord Peele had always possessed the pointed features of a rodent, but no more so than that evening, in Sterling's estimation.

"More money," Peele scoffed. "All they do is haul rocks and chip away at the ground. Can you believe they have the gall to demand more money for it?" He shook his head with incredulous disbelief, as if it was beyond his comprehension that the men wouldn't do such "simple" work for free. A few other heads nodded in grave agreement.

"I don't pretend to have ever been a laborer," Sterling said, slowly and evenly; "but I've enough understanding to assert that it is far more than just 'hauling rocks' and 'chipping earth.'" The head shaking stopped immediately. "In fact, these men do some of the most dangerous work in the kingdom, putting their lives at risk to line our pockets. I feel the least we can do is pay them a decent wage to make their risk worth it and, God forbid, provide for their families if the worst happens."

"We offer them employment." Peele's voice dripped with derision. "Do you not feel they are demonstrating ungratefulness by daring to claim their compensation is unfair? We bring industry to their far-flung communities and put a roof over their heads and food on their tables."

One of the men shifted uncomfortably from foot to foot; another found something fascinating about the chandelier over their heads. Either they agreed with Peele, but wanted to avoid contradicting Sterling, or they were made uncomfortable by the brewing disagreement. Regardless, Sterling believed them cowards.

"They feed and house their families through the sweat on their brow and the blood of their bodies. Sometimes with their lives. We are not doing them a favor by paying them for their lives; we are thanking them for their risk and their sacrifice, and I firmly believe their reward should be proportionate to this. We only live the way we do because other men put their lives in jeopardy."

A choked cough came from the lord who so clearly now regretted ever bringing up the topic of the mines. Peele, however, doubled down on his opinions.

"Are you saying we should be grateful to those we employ?" he scoffed, holding his hands in a supplicating manner as he glanced around for support. There was none to be found. "We are born to this, Morton. Some men are born to power, others are born to spend their lives dedicated to others, doing their small part to improve the world." There was a disgusted curl to his lips. "Some men are gods and some men are ants. They should be happy they aren't crushed beneath our boots—let alone have the temerity to demand we do more for them."

Sterling's blood chilled. His heart rate slowed to a dangerous, focused thrum. His eyes narrowed on one of the men who embodied the problem with Sterling's class. Men like Peele did not use their position for anything other than their own gain and privilege. Part of the reason Sterling had accepted his position in Ramsay's Spy Society was Sterling's desire to do more than the typical lord who sat back collecting rents. Managing his estates, his tenants, his employees was all well and good; it was what his father had taught him to do and there was no shame in that. He knew that was fine, especially when he might take his power to the House of Lords and enact real change. But he'd wanted to do more—get his hands dirty. So, when the opportunity presented itself, he took it. As a duke, he planned to do what he could on English soil. As an agent of the Spy Society, his impact might be far greater. He had spent years helping to ferret out foreign intelligence that saved hundreds—if not thousands—of lives. And he fully intended to bring all the lessons and skills he'd learned and the connections he had made home to make England a better place. A man's observant nature, charm, and talent with disarming words did not simply disappear when he returned to his normal life.

Sterling wasn't delusional; he knew he couldn't squash every roach in the peerage, but he could use his intimidating stature and notoriety to put them in their place every once in a while. Thanks to his connections and the information he'd amassed over the years, he knew more *ton* secrets than every tabloid and London gossipmonger combined.

Sterling met Peele's grin with a deadly smile of his own. He leaned forward and clapped the other man on the shoulder, allowing his hand to linger.

"I can see what you mean, Peele. I shall take your words into account as I move forward in my ventures."

"No trouble at all." Peele's grin spread to reveal rows of crooked teeth...but it faltered when Sterling leaned in to drop low, dangerous words in his ear.

"I will caution you that a single ant may go unnoticed...anger the colony and you may not live to regret it." He tightened his grip on Peele's shoulder. "And I strongly suggest you funnel some of your funds into paying fair wages rather than sending them overseas for illicit goods. There may come a time when the powers that be may decide you have skated by long enough."

With that, Sterling pressed his glass into the other man's chest, forcing him to take it lest it shatter on the floor, and turned away to find Alaina.

"PARDON THE INTERRUPTION, but I should very much like to steal away my wife." Sterling took an inordinate amount of pleasure at the surprise that crossed Alaina's face at the sound of his voice and...dare he imagine it...the warmth just barely flaring to life in her eyes.

"But of course, Your Grace," said the tall, curvaceous young woman with whom Alaina had been speaking, and she bobbed a deferential curtsy. "Please excuse me; I see my mother gesturing for my attention."

"I shall see you at our next meeting, then?" Alaina asked her.

The woman's sharp blue gaze briefly alighted on Sterling before she nodded. "But of course."

As soon as they were alone, Sterling gently pulled Alaina's arm through his. "Walk with me, wife." He didn't give her a chance to respond before he began to guide her around the room's perimeter.

"Whatever did you say to Lord Peele?" Alaina asked lightly, giving a little wave of her fan to an acquaintance.

"What makes you believe I said anything?"

"For one, you cannot threaten a peer in the ballroom of one of London's most notoriously nosey upstarts without someone noticing. Secondly, the man cannot take his horrified eyes off of you and he's whiter than a sheet."

Sterling wondered how successful Ramsay would be if he employed more Society women. It hadn't been more than five minutes since he'd left Peele and already Alaina was aware that something had transpired. This woman made him appreciate female strength and intelligence more and more each day.

"The man is a prig." He hadn't meant it as a joke, but he did so enjoy the bubble of laughter and sparkle in Alaina's eyes when she looked up at him.

"In that regard, we are in agreement." Her smile made his mouth go dry. "But I simply must know what you said to put him in his place." She leaned in conspiratorially and his pulse quickened when the side of her breast pressed against his arm. "You can tell me—I promise not to repeat it."

"I am no fool," he chuckled more nonchalantly than he felt. This comfortability between them was both foreign and delightful, and he wanted to prolong it as long as possible.

Alaina shrugged, not the least bit contrite. "Very well. I will probably tell Lady Sommerfeld and Lady Juliette, but that's it."

He cocked a brow and the bashful blush to her cheeks did a funny thing to his insides. He liked this Alaina. He liked this entire evening, as a matter of fact. She was carefree and confident in this setting, seemingly freer now that they'd been removed from the battleground of Morton House. And he loved their banter. It was almost shocking how easily they fell back into the habit of it. It felt like the two of them were against the world rather than being pitted against one another in an unwinnable war straight from a Greek Tragedy.

"Let us say that Peele may be rethinking some of his investments in the near future…and paying those employed in his mines something a bit closer to a reasonable wage."

She stared up at him with a mixture of disbelief and confusion, followed by understanding. Even if she didn't know the specifics, Sterling knew she recognized he'd called the man out for questionable practices. She was a sharp one, his wife.

"Shall we dance again?" he asked her, thinking only of being able to hold her in his arms once more. He was becoming addicted all over again to her lithe grace.

"We have already shared two dances, Morton."

"And?"

"There will be comments and titillation if we share another here tonight."

"I care not one fig what any of these people have to say." Alaina's luminous eyes widened at his words, but he could tell she enjoyed his bluntness. "I am enjoying myself tonight. With my wife."

His eyes were locked onto the way she pulled her lower lip between her teeth. His pulse quickened like a shot. "As much as I hate to admit it, I am enjoying myself tonight as well."

"You are allowed to have a nice time with me, Alaina. You are not betraying yourself and everything you felt and experienced in the last decade. Equal space can be held for the past as well as the present and future." He covered her hand with his and she focused on the gesture.

"I've felt several times this night that it was as if the time never passed at all," she whispered, as if uneasy about admitting such a thing aloud. "It has brought back certain memories."

"It has, has it not?" Sterling gazed down at her, his lips curled into a smile. What he wouldn't give to have her alone. He glanced up and took stock of their position in the ballroom, suddenly inspired. "In fact, I have another idea I think you may enjoy."

Sterling spirited Alaina through a side door and onto a small, unoccupied balcony overlooking the house's dark back garden. The evening air hung thick with the aroma of pruned shrubbery, earth, and rosebushes.

"What are you doing?" Alaina laughed as he backed her into the vee of the stone balustrade. He'd have preferred some sort of veranda or broader balcony with more space for concealment, but this would have to do.

"Wooing you, of course," he replied, head inclined to inhale her scent—so much more delicious than anything else he'd experienced in all his travels.

Alaina glanced around and he watched understanding dawn slowly at first, and then all at once.

"You said you would not force me."

"I am not forcing you, simply fulfilling my role as an interested suitor who has whisked his lady away for a private moment. Just like when we courted."

Alaina's small laugh was breathy and unsteady. "You never did that when you courted me."

"No." Sterling leaned in until his lips were a breath's space from her neck, forcing her to feel every one of his words as a hot puff of air on her exposed flesh. "I was too young, too stupid, too determined to do what I thought was right." Her shuddering breath caused a hot rush of heat to fly straight to his throbbing groin. "But I think we are well past that point. Wouldn't you agree, Alaina?" What he wouldn't give to run his tongue along the hammering pulse in her throat. Her low begrudging whimper was enough to fray his resolve dangerously thin. "Have I forced you?" he murmured into the sensitive skin where her neck met her shoulder. Alaina gave a mute, minuscule shake of her head. "All you need to do is say the word and I will stop." He crowded her more closely to the banister, the toes of his polished hessians sliding beneath the hem of her skirts, and he lifted his head until their mouths were nearly touching. "Do you wish for me to stop…or would you like for me to kiss you? Because I would very, very much like to kiss you right now."

"I—I don't know," Alaina stammered breathlessly.

"Yes or no. It's quite simple, really." Sterling couldn't take his eyes off hers, the dark pools of the sapphire irises, the blown-out pupils giving away her true desires. "Would you like me to leave you alone, or should I kiss you senseless?"

"Senseless?"

"Or at least as near to it as possible. I want to kiss you until your limbs tremble from it—until you ache for my touch as much as I ache for yours."

Her breath was coming in quick little pants now and she'd curled her fingers into the lapels of his coat. His cock was thick and straining with need at that point, his pulse beating in time to her shaky breaths.

"Mmm?" she hummed nonsensically, her eyes flitting to his mouth.

"Is that what you want, Alaina?" he whispered.

"Yes…" she finally exhaled. The word was still on her lips when he slanted his mouth over hers.

Sterling licked his way into her mouth, savoring her sigh as she allowed him in and met his tongue with equal fervor. They tangled and stroked, tasted and sucked. She surprised him by giving his lower lip a nip and his sanity fled like a stallion slapped on the haunches. An unbidden moan of delight slipped from his throat, and he felt the little minx smile against his lips.

Just for that, he closed the remaining distance between their bodies, cupped the back of her head, and yanked her hips flush with his using the hard band of his other arm around her trim waist. In response, Alaina slung her arms around his neck, simultaneously raising herself and pulling him down to meet her.

"Do you want me to stop?" he teased against her lips.

"No," she breathed. "No."

Sterling dragged his lips down her jaw, taking advantage to nibble the underside when her head fell back. He pressed hot, open-mouthed kisses to her throat and then licked his way back up to the delicate shell of her ear. He nearly groaned when she shivered as he nipped the lobe and then soothed it with a kiss.

"How about now?" he growled.

She shook her head and found his lips again, devouring him with deep, hungry kisses that set Sterling's blood on fire as if he'd been nothing but a bundle of dry powder until Alaina had come and dropped the spark. He swore he could feel every vein and artery in his body firing with that volatile heat.

As if with a mind of their own, his hands slid lower to squeeze appreciatively the perfect mounds of her bottom and then fist in the shimmering fabric of her gown. He flexed his hips and rocked the thick, hard ridge of his arousal against her softness. He was rewarded by her pressing back into him. She didn't retreat—if anything, her body seemed to reach for his and beg for more.

Sliding his knee between hers, Sterling pulled her up and over his leg so she straddled him. He nearly came just from the heat of her sex through the layers of their clothing. Trapping her between his body and the balustrade, she had no choice but to allow him to grip her bottom and drag her across his thigh in long, slow strokes. He slowed the pace of his kisses to match the languid teasing of her cleft. He knew he found the proper pace and pressure when Alaina's nails dug into his scalp, and she began to gasp and shudder.

"And now?" he asked wickedly.

"Don't...you...dare..." Alaina whimpered, clutching his head and his shoulders as if he were the only thing keeping her tethered to the world.

The pounding of Sterling's heart was deafening in his own ears as Alaina found the right angle and rode him. He wanted to bury himself deep inside her. He wanted to feel her body wrapped around his, to know how she felt with every drag and pull of their flesh. He had waited his whole life for Alaina, and it was killing not to lift her skirts and take her right then and there, but he knew she deserved better. His wife deserved better. Besides, he wasn't sure he wouldn't embarrass himself and finish instantly if she allowed him to take her fast and hard in a dark corner with others lurking not all that far away.

He'd add that to his mental list of all the ways he wanted Alaina, but it was not for them this time.

"That's it," he hissed through gritted teeth, trying with everything inside of him to hold onto the tattered remains of his sanity. "This is only a hint of what I could make you feel, Alaina. I want to explore together. I want to touch you everywhere, to learn your taste, to give you nothing but pleasure."

She sobbed deep in her chest and Sterling read it as she was nearing her peak. Quickly, he slanted his mouth over hers to muffle her cries, lest they be overheard and someone came outside to investigate. He held her flexing rear in a bruising grip as she worked herself over him. He helped her maintain her pace even when she faltered, her legs trembling too badly to provide the leverage she required. He needed her to find her climax even though he would deny himself that pleasure. This was about Alaina and showing her that she could trust him and that he wanted only to satisfy her, to give her the life she should have had for the last eight years.

Alaina's breath quickened and caught, but Sterling continued to urge the relentless pace. He nipped and nibbled her mouth, stroked her deeply with his tongue and she met him each time. She was his equal. She burned as hotly as he did, she pulsated with it just as he throbbed with need so painful it was nearly debilitating.

Suddenly, Alaina tensed and shuddered, her nails leaving crescent-shaped bites on the back of his neck as he kissed her deeply and drank her cries of joy. He crushed her to him, molding her soft, full breasts to his chest and running his hands along every one of her tantalizing curves, caressing and tasting her until her tremors stilled and her breathing gradually grew more even. Eventually, Sterling placed another kiss on her parted lips and then pressed his lips to her forehead, simply breathing her in.

Alaina melted in his arms and buried her face in his chest; Sterling closed his eyes and simply allowed himself to be. He reveled in her nearness, cherished the faith she'd placed in him, and struggled to calm his own raging arousal.

Alaina tilted her head back and his breath caught in his throat. His wife was glorious. "That was…"

"Amazing," he finished for her.

She pulled her lips between her teeth and lowered her gaze. Unable to bear the thought of her being at all ashamed of what they'd just done, Sterling crooked a finger beneath her chin and lifted her face to his.

"Just like kisses, it is your right to demand pleasure from me." His words were soft, but firm, leaving no room for her to misinterpret him. "And I heartily encourage you to ask for it whenever—and wherever—the fancy strikes. I am far from shy."

Alaina blushed in the most becoming way before she straightened her spine and disentangled herself from him. While she did her best to shake out her skirts, Sterling tilted his gaze to the dark sky overhead, and, placing his hands on his hips, he inhaled the thick night air deeply and tried to cool his ardor.

"I am hopelessly wrinkled now, thanks to you," Alaina grumbled, frowning down at the crumpled state of her skirts.

Sterling grinned at her. "A small price to pay."

"Do try not to sound so pleased with yourself," she bit out, moving past him to reenter the ballroom.

"How can I not when you can hardly walk a straight line?" Sterling caught up to her and leaned in closer so his breath tickled the nape of her neck. "Imagine what will happen when we finally get our hands on one another in privacy."

He was rewarded with a stuttering step and a vicious glare from Alaina when he caught her elbow so she didn't land face-first in the doorway. He couldn't stop his chuckle when she wrenched her arm away and plowed into the room toward a clutch of women.

She could present all the bluster in the world and Sterling would still know he'd made some headway with his wife. And he couldn't wait to be alone with her again.

THE CARRIAGE RIDE back to Morton House hadn't come quickly enough for Sterling. It was the wee hours of the morning before they were able to leave the Finchley home and, rather than take the rear-facing seat across from Alaina, he'd dropped down beside her. He felt her stiffen, but she didn't sidle away. He'd count that as another victory—his second for the night—tallying it up alongside his very pathetic number of wins when it came to Alaina and their relationship.

Overall, the evening had to be considered a success. There were no incidents, raucous arguments, or verbal sparring in public. That had to be progress, didn't it? And he'd been able to dance with her, hold her close, openly lay claim to her once again, announcing to all the *ton* that he was back, this was his wife, and he had no designs to go anywhere. After eight long, exhausting, dangerous years, he was finally where he belonged.

And that delicious interlude on the balcony would live on endlessly in his memory.

Sterling leaned back in the plush squab upholstered in rich ruby-red velvet, stretching his tired legs out before him and crossing them at the ankle.

"I commend your choice for a first outing," he said gently as they rocked into motion. He noticed out of the corner of his eye that Alaina was busy twisting her dance card in her lap. His fingers itched to reach out and replace the card with his hand, to feel the way their palms fit together, to tug her closer... Instead, he forced himself to settle for just being this near to her for so many consecutive hours without bloodshed.

As much as it pained him to acknowledge the truth of it, Alaina had been right about the speculation surrounding their marriage. He'd received a few stomach-churning insinuations that his return was solely to get a legitimate heir on Alaina before returning to his absentee ways; more still had inquired if he'd be willing to divulge some of his tantalizing stories. Cold set-downs had awaited those men. Barely banked rage met the one or two men who'd been uncouth enough to comment that Sterling's return would surely help bring the duchess to heel—that it would do her good to have a man's hand in her life. It was one thing for him to consider his wife a handful, and another entirely to have relative strangers take the liberty of saying such things.

It sickened him to realize that this was just a taste of all Alaina had endured in his absence. He was beginning to understand how she'd developed such teeth and claws. Necessity was a powerful tool of adaptation.

More than once, he'd had to force his hands to unclench. Laying an earl, knight, or obscenely wealthy businessman out flat in the Finchley ballroom would serve no purpose other than making him feel momentarily better. It would do nothing to erase incorrect assumptions and might add more fuel to the fire. Instead, Sterling had to tell himself that things would change now that he was home. Alaina did not have to face these boors and harpies alone. He'd meant what he'd said when he told her he would not leave her. Together, they would weather this cruel world; neither would be alone again, and he found that intensely comforting.

Not that it had been a chore, but he'd done his best to present that united front he'd expounded to Alaina. He'd gladly do so again and again until the practice became a habit for them both, and he was determined to extinguish the nasty rumors surrounding the Morton Dukedom and relieve Alaina of the burden she'd shouldered alone for so long, if he had to stomp the flames out himself one by one.

"Thank you," Alaina replied lightly, offering him only the shell of her dainty ear as she turned her attention to the passing scenery.

"Am I mistaken or is Miss Finchley one of the ladies from your reading society?" he asked about the dark-eyed, curvaceous daughter of their hosts with whom he'd done his polite duty and shared a dance. She'd been quiet and shy, providing only one-word answers to his inquiries, but she'd moved with all the grace and elegance of a woman who had spent years with a dancing master.

One corner of Alaina's mouth tilted in a bemused smile when she finally met his gaze. "She is."

"How appropriate."

She chuckled lightly, the throaty sound sending a shockwave straight to his groin. "You should count yourself fortunate that the company I keep is more understanding than most; they are not the usual Society lot."

"I do count myself lucky in many ways, Alaina."

When his knee knocked into hers as they took a turn…she didn't pull away.

STERLING ESCORTED ALAINA up the sweeping staircase to the floor where their bedchambers were situated. Side-by-side. Tantalizingly close.

And, when he stopped in front of her door, when she looked up at him with her wide, luminous blue eyes with her arm still wrapped through his, when just the edge of her lower lip was caught between her straight white teeth, he could almost fool himself into believing that they were a normal man and wife.

That life hadn't gotten in the way.

That she'd allow him to guide her a few steps further to his own door.

Or, better yet, that she would tug him into her room and shut out the rest of the world.

"Thank you," Alaina breathed.

He had to clear his throat before he could speak. "For?"

"For a lovely evening. It was surprisingly enjoyable."

"Surprisingly?" he scoffed lightheartedly. "I can see I have quite a bit of work to do if I am to elevate your expectations of me."

He knew she saw his eyes flit to her smiling mouth; he felt it in the way her fingers tightened ever so slightly on his bicep.

Just one taste.

He wouldn't go back on his word—he wouldn't press her for more, no matter how badly his body ached for it—but he could no more stop himself from leaning down and pressing a gentle, achingly slow kiss to her lips than he could his lungs from breathing.

He needed this.

He needed *her.*

Sterling forced himself to pull back just when he felt her leaning into him. It nearly killed him, but he knew it was necessary for his sanity.

Her gilded lashes fluttered open when he stepped back.

"Pleasant dreams, Alaina," he murmured as he retreated to his own door. He knew without looking back that she was as confused and frustrated as he, but he was honor-bound to hold true to his promise to her. He reminded himself to maintain his hope that she would come to him in her own time.

He just had to be patient…even if it killed him.

Chapter Fourteen

"A S YOU CAN see from this report, Your Grace, the textile manufacturing in the North has continued to exceed expectations, even with the conclusion of the wars."

"And the working conditions?" Sterling asked his solicitor as he perused the sheets of figures laid out before him. Thoughts of Peele's deplorable opinions of those who worked for him came rushing back to Sterling. He hadn't been simply paying him lip service when he'd claimed he intended to ensure those who worked his mines and factories would be paid fair wages for their efforts. It was vitally important to Sterling that he follow through with his father's example and teachings and do whatever was in his power to improve the lives of others, starting with those whom he could impact most directly.

"Your Grace?"

Sterling's eyes flicked up to look at the diminutive, graying, bespectacled man sitting across his desk, Mr. Bernard Bartholomew Bates of Bates, Bates & Bates (yes, Sterling had always enjoyed the excessive alliteration). The firm of Bates, et al, had been loyal to the St. John family for decades—since well before Sterling had inherited the title—and Bates had done an admirable job of maintaining and managing the stewards handling Morton estates and holdings in his absence. He'd religiously supplied Sterling with updates while he was away on the Continent and Sterling trusted his input in matters of business. When it came to the human aspect of business, however, Sterling doubted the man saw past the numbers in front of his nose.

"The workers," Sterling elaborated flatly. "In the textile mill." He located a stack of parchment they'd already discussed. "And the tannery and the coal mines, for that matter. How are the working conditions?"

"I—I assume they're as expected, Your Grace. The production remains—"

"Secondary to the health and wellbeing of those under my care," Sterling said, cutting off his solicitor. One of the downfalls of using Bates as his intermediary was the man hardly looked past his nose. He was satisfied if the numbers added up. "What good is production if it becomes sloppy from overworked or ill workers?" This seemed to baffle the other man. Sterling narrowly resisted an annoyed sigh. This wasn't the first time he'd asked this question of his solicitor and stewards, but it was the first time Sterling was in England to do anything about it and ensure his wishes were being met. "I wish to make plans to view the mills and the mines to see for myself that the workers are being treated well and their wages are fair for their efforts."

"Why, yes, of course." Despite his befuddlement, Bates used his quill to scribble furiously on a slip of parchment perched atop the portable desk laid across his lap. He would notify the stewards of Sterling's plans.

"And I wish to schedule a trip to see the sheep farms in Wales; the lands in Staffordshire, Surrey, North Yorkshire, Devon..." Sterling added thoughtfully, wondering if he might be able to convince Alaina to accompany him on this tour of sorts. He knew she'd traveled little prior to their marriage and he didn't believe she'd done much of it since; perhaps this might be a sort of much delayed honeymoon for them. A man could dream, couldn't he?

They proceeded to discuss the rest of the Morton holdings and estates; spent hours going over production, staffing, maintenance, repairs, and updates; and planned the sale of one of the lesser properties in Cornwall that Sterling had only visited once in his life and had no desire to spend the money on upkeep when there was already another interested party.

"And now, if I may, the household expenses," Bates added, flipping through the papers and pulling out the ones he was looking for before handing them to Sterling. Tidy rows of numbers and accounts filled the pages in a looping, floral script so unlike the other pages they'd reviewed thus far.

"Has Her Grace been keeping these accounts on her own?" Sterling asked, skimming page after page of the document.

"She has, indeed. But not without supervision, of course." The last was added as if he believed Sterling might find fault with his own wife managing the household accounts.

"Should I have cause to be concerned about Her Grace managing this?" Sterling cocked a brow, fixing his steward with a penetrating stare.

"N—No! Of course not! Every penny is always accounted for."

"Then I believe Her Grace has proven her abilities many times over by this point. I trust her calculations; you needn't monitor her every move."

The older man's mouth twitched, but he nodded in acquiescence. Satisfied, Sterling turned his eyes back to the documents in his hands. All seemed in order until his gaze snagged on a line indicating a sizable expense simply marked *Mrs. Worthy* with itemizations below it for books, fabric, a physician… He stared, trying to decipher what it could mean. It was in the same area of the ledger as the monthly donations to the foundling hospital and other charitable contributions, but he knew no one named Mrs. Worthy. It needled him, this unfamiliar charge on the account, and he couldn't fathom why Alaina would be sending that amount of money to her for these items. It wasn't one of the usual foundations the Morton Dukedom normally supported, but—he flipped back through the pages—it seemed to go back more months than he could count with Bates staring at him expectantly. Sterling tapped his fingers on the desk in thought.

What was Alaina hiding in plain sight? What was she coordinating?

His life was made of secrets—he lived and, potentially, died by them—but there had been something comforting for him to know Alaina was exactly who she presented. She was blunt, straightforward, and unafraid to show her teeth...but what if there was much more to her than he knew? This seemingly innocuous entry in the household account was disconcerting when compared to row after row of easily explainable expenses. The secrecy of it was like a pebble in his boot. It seemed innocent at first, relatively easy to ignore, but it would wear a hole if left to its own devices. It would lay in wait for him until the most inconvenient time to remind him of its uncomfortable presence. His nature would not allow him to leave the puzzle unsolved.

Sterling made a mental note to look into the item on the ledger. While the rest of the books demonstrated Alaina's aptitude for efficiency, he told himself he just wanted to be sure she wasn't being swindled or that something untoward was not taking place. He didn't doubt her intelligence in the slightest, but Alaina had demonstrated a bit of a bleeding heart in her adoption of Society's misfits and their championing of unpopular causes. Besides, he'd already vowed to do a better job of protecting her; this seemed as good a place as any to start.

It took Sterling a moment to realize Bates had resumed speaking to him. He pasted on a blandly interested expression and did his best to pay attention as they continued their meeting.

LATER THAT AFTERNOON, Sterling followed the sound of his wife's voice and strode into the drawing room. There, he found Viscount Sommerfeld and his fiery-haired wife sitting across from Alaina. Between them, the table was filled with a full tea service, sandwiches, biscuits, and other treats.

"Sommerfeld," he greeted the blond man with a smile.

"Morton," the viscount said in return and set down his plate. Sterling saved him from having to stand by striding over and clasping his hand in greeting. "My wife, Meredith Stratford, Lady Sommerfeld," he added, gesturing to the lovely woman beside him.

Sterling took the pale hand of the willowy woman dressed in a bright blue gown. Her dark blue eyes were striking and intelligent as he bent over her hand in greeting.

"Charmed, my lady; though I do believe we've encountered one another before."

Mischief danced in her eyes. "I might recall an instance; would you refresh my memory?"

Sommerfeld flashed a wicked smile at his wife's wit a moment before he could mask it. Clearly, the secret was out.

"I believe we've all had enough Shakespeare for the time being," Sterling replied good-naturedly before turning back to Alaina. "I hadn't realized we were having guests."

"I knew you were busy and—" she stuttered uncharacteristically when he took her hand and pressed her bare knuckles to his lips in greeting. "And you were with Mr. Bates all morning. I didn't think you wanted to be disturbed."

"You could never disturb me," he whispered, and she set her teacup down a bit more forcefully than she'd intended.

"Pardon our intrusion upon your day," Sommerfeld chimed in. "We only intended to stop by for a short time."

"I get a bit anxious whenever I need to leave the girls," Lady Sommerfeld explained somewhat bashfully.

"Well, I cannot blame you," Alaina reassured her. "They are absolutely darling."

"You have my most sincere congratulations, by the way," Sterling added earnestly.

The other couple beamed warmly, accepting his words. "Thank you; we're planning on having them christened in the next few weeks," said the viscountess. The way she and her husband squeezed each other's hands in a silent language all their own was not lost on Sterling. He glanced at Alaina out of the corner of his eye.

What would it be like to have that with her? Would she ever allow him in enough for them to develop such a bond?

Sterling cleared his throat and addressed the viscount. "While this is a lovely spread, I was thinking of heading to the study for a cigar. Would you care to join me?" The proximity with Alaina was too intoxicating for him to handle. He didn't trust himself to be so near to her with an audience—not when the memory of her coming apart in his arms was so fresh in his mind.

Sommerfeld looked to his wife who lifted her chin in silent agreement. "I think I just might, thank you, Morton." He snagged two more biscuits from the platter, pressed a quick kiss to his wife's temple, and used his cane to stand. Sterling took note of the leg brace the other man wore and, rather than hinder his movements, it seemed to lend him more strength and mobility than without it. Sommerfeld bowed to Alaina and thanked her for her hospitality before following Sterling from the room. Their wives resumed their conversation about the infant girls.

Once in the study, Sterling retrieved two cigars from their cherrywood box, collecting the cutter and matches and a crystal ashtray, carrying all of it over to where Sommerfeld had taken up a seat on the leather-upholstered armchair and propped his leg on its matching ottoman.

"May I offer you a brandy or scotch as well?"

Sommerfeld shook his head. "No, thank you." He concentrated on the glowing tip of his cigar, filling the room with its rich, thick odor. "But do not feel as if you can't enjoy a drink. By all means, man."

Sterling chuckled and waved it off as he sat back in his own chair.

Several minutes of companionable silence passed before Sommerfeld next spoke. "Pardon me for the observation, but I take it the wooing must be going well; it doesn't seem like Her

Grace wanted to draw blood when you came upon us in the drawing room."

Sterling exhaled the truth in an aromatic cloud of the rich tobacco. "It's actually going quite terribly." He smiled despite his words. "No doubt you heard about the scene at the last meeting of their bloody Reading Society."

Sommerfeld had the good grace to cringe. "I had, but I'd been trying to avoid mentioning it."

Sterling took the opportunity to give his account of the meeting—omitting only how arousing he'd found Alaina's defiant performance. Sommerfeld responded by laughing in appreciation of her cunning.

"She shows no mercy, does she?" the viscount chuckled.

Sterling shook his head in amused resignation. "It is a good thing I'm an infinitely patient man."

He'd waited eight years; he could wait a bit longer.

And he instinctively knew it would be well worth it.

MEANWHILE, BACK IN the drawing room, Lady Sommerfeld took her own chance to ask Alaina what had happened following the incident at the last Society meeting.

"I was more than a little surprised when Miss Finchley told me you'd both attended her family's ball. *Together.*" Lady Sommerfeld arched a cinnamon-colored brow and took a sip of her tea.

"As you can see, I'm quite alive and well...as is the duke."

"Well that much is obvious," Lady Sommerfeld said with a roll of her eyes. "The duke seemed bent upon murder—a stark contrast to today's more amorous presentation."

Alaina willed her cheeks not to flame. For all Lady Sommerfeld and the rest of Society knew, Alaina was well and truly Sterling's wife—and had been for many years. She shouldn't be embarrassed by her friend's observation.

She did her best to play it off with a tilt of her head. "He is either mad or insanely determined to get back into my good graces, neither of which I believe I can fend off forever."

"Is it really such a bad thing if you give in?" her friend offered.

"You sound like Lady Juliette," Alaina scoffed.

"If more than one source provides the same information, then it stands to reason there may be some genuine merit to the information."

"And now you sound like a scientist."

Lady Sommerfeld chuckled warmly and set down her tea to slide over and take up the cushion beside Alaina. She gently removed Alaina's cup from her hands and placed it on the table as well before clasping her long, elegant fingers around Alaina's.

"You *have* already lost eight years together…why continue to waste more time on old wrongs and stubbornness…especially when he seems to be doing his best to make things right?" She and Juliette were two of the only people who knew about Sterling's efforts these past few weeks, and Meredith was correct, their suggestions to her echoed one another, and that made them difficult to ignore.

"I despise it when you make so much sense."

Lady Sommerfeld's fingers squeezed hers.

THOUGH HE GAVE it a valiant try, Sterling was unable to sleep again that night, plagued by a persistent, violent arousal. Each time he closed his eyes, he could only picture Alaina's body, her smile, her lips, her flashing eyes, her graceful hands on his…

No.

Stop, dammit.

He wasn't a lad who needed to frig himself into sleep each night. He had more bloody dignity than that, didn't he?

Maintaining his patience and holding onto his hope that Alaina would eventually come 'round was slowly killing him. He'd made significant progress in living more civilly with his wife—she'd even allowed him those few kisses and caresses without clawing his face—but that was it. As badly as he wanted to move the process forward and have his wife once and for all, he needed to remember that the past eight years had been different for her than they had been for him. She'd suffered differently. And she couldn't know the depth of the truth that he'd never stopped caring for her, had held onto her image in his mind and his heart, throughout his absence. He had to give her time.

And if she never decided to allow him to be with her, then he needed to find a way to cope with his situation.

Frustrated and in need of a distraction, Sterling decided to empty the final trunk he had yet to unpack. His valet had attempted several times to empty the offending luggage, but Sterling had refused. It contained some of his important documents, personal papers, and other items he'd deemed vital enough to cart back with him from the Continent. Beneath a pile of books, he uncovered a carved ebony box at the very bottom of the trunk. His heart stuttered and he sat back on his heels. He knew what he would find before he lifted the lid.

Every single letter his wife had ever written to him was tucked safely away, protected and cherished.

The stack was thicker than his palm and surprisingly heavy, well-worn from countless readings.

He experienced no small stab of pain when he recalled his agonizing decision to reply to none of them.

It had been far safer for her that way—better to have any enemies believe his wife was inconsequential and unworthy of his time than one of the most important things in his world.

He knew Alaina's words as if they were his own. Her letters contained inquiries as to his wellbeing, little accounts of her days, and determination to hold onto the belief that he hadn't truly abandoned her and would return shortly. He'd been shocked to receive the first letter, forwarded by a neutral contact established by Ramsay. Even back then, Alaina had been feistier and more determined than he'd thought possible. The letters had begun frequently and then gradually tapered off after five years of determined scribbling.

Truth be told, it had deflated his soul when the letters had stopped altogether, but he'd repeatedly told himself it was all for the best. Though the words eventually rang hollow from overuse and provided little comfort, he continued to say them to himself.

Now that he was back home, however, these letters created a very interesting opportunity.

Sterling stood and carried the box back to his bed, settling in for a night of reading.

Chapter Fifteen

THE FOLLOWING MORNING, Alaina rose, dressed, and went down to break her fast a little earlier than usual. There had been something comfortable about her last few meals with Sterling and a part of her looked forward to a repeat that morning. They'd moved past the awkwardness of the early days and adopted something akin to the civility Sterling had pleaded for in the beginning. It felt like quite an accomplishment to look back and see how far they'd come in the weeks since his return. The shift in their dynamic was undeniable. Even if she hadn't completely forgotten their past, they were far closer to reconciliation than they had been.

She entered the morning room to find only Sterling. No footmen hovered on the edge of the room ready to seat her and prepare her plate. Instead, her husband stood and held his hand out to her. There was a new gentleness in his hazel eyes, an unexpected sincerity that stole her breath. He was dressed simply, but immaculately in a charcoal coat and matching breeches, a well-fitted deep blue waistcoat, and crisp cravat at his throat. The sharp line of his jaw was freshly shaven, and, in all, he was devastatingly handsome.

"Good morning," he greeted her. There was a velvety curl to his voice that made her stomach flutter.

"Morning," she replied automatically and allowed him to help her to her chair.

"I trust you slept well?"

"Yes, I—" Alaina's words died in the air when she caught sight of the small crystal vase on the table between their chairs. It was stuffed with fat, glorious peonies in various shades of fragile pink.

Sterling spoke beside her ear when it was clear she could not find her words. "They're your favorite flower, are they not?" His warm breath on her naked neck made her shiver.

"How did you—" She stopped speaking again when she caught sight of his confident smile mere inches from her face. The man was full of surprises. If he'd taken the time to figure this out, then perhaps he did care.

Perhaps he was telling the truth about all of it and spoke from his heart.

And, even if he hadn't expressly explained *why* he'd left her in the first place, maybe he had told the truth about his activities when he'd been away.

It was nearly impossible for her to swallow past the growing lump in her throat. She couldn't tear her eyes from his because she saw hope there for the first time in a very long while.

ALAINA SPENT THE rest of the day agonizing over the advice Lady Juliette and Viscountess Sommerfeld had given her. Sterling had made himself scarce following that morning's meal—whether because he had actual business to attend, or he wanted to leave her alone to stew and contemplate the appearance of the peonies at the table, she wasn't sure. Either way, that is precisely what he did.

And this suited Alaina just fine because the last thing she needed was a witness to her racing mind.

If her friends could have come to such a conclusion—that she and Sterling had already wasted far too much time—even without knowing the full extent of Sterling's confessions and this morning's efforts, then did that mean the answer was right in front of Alaina the whole time? Was her stubbornness preventing her from seeing the reality of the situation? Was she perhaps missing out on what could possibly be a future of contentment and wedded bliss if she could only climb over this hurdle? Could she truly forgive the last eight years and allow herself to admit there was more to Sterling than she'd believed? Could she accept the words he offered her and consider penance paid?

She spent hour after hour torn between desperately wanting to be left alone with her thoughts and wanting to face her husband to see if she still felt the same when confronted once more with his beautiful face. Only after a solitary supper in her rooms when Sterling sent word that he'd been held up in a meeting did Alaina find herself standing before the door adjoining their chambers. She'd listened to the now-familiar sounds of Sterling returning, the murmur of his baritone as he and his valet conversed, and the ensuing silence as, she presumed, her husband settled in for sleep.

Only this one barrier stood between them, and yet, it felt like the largest of chasms. Could she possibly consider setting aside her pride, taking the initiative, and moving to cross that void?

Her nerves were uncharacteristically powerful as she forced herself to turn the polished brass knob with clammy fingers. Unlocked, the door swung open on silent hinges. She didn't believe she'd made a sound, but Sterling immediately stirred nonetheless. He abruptly sat up, the deep blue coverlet slipping down his naked torso. The only light in the room was cast from the banked coals in the fire; the orange glow cast his angular features in mesmerizing shadow and relief. Her eyes drifted downward from the sharp lines of his face to the muscular planes of his bare chest, the defined ridges of his abdomen, the corded muscles of his arms as he propped himself up and ran a hand through his tousled chestnut hair burnished and glowing in the dim room.

"Alaina?" Her name in his husky voice sent an unexpectedly pleasant chill traipsing up her spine. "Are you well?"

She could only nod, unable to speak over the pounding of her heart when faced with her first naked man...her husband of nearly a decade.

Alaina hesitated another moment before entering the room and pressing the door closed behind her with a snick of finality, never removing her eyes from Sterling's face. Though his features were immobile, Sterling swallowed so hard that she could see the bob of his throat even in the flickering light.

"Alaina…" he whispered as she approached the bed; it might have been a curse or a prayer. Perhaps a little of both.

"How did you know about the peonies?" she asked more steadily than she felt. She'd mulled over the options off and on throughout the day. He could have easily enough learned the information from her maid or even one of her friends. If he paid attention, he'd have noticed she wore peonies affixed often enough to her bonnets.

His response, however, was nothing Alaina could have anticipated.

Rather than immediately respond, his hazel eyes burned into her for several prolonged seconds. Just as she was about to repeat her query, he rolled to the side, giving her a spectacular view of the flexing muscles of his expansive back, and reached for a pile of papers lying in an open wooden box set atop the small table beside the bed. He held out the stack to her but still said nothing. Alaina stepped close enough only to retrieve the papers and skim them in the flickering firelight. It took her less than a second to recognize her own handwriting, to be yanked back in time to the days she'd once been a young, naïve girl writing to her husband and hoping each day would be the one he'd return to the doorstep of Morton House.

Her letters.

He'd kept them.

All of them, judging from the heft of the stack she held, and what remained still in the box beside his bed.

"Your grandmother's garden was filled with peonies…but your favorites were always the ones so pale pink they were nearly white." His voice was at once soft and deafening. Her throat grew tight with unshed emotion, silencing her. "You used to collect the enormous blooms by the armful."

She looked up to see a faint, rueful tilt to his beautiful mouth just before her vision grew watery and blurred.

Her husband missed nothing.

It may have taken him time to figure things out, but he'd done it.

She heard him curse beneath his breath, and then the hasty rustle of fabric as he gathered the coverlet around his body and rose from the bed to close the gap between them in two long strides. Clutching the fabric around his waist with one hand, he gently pulled her to him with the other, cradling her against the warmth of his chest, his hot skin pressed to her cheek. The papers fell heedlessly from her fingers and fluttered to the rug at their feet like leaves in autumn. Her palms pressed against the hardness of his stomach, but not to push him away. Not this time.

"What did I do?" he asked, sounding both pained and baffled. "Please, tell me how to fix it."

What could she tell him? That simple flowers were the thing to split open her guarded heart? That her resolve to cling to the tattered remains of her animosity had been done in by peonies?

But it was so much more than that at the heart of it. To know he'd carried pieces of her with him in all his travels, and—even if he hadn't written back—they'd meant enough that he'd kept them, carted them around, held them, and read them repeatedly.

Alaina shook her head as best as she could with her face buried in his chest and looked up to meet Sterling's concerned gaze. Hot tears escaped her eyes when she witnessed the earnestness there, the vulnerability she hadn't been expecting. "You have no idea what it's like to suddenly realize that you do matter to someone—that you have always mattered…"

His mouth hardened, but his eyes grew softer than she'd ever seen before he pulled her against his body more tightly, as if wanting to absorb every ounce of pain she'd felt these past eight years. She inhaled the lingering delicious scent of his cologne, a hint of starch from his cravat lingering at the pulse in his throat, and the unique, clean musk of his skin. Alaina was suddenly keenly aware of his feverish flesh and nakedness, though it was absurd because how could she *not* be aware of this man's body and presence? If she'd learned one thing, it was that she was aware of his every movement and every glance. She was so tired of fighting this, so tired of being alone—especially when this man holding her would give her everything, had done so much to ingratiate himself to her once more. He'd met every one of her challenges with fire of his own. And he was strong enough to be calm and quiet when it mattered most.

The warmth of his eyes spread throughout her body with insistent tendrils until she felt it from her head to the tips of her bare toes.

"Will you kiss me?" she whispered without thinking.

"Always," he murmured, his pupils widening to nearly swallow their hazel rims. His hand snaked up to cup the back of her head, his fingers gently winding between the strands of her thick plait of golden hair to tilt her chin up. His warm breath tickled her lips, parting them on a sigh, and then his mouth grazed hers in an incredibly tender side-to-side skim.

He pressed gentle caresses to her top lip, then the bottom, then the sensitive corners, before finally giving her that which she ached for. His mouth sealed over hers, a perfect fit. Their lips mated in a perfect combination of need and tenderness, tasting and learning one another in a way that was so very long overdue. Sterling's tongue met hers, sweeping in deeply to tangle and stroke her until her joints grew weak. Though relatively untutored, she met his kisses and touches with her own, gradually losing her self-consciousness as the minutes ticked by. She stepped more closely to hold herself upright by wrapping her arms 'round his neck, stretching to her toes until her calves burned.

A hot, steely hardness pressed against her lower abdomen, through the layers of the coverlet, her robe, and nightshift. Long and thick, his member throbbed insistently, demanding her attention. Happy to oblige, she leaned in even closer. Sterling released a low, deep sound in his throat. Her leaden mind all at once snapped to attention. Even her practically inexperienced mind recognized what this meant. Her husband desired her, in no uncertain terms.

Alaina broke the kiss, pulling away just far enough to give their mouths a breath's space between. Her eyes darted down to the straining bulge between them. The ladder of his abdominal muscles above the edge of the sheet clenched convulsively, his chest heaved unevenly. She'd seen him shaken by arguments, practically vibrating with tension, but nothing compared to how tightly coiled he was just then.

Despite her burning cheeks, Alaina shoved aside all trepidations, bolstered her courage, and slowly reached forward to hook her fingers in the edge of the coverlet draped around Sterling's hips. The heat of his bare skin seared the backs of her knuckles most deliciously. Slowly, she began to tug the fabric from his grasp. There was only a moment's hesitation before he relinquished it to her, and she could feel his eyes upon her as tangible as a finger's touch. When the coverlet dropped to the floor, Alaina released the breath she hadn't realized she'd been holding in one long, slow exhalation.

He was a beautiful man, her husband.

Shamelessly, she admired the thick strength of his thighs, honed from years of riding; the lean cut of his calves dusted lightly with light brown hair; back up to the impressively thick column of his aroused sex where it sprang from a nest of dark chestnut curls, accentuated by the elegant wings of his pelvis. Alaina swallowed convulsively. *Oh my...* None of her friends had ever described the male member in such glorious, vivid detail as the one before her.

And she doubted any words could ever do it proper justice.

It excited her and made her nervous in equal measure. Faced with its jutting pride, its wide, blunt head and the soft, heavy sac beneath filled her with a confusing amount of anticipation. She knew as much that, should a man care to try, this part of him might bring her an unspeakable pleasure. And, if she'd learned one thing, Sterling would go to great lengths to do so.

It is your right to demand pleasure from me…

His words expanded within her skull until there was little room for anything else, like heady, intoxicating smoke in a closed room.

She dragged her eyes up along the thin trail of tawny hair that climbed toward his navel, across the defined ridges of his abdomen, the smooth planes of his chest and broad shoulders, the tenseness of his neck muscles as he held himself impossibly still and in check. His swirling hazel eyes watched her with an emotion she could not fully define. Desire was there, to be sure, but something else. A question?

"Alaina," he whispered almost painfully. She could only meet his eyes and curl her lips between her teeth as she waited in tense silence for him to continue. "What I told you earlier about there never being other women…" Her heart stuttered. Was he going to admit to a lie? *Now?* "There never was another woman. Not since the day I met you."

Alaina's mind stuttered at the admission, taking far longer than it should have to process it. "You mean…"

"When I told you none of the despicable rumors of my behavior on the Continent were true, I meant it. In all this time, no face has ever enticed me as much as yours, no mouth has drugged me so sweetly. I knew the moment I saw you, I wanted you; I knew the first time we spoke, I would never desire another." He spoke with bald frankness, though the slight pink on the crests of his cheeks was incredibly endearing. "I cannot lie and say I have never seen another woman bared before me, but I can speak with confidence when I declare there has never been another woman as beautiful as you, wife. And I hope only to bring you pleasure." His chest rose and fell with deep, broken breaths, as if his heart were attempting to break free of its cage. "You can touch me," he rasped. "Please, touch me. Put an end to my misery." She'd never heard her husband so near the brink of shattering. It was counterintuitively humbling to know she held all the power—even more so when she considered that, beyond all odds, this situation felt as if they were on leveler ground than they had been in years. He stood naked before her in both body and heart; he had yet to see her thusly. He was handing her control, and it was so tempting for her to relent and do the same.

Hesitantly, Alaina reached up and, with a feather-light touch, ran her fingers along the lines of his defined collarbone to the point where it melded into the swells of his broad shoulders. Her hands traced a tantalizing trail down to his flat nipples, so different from her own needy buds pressing so insistently against the soft fabric of her nightshift. Her nails grazed a path further to the undulating muscles of his abdomen, the defined wings of his pelvis, and, feeling unaccountably brave, through the crisp nest of hair cradling his member. She was utterly enthralled, and she was rewarded with a desperate inhalation from her husband. Still, he did not touch her in return. Her hands froze just shy of caressing that part of him that bobbed and strained so fervently for her attention.

Sensing her hesitation, Serling held himself even more still than she thought physically possible for a living, breathing man. "What is the matter?" he asked with a very subtle tremor.

"I—I am…" she trailed off, suddenly feeling very silly voicing her insecurities. "You are so beautiful," Alaina finally breathed, unable to meet his eye for fear of what she might find there. Few times in her life had she felt less certain of herself, and it was maddening. "And I am unsure."

Sterling crooked a finger beneath her chin and gently lifted it so he might look into her face. The corner of his mouth was tilted in a small smile, but it was far from mocking or unbearably prideful. It was reassuring. And what she saw in his eyes melted her all the way to her molten core.

"Come," he breathed and engulfed her hand in his before

turning to lead her across the room and, to her surprise, away from the bed. Her spiraling mind halted when she glimpsed the delectable swells of his rear, flexing with his every confident step. So distracted was she that she nearly collided with him when he stopped before the full-length looking glass leaning in the corner of the room.

Sterling's hands gently guided her to stand before him to face the polished surface. His beautiful eyes were deep green in the dim lighting when they met hers in their reflection.

"Do you know what I see?" he asked, standing so close she could feel the vibrations of his voice in her back. She forced herself to break his intense gaze and ran her eyes along her shadowed figure. She wasn't vain, but she knew herself to be reasonably attractive—at least, she'd been described as such in tabloids and by more than a couple of admirers taking advantage of her absent husband to boldly proclaim their admiration. She possessed a slim figure and had learned long ago how to accentuate her features with her fashion choices. Her golden hair glinting in the flickering light was considered desirable. Her nose was straight and had been described as fey. While taller than some women, she wasn't so tall as to be considered unattractively so, or to be intimidating to most male dance partners. Any grooming or dressing was merely a façade.

No man had ever seen her so unadorned, so without artifice. And now, as she stood before the mirror in her husband's bedchamber, she saw a woman who was nearing thirty years of age. A married virgin. A woman who wore no rouge and whose hair hung down her back in a simple plait affixed with only a satin ribbon. Her wrapper in a print of blue flowers was modest; the lace of her nightshift tickled the tops of her feet, and her bare toes peeked from beneath the fabric. She fought the girlish urge to bury them in the pile of the rug.

"Just a woman," Alaina replied with uncharacteristic meekness.

Her husband tilted his head, his lips curving further. "I see a woman of fiery passions and unparalleled intelligence." There was a gentle tug on her hair and his strong fingers tenderly unwound her plait. She watched him in the mirror, marveling at the intensity in his gaze and how it contrasted with his gentle touch. "A kind heart, but one unwilling to be trod upon." His arms reached around her and untied her wrapper in one swift tug. Her body began to vibrate with anticipation as the garment was slid from her shoulders and discarded. She caught where Sterling's eyes had locked and noticed the prominence of her aroused nipples was infinitely apparent through the delicate fabric of her nightshift. When she would have covered herself, Sterling caught her hands in his and pulled them back to place searing kisses on each of her palms. Her self-consciousness melted enough that she allowed him to weave her arms back behind his neck, arching her back to jut her breasts toward the mirror.

"Do not move," he ordered gently, causing an unexpected rush of liquid heat between her thighs. "I see..." he continued huskily, trailing his fingers down her sides, making her shiver and her eyes slide nearly closed; "a most desirable woman, in mind, soul...and body." His fingers twisted in the fabric at her hips. "This body," he breathed, "has driven me mad with desire since the day we met. And I have never wanted another." The words were like the release of a dam, losing a flood of need through her limbs. Her flesh was suddenly almost unbearably hot and her inner muscles clenched reflexively, aching for unnamed relief.

She was fascinated by the painfully slow raising of her nightshift's hem as Sterling continued to wrap the fabric around his hands. "I lay awake at night, hard and aching, thinking about these legs wrapped around my hips." She shuddered at the image; only her arms locked around the back of his neck kept her upright when she would have otherwise melted into a puddle on the floor. "When I can sleep, I dream of kissing every last inch of this perfect flesh." The fabric rose above her navel, revealing the glistening golden curls at the juncture of her thighs. So aroused, she was well past the point of modesty. She pressed her thighs together in an effort to staunch the delicious throb pounding there with every heavy beat of her heart. The fabric continued to rise, dragging against her sensitized nipples just enough to cause an unbidden gasp to escape her lips.

Sterling released an involuntary groan of his own. "And these breasts…divine isn't apt enough for their perfection." He gently unclasped her hands to pull the fabric over her head and dropped it to pool around their feet. He steadied her with one strong forearm around her waist, pulling her back against his chest, the thick column of his sex notching perfectly against her rear. He bent his head and pressed a hot, open-mouthed kiss to the soft flesh of her neck. "I have never stopped wanting you, Alaina," he groaned. "It kills me that you ever believed that was not the truth. I have always wanted every part of you with everything I am and everything I have. I swore it the day we stood before the archbishop, and I have never stopped believing it."

Alaina turned her head to look back up into his face. The raw honesty there was her undoing.

She tilted up and caught his mouth with hers, the first time she'd initiated a kiss with him. She felt consumed by his power and heat, and she savored it. She reveled in it. She wanted to lose herself in it and never resurface. She wanted to believe every one of his words and she allowed it to happen—to give herself over to this attraction simmering between them.

His large hand spanned her flat abdomen, stopping just below her navel, hot as a brand yet tender as a feather. His arm tightened around her ribs.

"May I touch you?" Sterling rasped in between kisses. "Please." The pleading in his tone made her fall apart.

She nodded jerkily, not fully understanding what he was asking—he was, after all, already touching her, the full length of his hard body nestled against her back—but she knew she wanted whatever he was willing to offer. "Yes." The word finished with a gasp as his hand already dipped lower. Tenderly, carefully, he parted the folds of her sex with one blunt fingertip. He traced her seam, spreading the dewiness there with every pass. When she would have been embarrassed to have him discover that wetness, the approving rumble from his chest bolstered her confidence. He liked what he'd discovered.

"Even more beautiful than I'd ever imagined..." Sterling's voice was barely above a growl.

His other hand rose from her ribs to cup the weight of her left breast, and a groan of stark desire rumbled like thunder from his body through hers until she felt it in her soul. When the calloused pad of his thumb found the budded peak, she shuddered at the desire lancing from that point throughout each of her limbs and back in time with his touch before it settled low in her stomach. He worked a gentle, insistent rhythm with both of his remarkably skilled hands; plucking her nipple and then soothing the ache, gradually stroking more deeply within her intimate folds until his finger met the very center of her tight core. Those skilled fingers of his circled there, spreading her slickness and making her throb until she involuntarily arched her hips into his touch, and then he suddenly retreated. Alaina would have whimpered in confusion, but his fingers slipped up several inches to discover an even more sensitive spot at the crux of her sex. The pad of his longest finger pressed just right and she gasped in shock at the intensity of the sensation, finally breaking their kiss.

Alaina's hazy vision caught sight of the intensely erotic image they made standing there before the mirror. His temple rested against hers, his fingers cupped her and lashed her close to his body, his other hand confidently worked between her legs as he made her knees tremble with his touch. Her spine turned to jelly, her thighs twitched helplessly as he added another finger to his machinations. The sight of his glistening fingers disappearing between her folds, stroking her where no one had before, should have scandalized her, but, instead, it served only to inflame her passion. Her breath hitched when she met Sterling's eyes in the mirror and she found them burning with an unnatural intensity.

Suddenly, his fingers dipped lower once more, pressing

against her entrance. Her body tensed instinctively.

"Relax, love," Sterling said against her neck, nipping at the lobe of her ear. She began to shake her head—how could she when she felt like a bowstring ready to snap?—until he caught her mouth with his, kissing her so deeply, possessively she felt it in every inch of her being. Her toes curled, her muscles went molten, and Sterling took the opportunity to press his fingers forward, invading her body in the most delicious way. She gasped against his lips and, when his thumb rubbed that secret pearl in time with the slow, shallow thrusts of his two longest fingers, she lost control of her limbs. Her head fell back against Sterling's hard shoulder, and her pounding heart was all she could hear...well, that, and the deep, pained rumble of Sterling's voice.

"So sweet," he growled. "So tight." He cursed. "I don't know how I shall survive."

She might have collapsed had he not insinuated a leg between hers from behind, helping both to spread her wider for his efforts and prop her up. She clutched at his forearm, her nails biting into the corded muscles, and panted frantically. Something was building. A crisis was coming. She didn't know how to stop it— what to do.

"Sterling," she whimpered.

"Look," he replied. "Watch yourself in the mirror. See how glorious and desirable you are as you come apart in my arms." His thick member throbbed against her back, the arching of her spine and rocking tilt of her hips earned her a guttural groan of approval from her husband. Despite her hazy vision, she did as he commanded. She focused her cloudy vision on the reflection in the mirror.

Who was that woman with the flush cresting her cheeks, the passion-glazed eyes, the kiss-swollen lips? The woman who was wantonly spread before a mirror as a man touched her most intimate of places, who held her bright pink nipple trapped in a tantalizing grip between two fingers of the broad hand spanning her pale breast? This woman who was so overcome with lust that she couldn't hold herself up without that man's assistance?

Alaina didn't recognize this confident, sensual being. And she had Sterling to thank for that.

One crook of his finger inside of her coupled with a firm circle of his thumb sent Alaina spiraling. She cried out raggedly as wave after wave of pleasure overcame her. Part of her was terrified of this loss of control, but she also never wanted it to stop. As if reading her mind, Sterling continued his ministrations, never slowing or stilling, murmuring harsh words of encouragement against her hair as she bucked against the heel of his palm where it continued its insistent pressure. She clung to Sterling, riding each pulse of her orgasm and allowing him to wring every last glimmer of pleasure from her body until she went limp, whimpering in shock and exhaustion, both of their bodies slick with sweat—hers from ecstasy and his from restraint.

As she floated down, Sterling continued to nuzzle her hair, planting gentle kisses and reassuring words to her hair. He held her up when her shaky legs would have given out; remained steadfast and strong when she would have given up and given over to her weakened muscles. He continued to hold her until the world was once more solid and steady—until she could find her footing once more. Still, however, he didn't free her. He allowed Alaina to turn within his embrace, pressing against the length of his body. Her eyes closed, she rested her forehead to the hard, sweat-dampened plane of his chest as he stroked her back from the nape of her neck down to the sloping curve of her rear and back up.

"We can stop here," Sterling finally whispered thickly. "If you wish." He seemed to hold himself impossibly still, barely daring to breathe…a hunter terrified of scaring off his target.

Though the tremors of her orgasm still rippled throughout her body, though Sterling had given her the most joyous physical experience of her life, Alaina couldn't help but feel as if something was missing. The throbbing juncture of her thighs ached for more…something she couldn't name but knew in the most primal part of her that it existed.

And, judging by the insistent throb of Sterling's arousal between them, he craved more as well.

Alaina looked up into his face, so gorgeously sculpted, taut with self-control. She didn't recognize the husky, sensual voice coming from her throat when she said, "Make me your wife in truth. Make love to me."

Chapter Sixteen

S TERLING DIDN'T DARE believe his ears.

Was it possible for a heart to long for something so greatly that the ears created falsehoods?

He'd heard of men in extreme situations of deprivation or torture so desperate for relief they became delirious from it. Could that be what Sterling was experiencing? Had he pined for Alaina for so long that his mind had attempted the mercy of imagining Alaina's words?

But no.

There was no mistaking the way Alaina's glittering sapphire eyes gazed up at him, the caress of her hands on his shoulders, the tantalizing press of her erect, mouthwateringly pink nipples against his bare chest, the teasing graze of her soft abdomen against the throbbing ridge of his straining erection.

"Please, Sterling," she breathed. He could do nothing but stare down at her in awe, both their souls laid as naked as their bodies.

His heart stuttered when he witnessed a flicker of insecurity and, not willing to allow her even that iota of it, he smoothly swept Alaina into his arms, holding her high against his chest, savoring the feel of her soft skin against him more than he had anything else in his life. He was certain she could feel the heavy pounding of his heart, but he cared not. If anything, he wanted this woman to know what she did to him—what she'd always done to him, and how he'd never stopped wanting her.

Despite their history, despite everything they'd put one another through these past several weeks, all of this had served only to draw them together more powerfully. For his part, Sterling was done fighting, done being held at arm's length and experiencing the bitterness that came along with it. He wanted to begin his life with this woman in earnest.

While it was tempting to say he wanted to forget the past eight years and start over, this would be a disservice to what they'd both endured and who they'd both become. Sterling had cared deeply for Alaina when they'd married, but this woman in his arms was more mature, more headstrong, and more outspoken in ways that infuriated him and made him step back and appreciate everything about her. He could love her with everything he had, if only she'd let him.

And, as he laid her in the center of his mattress, her long golden locks fanning out like an angel's halo and her blue eyes heavily lidded with desire, he found he wanted her even more than he had in even his wildest, most desperate, most feverish of dreams. His frame of reference was unfortunately rusty, but he instinctively knew she would surpass everything he'd dared hope. She'd already proven to be that and so, so much more.

He knelt beside her, drinking in every inch of her ivory skin, her long, lean legs and those utterly perfect pebbled nipples, more delectable than he could have imagined. His body trembled with nerves and desire. He needed a moment; he had to fight to regain some of his composure lest he do her a disservice. He took a shuddering breath and scrubbed his hand over his face, muttering her name as both a curse and a benediction. He wanted to spend hours learning everything about her body, practicing ways to drive her as unhinged as he felt inside.

"Sterling?" Alaina's soft voice cut through his admiring perusal.

"I want to do this moment justice," he finally said.

"You have already pleased me," she replied with a shy smile. He could now say with confidence that her blushes swept down her face, her throat, and the perfect flesh of her breasts. It was glorious. *She* was glorious.

"I want to please you more. I want to commit all of this to memory to revisit again and again. I want it to be the last thing that crosses my mind when I take my final breath."

"So melodramatic of you." She smiled, but her humor faded when she read the sincerity in his eyes. Alaina reached up one small hand to him, welcoming him into her arms, and he was undone.

Carefully, he covered her body, fitting them together like two long-lost pieces of the same puzzle. The underside of his arousal glided against the smooth flesh of her stomach and thighs, and he barely bit back a groan. His body was long past finished with waiting and he'd imagined this moment with such vivid intensity for so many years that he could only pray he didn't make a fool of himself. To spend before he even got inside her would be the worst sort of embarrassment.

Instead, he took his time, dropping languorous kisses to her lips, savoring her sweet flavor, inhaling the scent of her hair and skin, his chest swelling with pride when she tilted her hips for him. Accepted him. She was untutored and eager, both qualities that added another notch to Sterling's long list of things about his wife that drove him mad with desire.

He reached between them, his fingers seeking and then finding the part of her he most ached to touch, to taste, to possess. She sighed against his lips, her knees falling open as he stroked her. She was so wet for him, so ready from her earlier climax. She felt like the hot, honeyed nectar of the gods. His mouth watered for her; his body trembled. How could she make him feel so weak and so powerful at the same time? He'd never known such a juxtaposition was possible, but there they were. She might have been the one lying prone, but Alaina had him at her mercy.

He wanted this to be good for her—no, better than good. He wanted this to somehow be the beginning of his making up for abandoning her. He wanted this to be transcendent, the true start of how he'd spend the rest of his life worshiping her and making Alaina realize just how much he cared. Though his body screamed for release, his muscles twitching with need and his cock throbbing with desire, weeping with it, he was determined to take his time.

Sterling slid down her body, slowly running his tongue along the virgin flesh on the underside of her breasts, memorizing the flavor of the sweet musk of her skin. His hand dipped lower to caress her folds, pressing the heel of his palm to her pearl. Already sensitized from her first climax at his hands, Alaina quickly responded to the steady rhythm and pressure he applied, making her shake with need. She gasped and undulated against his hand, moving in time with him, tangling her fingers in his hair and holding his mouth to her breast as he laved the puckered tip, kissing and nipping, licking and suckling, strumming her to impossible heights all over again. He loved the sounds she made; he loved how uninhibited she was with him—how she trusted him with her body and her pleasure. Sterling's cock throbbed painfully with every one of her gasps. His jaw clenched as he clutched futilely at the last shred of his sanity, slipping through his hands like water. Her moans and gasps continued to work him higher until he was forced to grind his pelvis against the bed to try to relieve some of the maelstrom overtaking his every nerve.

Her body gave and gripped his fingers as he slid two, then three inside of her. She was impossibly tight, but her liquid arousal eased the way. God, if she felt this unbelievable on his fingers, he could only imagine how she would feel riding his cock…

Unable to take it any longer, Sterling took his member into his hand, running the head through her slick folds, groaning at how good it felt—how good *she* felt—and positioned himself at her tight entrance. He looked back up her body to her flushed, elegant face, reveling in her passion-hazed gaze—something primal roaring with triumph from the knowledge that he'd given that to her—and began to flex his hips. Slowly. Gradually.

Holding his breath as she allowed his intrusion inch by excruciating inch, he paused only when he felt her body tense. His arms trembled with the restraint he employed and it took everything in him not to give into the tingling at the base of his spine begging for release.

"It's alright," he shakily reassured her, placing a kiss upon each of her tightly closed eyelids. His body screamed to thrust home and pound into her, finally claiming his wife as his, but he held it at bay.

"I can't—" Alaina panted and flinched. She was too tight and he, too large. He'd hoped not to cause her pain, but it was now evident that it was inevitable.

"You can," Sterling reassured her before he took a deep breath and lowered his chest to hers, bracing his forearms on either side of her head. He began peppering gentle kisses across her face even though his every nerve was wracked with luscious agony. He steadfastly held his hips still to allow her to accommodate his girth. He felt her relax in increments as she returned his kisses, wrapping her arms around his neck, twisting her fingers in his hair, and running her nails across his scalp.

She held him there, meeting his lips and teeth and tongue with her own. They took turns suckling and nibbling, trading erotic sighs and moans. Finally, Alaina's thighs fell apart, but still, she was too tense. Sterling reached between them once more and caressed where their bodies were joined. He circled her clitoris, working her arousal toward its peak once more with careful strokes and plucks. She whimpered and moaned his name, her body teasing his cock, pulling him deeper, beckoning him home until, finally, Sterling could take it no more and he breached her maidenhead, fully seating him to the hilt. Alaina gasped in surprise, but it quickly melted back into passion as he began to move.

Sterling reveled in the possession, the way they fit together, the way they completed one another. She was so wet for him, slick with the nectar of her arousal, and it eased his way. Every ripple of her inner muscles was the most divine torture, holy and hellish all at once. He ground his hips against hers, trailing his hand along her thighs and encouraging her to wrap those long legs of hers around his hips.

This is what he'd waited for...this night with Alaina in his arms. She was astonishingly gorgeous, brilliant, and his in every way. Just like he was hers.

Nothing could measure up to Alaina.

No one could measure up to her.

The profound relief at finally having her in his bed, of having her welcome him with open arms, of claiming her from the inside out was nearly overwhelming. She overtook every one of his senses—made the rest of the world disappear.

"Yes," he growled, burying his face in her floral-scented neck. A delighted curse slipped from his lips when she tilted her hips just so. What she lacked in experience, she made up for in pure instinct. "God, Alaina," he groaned. She felt so good, so right, so safe.

She was his home.

Her nails raked his shoulders in white-hot streaks of need; they plunged into his hair and bit his scalp as she yanked his head down for an open-mouthed kiss. He gladly obliged her, and they traded sighs and cries and groans.

Undulating against her, their sweat-slicked bodies meeting at an increasingly frantic pace, Sterling felt the beginnings of a powerful climax building again at the base of his spine. He needed her to come; he needed to feel her orgasm pulse around him. He needed confirmation that it, too, was more than he ever could have imagined.

Sterling leaned back and adjusted the angle to stroke a new place inside of her. In response, Alaina's head tossed from side to side, and she muttered incoherently as if she were overcome with fever. Her body fluttered and clenched him most deliciously.

"That's it," he ground out. "Let go," he commanded. Alaina's body tensed and then trembled as she shattered. She dug her heels into his arching back and released a gasping cry which culminated in his name being torn from her lips in a delighted sob. Her sheath milked every last shred of control from his body and Sterling was lost. A series of deep, jerking thrusts signaled his climax, a guttural roar underscoring his utter and complete surrender. She may have been limp and sated beneath him, but Sterling knew, in that moment, Alaina owned him, everything he was, and everything he would ever be.

ALAINA AWOKE TO the caress of large, calloused hands massaging her back in languid strokes. The slow, warm movements seemed to find and lavish just the right amount of attention to each sore muscle. From the base of her skull to the indentation of her lower back, everything was given its due consideration until she was practically molten from it.

She released a little involuntary moan of delight, relishing in the unfamiliar—yet far from unwelcome—treatment. She didn't open her eyes, instead, savoring the strong fingers and broad palms and the pleasure they wrought. She stretched out on her stomach and allowed herself to be engulfed in Sterling's scent left there both from sleep and their earlier sweat-slicked lovemaking.

"Do you like that?" her husband asked in a low whisper.

"Mmm…" was the only reply she could manage.

She buried her face in his pillows, inhaling deeply as his hands worked lower to stroke her buttocks and the muscles of the backs of her thighs.

"Do you have any idea how beautiful you are?" Sterling asked though it was clear he didn't expect a response. "I could simply stare at you for endless hours and never grow bored. I ache to learn every freckle and hollow, every curve and place that makes you sigh." She felt him trace a triangle on the very center of her back. "Did you know you have a trio of flecks here?" There was a light rasp of midnight beard and the warm press of kisses along her spine. "And do you realize how much I love knowing that I'm the only man who has seen them?" Despite her better sense, the possessive heat in his tone was intoxicating...because she liked the same things about him. It was heady to know that he'd waited for her all this time; that Sterling had wanted only her for all this time. This, coupled with the earth-shattering joy to which he'd introduced her, could be enough to make her lose her mind and her heart.

The last thing she'd expected that evening had been winding up in Sterling's arms and his bed, but she couldn't say she was sorry about it in the least. They'd learned together, found the right rhythm, and discovered bliss in one another's arms. She could hardly believe that it could only get better from there when she was utterly boneless when she was in his arms.

Eventually, Sterling's caresses became less and less innocent; the circles he drew with his hands grew wider and wider to encompass the curve of her waist, the sides of her breasts, the cleft of her bottom. He nudged her thighs apart and she obliged as his fingers moved slowly, teasingly closer to where she already throbbed and ached for him all over again, but never quite touching her there. She was slick in anticipation; her body preparing for him to fill and overwhelm her. Just the thought of having his thick, hot flesh between her legs once more made her moan.

Still, Sterling continued his patient ministrations for what felt like an eternity until Alaina finally arched her back with a whimper, wordlessly begging him for more.

More of everything.

He paused in his kisses and she felt his wicked smile against her shoulder just before his fingers delved between her thighs, parting her dewy folds to find that pearl of pleasure he'd discovered some hours earlier. He continued to stroke her, the broad head of his sex twitching against her thigh, insisting upon its own desires and exciting her beyond reason. He rubbed her from her clitoris to her entrance again and again, teasing the swollen flesh and spreading her slickness until she rocked back against him. Her nipples grew taut and hard against the mattress, and her entire body overflowed with anticipation, humming with it like a harp string. Each pass of Sterling's fingers thrummed against that cord, sending tingling vibrations to her fingers and toes, and back again. Fisting the bedclothes, she felt herself climbing dangerously high to where the air thinned, and she had to gasp to pull enough air into her lungs.

Just before she tumbled over that precipice, Sterling removed his hand. Ignoring her whimpering complaint, he grabbed her hips and hauled her back against his front so they both lay on their sides. Curling one large hand around her thigh, he brought her leg over his hip and, with one swift, decisive thrust, he slid home to the hilt. They groaned in unison.

Alaina's body was sensitive and slightly sore from their earlier exertions, but, when Sterling began to move, it all melted away on a tide of pleasure. She loved the sounds he made, the uncontrolled desirous grunts and moans, the erotic words he whispered into the shell of her ear—how he reveled in her body, how her sharp tongue drove him wild, how much he loved being inside of her. Even the collision and pull of their wet flesh gliding together drove her higher. He wrapped a strong corded arm around her waist to hold her in place and ground against her, pressing his teeth into the curve where her neck met her shoulder with just enough pressure to mix pain and eroticism.

It wasn't long before Alaina's climax was upon her. She tensed and trembled, arching back into his thrusts, crying out Sterling's name as he increased his speed and ferocity. He pounded into her from behind, claiming her, and followed her shortly, filling her with more and more of his hot seed with every pulse of his orgasm.

They lay like that for many minutes, savoring the throbbing aftermath of their lovemaking, the air filled with their heavy breaths and pounding hearts, until Sterling slid from her body and tugged her flush to him. He enveloped her with his limbs and buried his face in her unbound hair. There, cradled safe and close in the arms of her husband, Alaina drifted off to sleep once more.

STERLING ROSE SOUNDLESSLY and stealthily from the bed early the following morning. The sight of a sated woman—*his wife*—still lying there sound asleep, buried in a nest of pillows and a rumpled cobalt coverlet was one of the most satisfying sights of his existence.

Waking there with her beside him, curled against his side like a deceptively peaceful cat…he hadn't felt so warm and content in Lord only knew how long. He committed the curve of her cheek, the fan of her long, tawny lashes to his memory, and went to summon his valet to his dressing room so as not to disturb Alaina's slumber. He planned on enjoying breakfast while fully savoring the knowledge that she was content and in his bed at last. He made a mental note to ask for a tray to be prepared for her later so she could rest as long as she liked. Nothing was quite so gratifying as having one's wife as safe and secure as Alaina was in his bed.

His life was finally falling into place, and it was better than he'd ever dared dream.

Chapter Seventeen

THE MARRIAGE OF the Duke and Duchess of Morton progressed quite quickly after that first evening. This was, of course, not to say the two did not have their disagreements—the intercourse was astonishingly wonderful, but it was not magic. Alaina remained her feisty, strong-willed self and Sterling continued to learn patience; still, they wound up panting in each other's arms every night and then curled together in sleep.

Perhaps Sterling's greatest character reference was his ongoing determination to continue wooing his wife even though they'd finally shared a bed—he was convinced nothing would ever be enough for him where she was concerned. The letters Alaina had written to him continued to prove useful in that regard.

He scoured them like a man possessed, filtering through the words for hidden tidbits that might further endear him to his wife. Of course, he'd read them all time and time again but viewing them through a new lens was proving highly informative.

He'd already been reminded of the peonies and continued to ply her with a steady supply of them with a standing order that Morton House be filled with them no less than twice a week. He discovered the name of her preferred bookseller and—after making a trip there and meeting with the manager—he was able to discern which books were her favorites, which she already owned, and which new ones she might enjoy. Those he left waiting for her in her favorite sun-drenched spot in the library and on the cushion of her bedchamber window seat. He snuck to the kitchens and asked Cook to surprise Alaina with her favorite chocolate tart for dessert one evening; the reception that gesture had received was warm, indeed. His favorite had been the trip to the theater.

There was a production of *Hamlet* being put on by the renowned troupe at The Mask & Lyre. He'd simply requested Alaina dress for the theater and be ready at the appointed time. She'd been utterly breathtaking in her emerald green gown with gold embroidered flowers and vines. She glittered, his wife. And when she allowed him to hold her hand in his during the carriage ride from Mayfair to the East End, he could have crowed with pride from the rooftops.

They'd rolled to a stop in front of the building with its dramatic doors and buzz of excited activity and Alaina had finally asked him what they were there to see. The anticipatory glimmer in her eyes nearly made him swallow his tongue.

"Hamlet," he replied. "I realize it's not *The Taming of the Shrew*, but I figured another Shakespearean work might suffice." Her grin had been blinding, her bubble of laughter had been infectious, and the long, unabashed kiss she placed upon his lips had nearly ended the evening far earlier than anticipated.

Sterling spent the evening watching his wife instead of the performance. From what little he did see, the production was of excellent quality. He was far more entertained by the rapt expression on Alaina's face, the thoughtful tilt of her expressive and utterly kissable mouth, and the warmth of her thigh beneath her skirts when he rested his palm there during the play's climax. She held him utterly bewitched.

Nothing, however, compared to the carriage ride home following the performance.

Alaina had lifted the velvet curtain and was staring out the glass of the window at the passing buildings and the occasional golden orb of a streetlamp cutting through the misty night.

Without turning her attention from the scene outside, she spoke in a very soft, casual tone, "Last night, when you kissed me...down there. Is that something that would bring you pleasure as well?"

Sterling's entire body flushed with heat, and he had to clear his throat before he could speak. "Yes. I enjoyed that a great deal." That had been putting it mildly. He was ravenous for her—couldn't wait to taste her sweet ambrosia again and feel her lean thighs grip his head as she came apart and ground against his mouth.

"No," Alaina said, finally turning to face him where he sat beside her. "I mean, would you like it if I did that to you?"

Sterling nearly choked from the instantaneous lust that overcame him. He was overwhelmed by the image of Alaina's blond head looking up at him, her graceful hands working between his legs. To have her mouth on him...that was not something he'd ever thought to ask for—no matter how badly it made him ache with want. He'd witnessed the act more than a handful of times during the debauched parties on the Continent (and far worse, if he were honest), and had certainly imagined receiving such treatment, but to request such a thing of his wife felt like overstepping. If she started the conversation, however...

"You do not need to," he replied somewhat unsteadily.

"That isn't what I asked." Her sapphire eyes met his unflinchingly. "I asked if you would like it; if it would please you." It was nearly impossible for Sterling to breathe. "I want to taste you—"

"Yes," he croaked. "Yes, it would please me. Greatly."

Alaina nodded once very thoughtfully, and then shocked him to his core when she hiked up her skirts and spun to kneel on the floor of the carriage as best as she could in the cramped space.

"Oh, God, Alaina..." Sterling gasped. "Now?" Her fingers were already working on the fastenings of his breeches, her knuckles and the back of her hand brushing the thick ridge of his immediate, raging arousal. He didn't know if he'd ever become so hard so fast before—it left him lightheaded. She batted his hands away when he would have stopped her. Very little would have pleased him more than his wife so overcome with passion for him that she cared not when or where the act took place, but the last thing he wanted was for her to feel obligated.

"Whyever not? By my estimation, we've plenty of time before we reach Morton House." The wicked gleam in her eyes was—would forever be—his undoing. "Would you deny me?"

"Never." And it was the truth. Sterling was at her mercy, body, heart, and soul.

The ruddy head of his sex sprang free from the confines of his clothing, proud and erect as it begged for her attention. Alaina's nails raked along his thighs, making his cock twitch in anticipation. Her eyes widened at the sight, but she was far from backing down.

Ever the brazen intellectual, she carefully wrapped her fingers around his length, testing his girth and the slide of the silken skin over the hardness beneath.

"Like this?" she asked after several seconds of tentative strokes.

Sterling grunted in choked delight.

"You can grip me tighter," he ground out as he braced his heels on the rocking floor. He covered her hand with his to demonstrate.

"So hard? I do not wish to hurt you."

"Darling, your cunny is twice as tight as that little fist of yours and I've survived that several times over." His low growl finally served to sway her composure. Her cheeks flared a brilliant pink evident in even the carriage's poor lighting. Sterling sat back and allowed her to find a rhythm; he couldn't watch her too closely or the sight of his wife touching and stroking him would quickly send him over the edge.

He almost lost himself entirely when he felt her hot breath on the sensitive head of his member and then a sweet, tentative kiss on the slit.

"Bloody—" He made a strangled curse and slammed a fist on

the squab beside him.

"Did that hurt?" Alaina almost backed away, so he responded hastily.

"No! No. It didn't. Keep going. Please."

Satisfied, Alaina leaned forward once more and peppered his sex with slow, tender kisses, beginning to stroke him once more while she did so. He trembled when he heard her inhale the scent of his skin; he nearly died when her lips parted and her tongue darted out to taste the little pearl of moisture beading there.

When her mouth closed around the head, he saw stars. She was warm and wet and sweet, so deliciously delicate as she began to lick and suck. Head falling back in helpless abandon, Sterling gave himself over to Alaina's ministrations. She was bloody amazing, his wife.

She'd already learned to listen to his moans and growls, continuing what made him squirm and his hips buck. It was everything he could do not to thrust himself deeper into her throat until she took all of him.

His hand flew to her head when she performed a particularly creative swirl but stopped just shy of wrapping his fingers in her locks and holding her there. He made the mistake of looking down to see her wide luminous eyes and golden blond head as she looked up at him from where she knelt between his spread legs. Her cheeks hollowed as she sucked him, her dainty fist working in tandem with her mouth from root to tip. Then, she did the unthinkable and reached up to bring his hand to her hair, letting him know it was alright to touch her. And Sterling was lost.

He cupped the back of her head and helped guide her in a rhythm that quickly had his hips bucking, thrusting as deeply as she could take him. "You are amazing," he panted. "Your mouth...God..." A gasp was wrenched from his chest. "You have all of me, Alaina. Every bit. I am at your mercy. I am yours..." He continued his praise of her and desperate, nonsensical pleas as she continued her relentless worship of his body.

When she moaned around him, the vibrations tickled every inch of his glistening cock. It took him only a few more thrusts until the telltale tingling began in the base of his spine.

"Alaina," he growled. "Alaina, I'm going to—" Clumsier than he'd ever been in his life, he tried to pull her off of him so he didn't finish in her mouth, but she steadfastly continued her pace and met the desperate digs of his pelvis. His body throbbed and she took him as deeply as she could just as his orgasm ripped through him with violent abandon.

His legs may have been numb, the rest of his body may have been left weak and depleted, but Sterling still managed to haul Alaina into his lap and kiss her deeply, savoring the heady saltiness on her tongue.

He loved Alaina.

He loved this woman, and he suspected he always had.

But he stopped before the words passed his lips. There were still repairs to be made in their relationship and he didn't want her to feel any unnecessary pressure. He was truly content in that moment, and he was more than happy to have her in his arms while he marveled at how far they'd already come and looked forward to where they would go.

STERLING TOOK EVERY opportunity to make passionate love to Alaina. They frequently spent hours exploring new and exciting ways in which they could worship one another.

Not that he'd doubted it, but Alaina proved to be just as voracious and intense in the bedroom as she was outside of it. And it delighted him to no end.

He'd allowed his wife so far beneath his skin that even the men at his club had commented upon the spring in his step. The Duke of Morton was a man obsessed, and he cared not one bit who knew. He'd waited his entire life to feel settled in marriage— to feel like he had someone by his side—and he'd be damned if he didn't enjoy it.

Currently, Sterling was seated at his desk in his expansive

study. It was often difficult to focus on the orderly columns of numbers and ceaseless parade of correspondence on a good day. However, with Alaina perched upon his lap, her bottom nestled securely against his rapidly swelling groin as she ran her lips along the lightly stubbled edge of his jaw, well, it was damn near impossible to see straight, let alone do anything productive.

His hand flexed against the soft flesh of her hip as she nipped the point where his jaw met his throat. She'd pay for that, to be sure. In fact, he quite looked forward to bending her over this desk and—

A knock at the study door rudely interrupted Sterling's train of thought. He barely stifled a groan of disappointment and had to clear his throat before he could speak…all while his wicked wife continued her teasing.

"What?" It came out more harshly than he'd intended, but it was difficult to maintain any composure when she wriggled against him like that.

Overall, the servants seemed to have caught on to Sterling and Alaina's reconciliation and called a silent truce with his presence in the house. In response, they'd gradually come to respect his word and afford the two of them a much greater level of privacy Sterling sincerely appreciated.

Thank God.

"A gentleman is here to see you, Your Grace," came Maxwell's voice through the door. The man was aware Sterling wasn't alone or he would have otherwise opened the door rather than raise his voice to be heard through the barrier. "A Mr. Grey. He has no card, but he insisted you were expecting him."

Sterling sobered at the name and his body grew taut for an entirely different reason. "Five minutes and then show him in, Maxwell."

Sensing the abrupt change in his demeanor, Alaina leaned back. He met her arresting eyes and, though he was loath to do so, he gently removed her from his lap and set her on her feet.

"I need to see what the man wants, darling."

"I understand." Alaina sighed dramatically, straightening the skirts of her bright blue morning dress. He received a rather glorious view of her breasts and the valley between them as she bent to do so. She was wicked enough that she likely did it on purpose. "I have correspondence of my own I've been sorely neglecting," she added with a rueful sigh. Sterling caught her hand before she could step away and pressed a kiss to her palm.

"I'll find you when I've finished."

She cocked a haughty brow at him. "And who is to say I'll have time for you? I am, after all, a very busy lady." Her coy smile followed by the elegant sway of her hips as she left the room sent a new knife of lust straight to his cock, and Sterling was forced to remain seated and use the desk to mask his arousal until his ardor cooled.

The butler shortly thereafter showed in the tall, dark, caller. The man went by many names, each one suiting a persona and geared toward a singular aim. To call him a gentleman would be considered laughable amongst the titled elitists; he had no breeding to speak of and little formal education. Sterling, however, trusted the man with his life and had done so and more for the past eight years.

His cold gaze met Sterling's, both of them remaining silent until the butler's footsteps could be heard retreating down the hallway.

Sterling hadn't expected this unannounced visit and had—thanks to Alaina's considerable charms—all but forgotten he'd sent a missive to the man to take a discreet inquiry into some of the numbers Sterling had come across in the ledgers. The abrupt change in Sterling's marital situation had created a hazy effect on the rest of his world. It wasn't smart and it wasn't safe, but it was a pleasant change from the constant stress and dangers he'd endured while on the Continent. He had rather enjoyed the unguarded way he could simply *be* with Alaina—when she wasn't trying to take off his head, that was.

"A drink?" Sterling offered and gestured to the upholstered

seat on the opposite side of his desk.

"Thank you, no," was the curt reply. The man's eerie silver eyes darted around the room, examining the gilt finishes, the polished wood, the expensive woven rug beneath his feet. It was odd having both of Sterling's worlds colliding at once—his past and his present mixing together like disparate paint on an artist's palette. "I've other business I need to address."

"I take it you're only passing through Mayfair, then?" Sterling tilted his head and leaned back in his chair, affecting a more relaxed persona than he felt.

The other man eyed him for several silent moments before his mouth split into an expression as close to a smile as Sterling had ever seen from him. "You know how it is. Besides, I'll develop a rash if I spend too long a time amongst all this frippery."

Sterling chuckled. "You never were comfortable on this side of the servants' doors. How is it being home? Settled back in yet?"

The two of them had spent every single day in each other's company for the last eight years. They knew one another better than some siblings and watched one another's backs more closely than brothers. Their lives had depended upon complete and utter vigilance and honesty. Hardly any moment passed where Sterling hadn't been grateful that Ramsay had paired the two of them together. Their first meeting had been mere weeks before Sterling and Alaina's wedding. Ramsay had informed him that this man would accompany him on his travels by playing the part of his valet. Where Sterling would obtain information from the noble and wealthy, his partner would have access to back rooms and gossiping servants. This turned out to be a masterful arrangement with one or both of them able to acquire valuable intelligence and report back to England. Working so closely together for so long necessitated a deep level of trust—one that did not simply disappear because the mission concluded. They came from two very different worlds, yet they'd become as close as brothers bonded by blood.

The man lifted one shoulder in a shrug as he strode forward and dropped into the chair to which Sterling had gestured earlier. Despite his impressive size, he moved with the innate grace of a jungle cat. "I'm no more at home here than I was on the Continent. Not all of us have a life and a home like this to return to. Or a wife such as the duchess." With that, the man pulled some folded papers from the inner pocket of his coat and placed them on the desk between them.

Sterling eyed them as if a barn cat had just dropped a dead rat at his feet.

"You always were one to get straight to business, Black," Sterling commented flatly. Oliver Black, alias "Mr. Grey" (among numerous others), former street urchin, one-time gang runner, and current espionage professional specializing in undercover assignments, was the only man Sterling knew he could trust with the task of tracking down his wife's movements and where, exactly, she was funneling money…who this Mrs. Worthy was.

He'd known there were few men skilled enough, subtle enough to ferret out the information he'd requested without sounding an alarm…he just hadn't known how badly he'd hoped to be disappointed until that very moment. Never in his life had he considered preferring ignorance to knowledge.

As if sensing Sterling's hesitation, Black leaned forward and placed his fingers on the papers between them. He began to drag them away slowly. "You know, this can disappear even more easily than it was acquired."

Sterling's hand smacked down atop the corner of the stack and they both froze, the sound of his palm on the wood echoing in the room. Black sat back once again while Sterling pulled the papers toward him and began to skim the information scrawled there.

He learned that "Mrs. Worthy" was a South Bank all-girls orphanage and Alaina had been making substantial donations for a number of years. On its own, this wasn't an odd thing for a titled woman to do, but it was interesting that the payments were being made outside of the funds directly earmarked for donations.

Sterling's family had long been benefactors of various charities. Technically, he was even on the board of a couple of foundations, though he'd never even met the members or attended functions—the position was more ceremonial than anything. He had no qualms about making donations and, in fact, there were sums set aside in the Morton accounts for just such things. Surely Alaina knew this...it wasn't exactly a secret, and she tallied the household accounts herself.

Why, then, did it seem as if she paid special attention to this orphanage? What vested interest existed?

Even stranger, there were notes that she made near-weekly visits to this particular girls' home and stayed for several hours each time...and she'd never mentioned it to him before. In fact, he quite vividly remembered at least one of the recorded dates where she'd told him she had a meeting with her modiste. He ran a mental recap of her schedule and, sure enough, there were a few other times he recognized where she'd been out, or he'd been attending to business and hadn't been around to witness her comings and goings.

"This orphanage..."

"Clean. Well-appointed as far as those places go." Sterling watched over the edge of the paper as his visitor sat back and crossed his arms over his chest. "When asked, the matrons and teachers alike had only the most wonderful things to say about the duchess. In fact, they seemed more than a little wary about any man's intentions that he would inquire after her. She appears to be quite the dedicated and charitable woman."

Sterling heard Black's words, the compliments he paid Alaina, but his mind spun and spiraled. The pebble in his boot returned to prod him with a vengeance. Any number of possibilities flashed before his mind's eye—everything from the innocent to the absurd. Alaina could simply be going above and beyond the normal expectations of a titled lady with charitable inclinations, couldn't she? The donations were so large; could she have been blackmailed into making them? Could "Mrs. Worthy's" be nothing more than a disguise for the deposit of the funds? He'd seen stranger things in his life…but it made no sense. Why, then, would she make such religious visits to the girls' home and stay? What drew her there?

His wife addled him, spun him around, turned him upside down. He was not a man who normally lacked in confidence, but she shook him. The fact that he'd been blind to these activities of hers—had dropped his guard enough for this to slip by him—was more than mildly unnerving to a man whose very life had depended upon his ability to remain observant. That she'd continued to hide these behaviors from him despite their recent rapport shattered the illusion he'd begun to craft that his wife was starting to care for him…to forgive him. Her trust in him was nothing compared to what he'd placed in her. Foolishly.

Sterling's stomach crashed through the floor as if it were attached to a lead anchor. His mind began to flail and scramble for purchase most uncharacteristically; he turned his eyes back to the words on the papers before him but saw none.

So much of his life had been nothing but secrets. His relationship with Alaina had been riddled with them, but he finally knew what it felt like to be on the receiving end of one and he liked it not one bit. It set him back on his heels. It made him lose sight of what he thought he knew and the truths he'd held onto fiercely for eight years. He didn't know his wife. They'd laid themselves bare, and still, she withheld something from him.

To be fair, he'd done the same to her.

His eyes focused back on the most damning bit of information listed at the top of the very first page: The donations began a little more than three years prior…right around the time her letters to him had stopped.

He didn't believe this to be a coincidence. Something about Mrs. Worthy's had absorbed her attention and a not-insignificant amount of money.

Fed up with subterfuge, Sterling knew he needed to go to the source.

Chapter Eighteen

BLACK TOOK HIS leave shortly after delivering the information he'd obtained, but Sterling remained in the study in stony, agonizing silence. He slouched back in his chair, propping up his tense jaw with his white-knuckled fist, his gaze boring holes in the sheaves of paper still laid out on his desk.

Black had been right.

This information could disappear.

He could feign ignorance.

He and Alaina could go about their new life; he could pretend that their bubble of peace hadn't been pierced by the harsh pin of reality.

No.

He couldn't live like that...not when he'd been as honest as he could be with her.

It wasn't so much the money that bothered him, it was the lie of it all. For her to have duped him so successfully was more than galling.

It was bile-inducing.

It was humiliating on a deeper level than any public shaming of him she'd attempted.

She made him *love her* and still, she hid things from him.

Because he did love her.

He'd begun to suspect it whenever his heart stopped when she smiled at him, when he counted the hours and minutes until he could see her again, when he struggled not to touch her at every opportunity, how he wanted nothing more than to hold her against him and shut out the rest of the world. She'd charmed him with her strong will, bewitched him with her body. He'd thought they'd finally reached a point where they might plan for a future, but how could that be the case when she continued to lie to him? What was keeping from him? His mind spun with the possibilities. He's seen enough of the dark side of human behavior in the last eight years that his mind automatically went to the worst possible scenario, even though he realized he was being ridiculous. Still, he couldn't let it be.

He rationalized that his lies were all in the past—that he hadn't been anything but as honest as possible with her since his return—but she clearly could not say the same. After all he and Alaina had shared, she still didn't trust him.

Anger fueled by pain boiled within his breast until it threatened to overflow. He was cut more deeply than any physical wound he'd ever endured in his years of training beneath Ramsay and the rest of the masters in his spy society. He'd made no secret of wanting to give Alaina everything, yet she couldn't even be honest about where she went. And who she might be involved with.

How dare she?

His actions decided, Sterling shoved himself to his feet and snatched up the papers in his fist. He flew from the study like a furious hurricane and stormed up the stairs and down the hall with his boots falling like thunder until he reached Alaina's private study. He saw none of the vibrant furnishings, the small oil paintings she'd selected so carefully, his eyes only focused upon the woman seated at the dainty writing desk. The smile upon her face when she saw him—the moment before she registered his barely masked rage—fully shattered what was left of his heart.

Her expression fell and she set aside her quill. "Sterling, whatever is the matter?" The concern in her tone served only to chafe the wound in his soul.

"The orphanage," he demanded in a low, dangerous tone.

"I beg your par—"

"Mrs. Worthy's. The donations." He held the crumpled sheaves of parchment in her face. "Tell me about your donations to the girls' home," he growled, sounding more like a monster every second, but he cared not.

Alaina shook her head. "I don't—"

"Don't lie!" he demanded, one decibel below a roar. "No more lies." He shoved the documents at her until she had no choice but to take them.

HER HEART POUNDING in her ears, Alaina could only skim the pages Sterling had shoved into her hands. He paced furiously back and forth, raking his hands through his chestnut hair and making it stand up in odd tufts. A deep notch was carved between his brows, and his mouth was set in a grim line.

Rather than explain his agitation, she grew only more and more baffled as to how he'd discovered so much about her schedule. Somehow, he'd tracked her movements to and from the girls' home, down to the minute. The notes listed the names of the matrons and staff with whom she was most closely acquainted; there was an accounting of her donations made directly to the orphanage. Her confusion swiftly grew to anger when the full realization of what she held struck her.

He'd had her followed.

He'd had reports written up on her like some sort of errant employee or suspect of a crime.

Despite his words of honesty and sincerity, it turned out that he trusted her less far than he could throw her.

It was Alaina's turn to twist the papers in her fists. "How did you obtain this information?" she ground out.

"What does it matter?" Sterling whirled on her, though he

was unable to meet her gaze. It was telling that his hazel eyes were evasive, aimed at a point above her left ear. How had they once looked upon her so warmly and now they reflected only frigid fury?

"It matters because you had me followed!"

"Clearly, with good reason."

"Good reason?" she scoffed incredulously.

"It is obvious you were hiding something."

"If this is about the funds, then you know I tracked them in the household accounts. I balanced the funds from my unused pin money, so I took nothing that was not mine—"

"Damn the money!" Sterling snarled. "It is not a drop in the bucket. I gave you a chance for honesty; I might have forgiven you had you told the truth weeks ago. I deserve to know why my wife is lying to me about her whereabouts!"

The words hit Alaina like a swift slap to her cheek.

Her arms fell limply to her sides.

"How dare you?" she whispered, no longer recognizing the man before her as the one who'd held her so tenderly, who'd confessed to her his devotion unwavering. It was a lie. The man she'd believed him to be was a lie.

"I have a right to know," Sterling insisted, thumping his chest. "You were making secret visits to a girls' home, funneling money into it. It makes one wonder what else you're hiding."

All sense of decorum fled Alaina at that point. Her husband's irrational rage doused any tenderness she'd begun to hold for him. How foolish she had been to ever consider forgiving this man. It was mortifying that she'd allowed her guard to fall, that she'd welcomed him into her bed, that she'd done those things to his body to return the pleasure he'd shown her, that she'd allowed him to seep through the cracks in her heart and fill the spaces with what she might have one day considered love. The illusion was so easily crumbled to dust that it was clear now to her how fragile the façade had been.

Furious, she sprung to her feet and stalked toward Sterling.

"The donations helped fund a library at the orphanage and paid tutors for the girls. Do you know that many of them were leaving the home with little to no education to speak of and couldn't even write their own names? What kind of preparation is that?" Her voice continued to rise, but she cared not who heard them. Let the servants gossip. Let them whisper about her volatile marriage. As far as Alaina was concerned, Sterling had just toppled every pillar upon which they'd begun to rebuild their life together. "To speak of the funds, you were *so generous* as to provide me with more pin money than I could ever spend. I decided to put the money to good use and directed it where it was more needed. I might have been a good little wife and begged your permission to add Mrs. Worthy's to the estate's list of charitable funds, but you'd never responded to my letters before…how was I to hope for a different outcome if I made such a request? And I'm sure you can tell how receptive Mr. Bates is to my involvement with anything related to accounts. I practically had to wrestle the books from his hands months after you and I were wed, so I would have wasted my breath had I asked him for his approval in adjusting the budgets.

"The ladies of my Reading Society and I regularly take up donations for Mrs. Worthy's. We pool what funds we can, and I made it my mission to fill in the gaps in their needs when and where I could. The home has no formal board, so I have done what I can to help them.

"As for the visits you have so kindly tracked and outlined, they were so I could personally inspect the facilities and make sure they were up to my standards. Sometimes, other members accompanied me; other times I went on my own. I wanted to be certain the funds were being used as allocated." Alaina exhaled a shaky breath. "And I read to the smaller girls… I, of all people, know what it feels like to be abandoned without explanation. I thought only to make the children feel a little less lonely and unloved and unworthy…and here I am being crucified for it."

AS SHE SPOKE, Sterling felt a knife plunge into heart and twist. His rage cooled, his vision slowly cleared, and he began to see reason…and what an ass he'd been. All the progress they'd made came crashing down around his ears in a matter of seconds with his accusation. It would have been easy for him to blame Black for it, but the information had been flawless…it had been Sterling's own rash reaction that had been faulty.

"Five years I've been championing Mrs. Worthy's—among other charities and causes—and now you choose to take issue?" Her eyes glistened with unshed tears. "What changed?"

Sterling wanted to say that she'd done something wrong in sending funds to the home. He wanted to take issue with the charity she was performing. But how could he begrudge her reading to girls and ensuring their wellbeing and education?

In truth, it was the perceived lie that had added fuel to the fire. He'd hidden behind secrets and half-truths for so long that it had been a relief to feel as if he was moving past all of it—that he'd left behind that constant uncertainty for a life with a woman who was made of candor. And, when he'd felt that had been threatened, he lost his whole sense of self. He lost his head.

His only close example of a marriage had been his parents. They'd cared for one another and adored him, but they'd lived a life of companionability and not love. There had been no volatile fights, but there had also been no outward passion. Upon the announcement of his engagement to Alaina, he'd been warned by older members of his club that marriage could cause a man to lose himself. All the books and poems and plays he'd been exposed to had echoed shades of this. Love was a powerful, all-consuming emotion that often guided men astray; it could cause the sanity of even the most logical person to slip.

And it was precisely why members at every level of the spy society were strongly discouraged from forming strong attachments that might lead to love—why Ramsay had displayed so much displeasure when Sterling had announced his intention to marry Alaina before he left for the Continent. A man in love was a man who made mistakes. He understood that first-hand now.

All of this spun over and over again in his frantic brain, but no words came as the noose tightened around his throat. His outburst had been disgusting and pathetic, but it was clear remaining levelheaded was hardly ever an option when it came to the woman he loved…that he'd never stopped loving.

"Is this the first time you've had me investigated? Followed?" Alaina demanded. She whipped the papers at him, though they fluttered uselessly to the ground before reaching him.

Though he knew the truth would damn him further, he couldn't help but admit to everything. He owed her that much at that point. Atonement was often a painful, rocky path, but one worth traversing.

Sterling shook his head.

There were several seconds of stunned hesitation. "Who?" she scoffed in disbelief. "When?"

"I needed a source of consistent, personal updates on you—information about how you were faring behind closed doors while I was abroad," he admitted evenly, keenly aware of the growing danger. She crossed her arms over her chest, holding herself as she waited, and Sterling took a bracing breath before he continued. "I had contacts here in London. When they could, they provided me with information as to the events you attended and your public activities—it is how I learned about the notoriety of your Reading Society while I was away—and they also directed some discreet inquiries to the household staff. This was more difficult because you've managed to garner quite the loyal staff; still, I was able to glean enough information that you were safe in my absence, even *thriving*." That had been a dagger to his gut if ever there was one. It had been part of the reason why he'd come back so determined to prove that he could be necessary to Alaina's future—that she needed him.

"You—you had strangers prying into my life to help assuage your guilt about abandoning me?"

"Not strangers," he sighed with resignation. "These were

people I trusted."

"Apparently, they weren't reliable enough to provide you with the reason for my visits to Mrs. Worthy's!" Alaina snapped. The fire in her eyes would have been beautiful if he hadn't sensed the potential for it to burn his world down. And he was the one who sparked the tinder.

"You are a woman who garners loyalty wherever you go, Alaina. Your staff was incredibly reluctant to divulge any information." Alaina scoffed, but he forged on. "I couldn't have you watched the entire time, not without raising suspicion or planting someone with questionable morals in your household, which was never an option." This, of course, didn't mean staff didn't chatter amongst themselves and let slip a few tidbits here and there to delivery men or others they believed to be their partners in service. They could be a wealth of information if one knew how to place the proper inquiries, but even they had their limitations. "You managed to acquire one of the most loyal staffs in all of London." The termination of her letters to him, the secret donations and frequent visits to the girls' home, and his own wavering confidence that leaving Alaina had been the right thing to do meant Sterling was primed for a wildly outrageous and unfair judgment of his wife. An overreaction.

Disbelief, anger, and sadness flashed across Alaina's face in a carousel of emotions, finally landing on incredulity. "So…you cared enough to hire people to ferret out information and feed you snippets of my life for eight years, but not enough to enquire after me yourself? You knew I wrote you all those letters and you never responded to a single one. I overlooked this fact because you were making such an effort now, but…Sterling…surely you must see how upsetting and backward this is."

He barely suppressed a flinch. Hearing his name on her lips was something he'd never grow tired of, but the circumstances transformed the word into a blade. "I couldn't, Alaina," he insisted. "It was unsafe."

"Why?" she demanded and advanced on him, prodding his

chest above where his heart had once resided. The organ was now singed to ash fine enough to blow away on the breeze. "No more secrets; we've had enough of those for a lifetime, and I will scream in earnest if I am forced to endure any further hypocrisy from you."

Sterling's eyes looked heavenward and slid closed.

It was now or never; he would divulge his secrets, or he would die alone with them.

"I was sent to the Continent by the Crown as a spy," he began evenly. "I could not let on that I had a wife at home whom I cared about in case my true aim was discovered. Your existence could have been used against me. You could have become a target and I refused to put you at risk."

To his dismay, Alaina laughed in disbelief and turned to flee the room. Sterling's hand darted out and grabbed her wrist to stop her. She'd demanded the truth and he'd be damned if he didn't give it all to her now that he knew they walked a razor's edge between understanding and utter disaster.

"It is the truth." The sincerity in his gaze must have given her pause because she ceased tugging at his grip. "I realize it sounds unbelievable, but I swear it is the only thing that could have dragged me from your side all those years ago.

"I was a diplomatic spy in the courts of Europe, chosen for my looks, youth, and title. I could misbehave and assume the role of debauched young duke, all while never drawing any suspicion. My title granted me access to inner circles in high society and my carefully cultivated reputation endeared me to my targets. They believed I was an immoral fop. It was all a façade; I swear it. What I told you before about my time on the Continent was the truth. Everything the tabloids reported was a lie. There were no other women…ever. The life I led was all for show." He chose to take it as a good sign that her furious eyes never left his face. At least she was listening, and he was determined to plod on.

"I was recommended by one of my professors at university and my training began before my eighteenth birthday. I was too busy to chase skirts like my peers, which is why I'd avoided any romantic entanglements. I never counted on meeting you…of falling in love with you, Alaina." His heart skipped a beat at her sudden intake of breath. "Our engagement had already been in the works by the time they'd deemed me ready for the plans they made, and I received my orders. I was strongly encouraged to break off our relationship…but we both know how well that turned out.

"Instead, I insisted upon having enough time for us to marry and…convinced them it was vital that I get an heir on you in case the worst happened…but I just couldn't go through with it. I was a coward who couldn't chance the possibility of leaving you with child before I fled to my mission and naïvely rationalized that I could at least give you the security of my name and wealth. I was young and stupid enough to believe it was kinder to simply leave than sleep with you and disappear knowing the possible peril involved in the role I'd have to play on the Continent."

"I—I need to sit down," Alaina murmured, but she swatted Sterling away when he would have helped her to a chair near the hearth. She dropped into it and took a shaky breath before looking up into his face once more. It broke his heart how beautiful and broken and small she looked. "You truly didn't leave me because you wanted to, but because you were ordered to? Everything I've read, everything I've believed about the past eight years was all a lie?"

"All an act. There were never any other women," he replied definitively, reiterating what he'd already told her several times over and fully prepared to do it as many times as she required to believe it in her soul. "I arranged much of it, but never truly took part. The women were hired. I would put on a show, never exchanging more than a reluctant kiss or two to maintain appearances, and even those left me guilt-ridden. You must believe me; I had no choice. I'd committed to the role and I couldn't simply break away from it."

He looked deeply into her eyes, willing her to see the truth.

"The entire time, I never stopped thinking about you. Not for a single hour."

RATHER THAN REASSURE Alaina, Sterling's words served only to fan the flames of resentment and pain expanding deep within the pit of Alaina's chest. His every explanation—every excuse—gradually enraged her more and more…made bile rise to the back of her throat. Everything she'd believed she'd known about her husband these past eight years was a lie. All of it. And he had the gall to accuse her of lying when she wasn't even sure she knew the barest of truths about him.

And if he'd lied so smoothly for so long, then who was to say there weren't still a thousand other lies littering the space between them?

"You never even considered telling me the truth?" Alaina's voice shook more than she cared to admit. "With everything you've said, not once did you say you'd weighed the option of simply telling me why you had to leave."

"I couldn't, Alaina; it was not safe."

"No!" she snapped. "Stop making yourself out to be some hero. You simply didn't once consider that I might have respected your duties and been better equipped to handle the years without you had I had the bolster of the truth to prop me up in my darkest moments. It is quite obvious that you didn't trust me enough or think me worthy of your secrets." She jutted her chin in the direction of the paper detritus scattered where they'd once stood. "Your *investigation* was evidence enough of that. You formed your conclusions too hastily—not a trait I would think someone with true espionage experience would possess."

"Everything is different with you, Alaina," Sterling interjected through gritted teeth. "I—I cannot think properly when I am around you."

"Is that supposed to be a compliment?" She sniffed and then shook her head. "Whatever the truth, it is now impeccably clear to me that all of this was a mistake. *All of it.*"

ALAINA STOOD AND smoothed her skirts. It was clear she was done meeting his eyes, no matter how hard he silently pleaded with her to do so…to not turn and slowly, woodenly stride from the room. This new stoic side of her unnerved him more than her anger—at least when she yelled at him, she saw him as worthy of her time and emotions. Her ice queen facade slid back into place, and he was frozen outside of an impenetrable wall.

"Where are you going?" he croaked out through his tight throat.

Alaina paused and spoke over her shoulder, never once raising her eyes. "I will be making arrangements to stay elsewhere for a while," she murmured coolly. "I cannot be around you right now." She turned once more to leave.

Sterling could no more stop his legs from closing the gap between them than he could his heart from beating. "You cannot just abandon this marriage."

She froze, her back ramrod straight. This time, she didn't bother turning her head. "Can't I? It seems like abandonment is a rather common theme in our lives."

He violently cursed his poor choice of words as Alaina slipped away. His emotions for his wife had turned him into the worst sort of overbearing husband. He was mistrusting when she'd truly given him no reason to be that way. He was irrational where he'd once prided himself on his level head. He'd become the worst sort of hypocrite for calling her out for walking away when that was precisely what he'd done on their wedding night.

He'd come to know Alaina fairly well since his return…short of bodily restraining her, there was no preventing her from leaving. He also knew he couldn't be present while her things were packed. While she walked away. The mere thought of it sent a wave of nausea crashing through him with such force that he nearly staggered.

He had to let her go, even if it killed him. She needed time and space to consider whether the depth of his sins was worth overlooking, and he owed it to her to allow her that much.

Not knowing what else to do, he stormed down the stairs and bellowed for his hat and cloak. He'd go to his club and drink himself numb. It was the only chance he had at sleeping without her in his arms.

Chapter Nineteen

STERLING LURKED IN a distant corner in a room at White's like a vengeful spirit, watching life but not part of it. When men made eye contact or dared inch toward him, he glared until they turned away uncomfortably. He relied upon his seething, brooding countenance to warn others away, woe be to the man too dense to notice the danger. He was poor company, in no mood for any social niceties, and couldn't stomach inquiries at the moment. He'd have been better off drinking at home, had everything not been a reminder of his wife and all the mistakes he'd made.

The worst part was that Sterling knew he deserved it. He deserved to spend the rest of his days a lonely bitter man suffering the consequences of all the poor choices he'd made and seemed to continue to make where Alaina was concerned.

For several hours, he tossed back drink after drink and contemplated the great, disgusting mess of his life.

On one hand, he'd made significant accomplishments in his position as a diplomatic spy. He'd earned more than one commendation (albeit, secret ones) for his bravery and cunning; however, it had always felt like such a farce. Who was proud of awards earned from behaving as a dense, spoiled, debauched young buck? It mattered not that he'd ferreted out vital information in foreign courts and likely prevented assassinations and at least two wars. It felt like a joke. *He* felt like a joke. And he'd been looking forward to exacting some real change at home in

England where he might directly impact the lives of others using his true voice and soul.

On the other hand, Sterling had wound up losing a part of himself in the process. The weight of his sacrifices to his personal life and personality was far greater than he ever could have anticipated as a younger man eager for adventure and excitement and serving his country. Aside from the unforgivable sin of abandoning his wife on their wedding night, he'd been forced to become someone else—to adopt a persona and do things he found more than a little distasteful. The *ton* had always shaken their heads over his decision to wed so young, but they didn't know him, not truly. Debauched parties and hell-raising had always held little appeal for him. Having lost his parents so young to illness, he'd formed in his head the vision and hopes of a comfortable, stable home with a loving wife and a passel of children. That had always been his goal. Along the way, the sense of duty his father had instilled in him from the cradle had gotten in the way; he viewed quantity of the impact over quality and saw helping England as a spy was of greater use than being just a duke in the House of Lords. He'd always told himself there would be time to achieve his dreams—that he had a wife who was waiting and seemed fine with doing so because she hadn't attempted to annul their marriage—but as the years dragged on and Ramsay's society deemed his presence on the Continent more beneficial than back in England, he'd put off that dream in the name of responsibility.

Now, he saw what it had truly cost him.

He realized just how fortunate he'd been that he had been able to begin salvaging his marriage—the one thing he'd wanted above all else—however briefly. It was as if his past had come back full circle to bite him.

He couldn't escape all that he had done...all the decisions he'd made and impulses he'd followed had led him no closer to the life he'd wished for. If anything, he was further away now than he had been a few weeks prior.

He asked himself for the hundredth time why he hadn't simply divulged the true reason for his absence to Alaina all those years ago or any time since, and he came to the same conclusion he always did—he was trying to protect her. Alaina having knowledge of his movements and his motives could have placed her in danger with anyone seeking to harm him or do damage to the Spy Society. One of the first things he'd learned in training was that England wasn't without its own dangers. If anyone was aware of how much she meant to him, then she might have become a target if it was discovered that Sterling was spying on some of the most powerful and dangerous people on the Continent. England still reeled in the aftermath of the Napoleonic Wars, and he would do whatever it took to neutralize threats before they could present another threat—be it from Spain, Italy, German princes, Russia, or any number of other European powers. He couldn't regret the lives he'd saved with his work, but he absolutely regretted the life he'd lost with Alaina.

His fingers clenched around the cut crystal glass with dangerous force.

Just then, a man (either foolishly brave or utterly stupid) appeared in Sterling's periphery. He could sense the rest of the room grow quiet as the other members waited to see if there would be bloodshed.

Sterling refused to move, choosing instead to glare at the dark figure out of the corner of his eye.

The man remained motionless for several irritating minutes.

Finally, Sterling turned and fixed the man with his most ducal glare.

In the face of his expression, the man bowed bravely and took up the seat beside Sterling. His graying hair was slicked back. His clothes were fine, if simple. He had a face unfamiliar to Sterling and yet…there was something intentionally unobtrusive about his appearance. Something nondescript. Something everyone would see, but no one would notice. Black was a master of this—blending in while in plain sight.

"Do I know you?" Sterling growled with derision, his every sense suddenly on alert and overcoming the alcohol he'd imbibed.

"No, Your Grace," the man said softly with a single shake of his head; "but we have a mutual acquaintance." A cold chill danced across Sterling's skin, and he sobered immediately. "The Phantom would have performed the introductions, but he finds himself indisposed." The man held out his hand, palm tilted toward the floor. Sterling eyed the appendage as if it might strike like a cobra, but he couldn't ignore it. His sense of duty demanded it. He took the man's hand and felt a small, sealed note from Ramsay slip into his palm. Sterling concealed it within the cuff of his sleeve with the ease of habit.

"Our friend hopes you'll meet him in the usual place in one week's time."

The man stood and tipped his head deferentially and took his leave.

Conversation gradually resumed around Sterling, but he heard none of it. The corner of the note pricked the inside of his wrist. He didn't need to read it to know his wife would have her wish granted, and a part of his soul would wither and die forever.

She'd be rid of him.

"WHA' 'APPENED TO the princess?" demanded a little voice so shrill with excitement that it was all Alaina could do not to flinch.

"Yes!" another child chimed in. "Tell us, m'lady!"

No less than half a dozen girls aged between four and nine years of age danced about Alaina's skirts, tugging at her hands and practically dragging her to the chair near the hearth from which she usually read to them.

"Girls!" fretted Miss Smythe. "We mustn't pull on the duchess!"

"It's quite alright," Alaina reassured the poor, harried young woman with a light laugh. Despite her aching heart, it was difficult not to allow the girls' infectious joy to wheedle its way in. She had been right to seek solace within these walls. Less than five minutes in their company and she already felt marginally better about her day. There was nothing like the honest adoration of a child. They possessed no hidden agenda, they didn't ask her to be someone she was not, and she and these girls shared the unfortunate kinship of being adrift in the world. "I'd be anxious, too, if I didn't know whether the prince was able to conquer the Black Knight."

Miss Smythe smiled with tired eyes. Younger than Alaina, her habitual simple black dress, severe chignon, and intense dedication to her wards left the unmarried woman with a constant look of exhaustion far more advanced than her years. Alaina had come to know her quite well through her consistent visits to Mrs. Worthy's Home and School for Girls, and there was an unending well of kindness behind her blue-grey eyes. Not a visit passed where they hadn't shared a kind word and Alaina could always count on Miss Smythe to provide the most thorough information about the children in residence, the schooling, and the facilities. Alaina had always felt it extremely admirable that the young woman had dedicated her life to the raising and education of these unfortunate children when she, by all accounts, was sweet, intelligent, and pretty enough to have found a husband with ease. All the better for the children to have her as an advocate, though. In the five years since Alaina had first arrived unannounced and carrying a basket overflowing with sweets, books, and toys, she and Miss Smythe had enjoyed one another's company on numerous occasions and worked together to implement necessary updates and reforms to turn the home into what it had become.

"Thank you, Your Grace. I'll just work on some mending," said Miss Smythe, retrieving the basket from the corner of the room and setting herself up near one of the tall windows overlooking Westminster Bridge Road. Unfortunately, most of the windows remained closed even in nice weather because the proximity to the Thames left a lingering odor if one wasn't careful. The building, however, was in good repair and the grounds were well-kept.

About three decades prior, Mrs. Mary Worthy—former orphan and wife of a shipping magnate—and her husband purchased the horseshoe-shaped home from a lord with a gambling problem and converted it into a refuge for disadvantaged girls. Patronage of the Home had passed to Mrs. Worthy's daughter upon her death and then her grandson following that. When it was clear the grandson had no motivation to improve upon his family's legacy, Alaina had made it her personal mission to assume the position of informal patroness, providing time, necessary items, and funds whenever she could. Her first visit to the home exposed her to the need these girls had for warmth in their lives. Having no children of her own and only an absent husband, Alaina sympathized with them and became a mother hen.

The home had first gained Alaina's attention at an event for an entirely different charity. Mrs. Worthy's was mentioned as one of the homes that would benefit greatly from an event such as the one being held that evening. Many homes and schools for orphaned children were parish-run, but independent ones like Mrs. Worthy's required additional support from patrons and an efficient foundation. Her first meeting with Mrs. Worthy's disinterested grandson was all the urging Alaina needed to take the home and its wards beneath her wing. Without the official approval from its current patron and little desire on his part to put effort into the creation of an appropriate foundation and board, her position was informal, though that suited her just fine since it allowed her to act without any real supervision. Gaining the trust of the matrons who ran the day-to-day operations had been difficult at first, but she proved through her time and her efforts that she was no fickle duchess seeking to make a great show of helping the less fortunate only to wander away when it no longer suited her.

Alaina's greatest joy came from seeing the girls grow into

young women who, at fifteen years of age, possessed the skills that would allow them to be apprenticed out in households and earn wages to support themselves. Not only that, but the additional education for which Alaina advocated meant they would also be able to read, write, perform arithmetic, and have a better chance at holding their own in the world.

For now, the littlest girls crowded around Alaina, jostling for places of honor closest to her, far less concerned with their futures or their tragic pasts than they were in the Medieval tale of chivalry and love. Scooping up the smallest child—a doe-eyed little doll named Mary, as many of the infant wards were named upon arrival both in homage to the Virgin and the Home's founder—and situated her in her lap. The girls were checked for lice each week, so Alaina had no concerns when the child curled up against her like a kitten and popped her thumb into her mouth to await the story.

Alaina had a difficult time swallowing past the lump in her throat and her eyes burned suspiciously.

Do not cry, she admonished herself. *Do not cry in front of the girls. No matter how broken your heart is, it is nothing compared to what these children have endured.*

She took a bracing breath, found the page in the book another of the girls handed to her, and she used her words to carry them all off to a much happier place.

AN HOUR LATER, Alaina descended the steps of the Home and ducked into the Morton carriage awaiting her. She gave the driver instructions to take her to Lady Juliette's townhouse—it was on her way back to Mayfair and she wasn't quite ready to chance a meeting with her husband just yet.

The tears which had threatened her since that morning reemerged with a vengeance. She had managed to sink into a pool of numbness and shock following the abrupt turn her marriage had taken, but that tactic was quickly wearing thin. She focused on taking slow, even breaths as they clattered across the bridge toward Westminster. Her foot tapped restlessly, and she tried not to contemplate how she'd been betrayed again...how bloody foolish she'd been to believe Sterling could be the man who could enrich her life rather than hinder it. She didn't *need* a husband to feel fulfilled—the last eight years had proven that time and time again—but it had been so nice, for however brief a time, to feel like she didn't have to handle everything on her own.

She was so lost in her thoughts and trying to keep her composure that she hadn't realized they'd arrived at her friend's home until a footman opened the door and reached inside to offer her his hand. Before she knew it, Alaina was shown into the sitting room by the housekeeper, where she promptly fell into Lady Juliette's arms and allowed the tears to finally flow freely.

There, sitting tightly side-by-side on the sofa, Alaina explained everything. The story started off painful, like the reopening of a wound, but the words came more easily as she described the truth of her marriage, how Sterling had left for the Continent without consummating their marriage, about the letters she'd written to him without response, how much he'd tossed her life upside down since his sudden return, and his assertion of celibacy—though she omitted Sterling's claim that he'd been sent on an espionage mission for which he'd supposedly trained for years; there was no sense in dragging her friend into that mess. She detailed all of his concerted efforts to woo her all over again, the glimmers of hope she'd had at a future with him, the ways he'd proven to her that he did, indeed, care. And then she told her how it had all come crumbling down with the evidence of his lack of trust in her...that he'd also had Alaina followed and had spied upon her for years.

"Oh, my dear..." Lady Juliette crooned as she patted Alaina's back and handed her yet another handkerchief.

"And now, I feel as if I've been shattered all over again," Alaina said with a very unladylike sniffle. "He speaks of trust and civility and moving forward with our lives, yet he does things like this."

"Men are often not the clearest thinkers."

"To say the least."

"And I had such high hopes for him after the last Society meeting…" Lady Juliette sighed.

"I am furious with myself," Alaina groaned and swiped at her eyes again. "How could I fall for everything he said? I am a more intelligent, more self-reliant woman than that."

"This has very little to do with brains or self-reliance."

Did it? Alaina didn't feel that way. She'd long prided herself on not needing a husband around to support her emotional needs. With Sterling, however, all of that seemed to have changed in an instant. She hadn't needed to be so strong. Someone had been there to let her know she was seen, she was heard, and…she was loved.

A fresh wave of hot tears threatened to spill over. "He said he loved me. But a man who loves someone does not do the things he did. He does not have his wife followed, for goodness' sake!"

"He said he loves you?"

"Yes. Though I suppose it was likely another of his falsehoods as he tried to endear himself to me once again."

"Alaina," Lady Juliette squeezed her hand. "The duke has made several mistakes—ones I fully believe for which he should be held accountable, and apologies are in order—but mistakes do not negate love. At least not real love."

Alaina scowled. "The man was disproportionately upset about my involvement with Mrs. Worthy's. He asked me to trust him but didn't hold me in the same regard. He uncovered information through underhanded means and, rather than discuss it with me, he believed the worst."

"We all believed the worst of him for many years, did we not?" her friend asked evenly. "And none of us trusted him. But now we have all seen the way he looks at you and…Alaina…that man *loves* you."

Her heart leapt into her throat.

"Do not shake your head at me," Lady Juliette admonished with a playful note. "Someone can make terrible mistakes and still be in love. Someone can be an utter imbecile and still be in love. If anything, love often amplifies a person's other emotions and makes them far less rational than they normally are."

"That sounds like an excuse to behave poorly."

"It is not an excuse; I am speaking from experience. Men like to pretend they are noble and sensible, but it all flies out the window when love comes into play. Level-headed men act like fools, calm men run wild, hardened men turn soft." The empathy in her friend's eyes began softening Alaina's resolve. "He was hurt, he jumped to a terrible conclusion, and it spiraled out of control. It was wrong that he did not trust you after asking you to place your faith in him, but it sounds like he regrets it. Did he regret it?"

Alaina pictured Sterling's pleading hazel eyes, the utter devastation on his face when she told him she would be staying elsewhere. Part of her wanted to say he regretted it only because he'd been called out for his mistrust of her, but she knew him better than that. Alaina looked down at her lap and nodded.

"That's a start." A thoughtful silence dragged out between them before Lady Juliette continued. "You know, through this all, you have yet to tell me how you feel about him."

Alaina's head whipped up. "I am furious with him, of course! And I am hurt."

"Understandable." She tipped her head and lifted her brows at Alaina as if to say, *And...?*

"I thought...maybe...that is, no one ever made me feel like Morton has. I hated him for leaving, but I loathe him for returning and giving me hope—" Alaina's voice caught on the last word. "He gave me hope for things I thought I'd lost forever. Companionship. A family."

"Why must we lose all hope?" The words were a whisper floating on the air before lodging themselves within Alaina's subconscious.

Was all hope lost? Had she and Sterling really tread into lands from which they could never return?

More importantly, could Alaina go back to a life without her husband?

Chapter Twenty

ALAINA LEFT LADY Juliette's home after plenty of sweets, tea bolstered with a splash of whiskey from Dr. McCullom's sideboard, and more comforting conversation. She invited Alaina to stay with her if she desired to place some space between herself and her husband, but it was clear Lady Juliette didn't wholeheartedly support the idea. Promising to consider everything they'd discussed, Alaina returned to Morton House intending to take a long soak in the tub before she made any decisions. Unfortunately, her return home was not without incident.

Her maid, Penny, was among the first to arrive in her rooms to help prepare the bath. Alaina was instantly transported back to the moment when Sterling had admitted to manipulating her staff to obtain information about her. It was mortifying, and she hadn't felt so alone since the night of her wedding.

Cheeks flushed from embarrassment and anger, she silently allowed Penny to help her undress as the other maids worked in tandem to fill the brass tub in the bathing room with water boiled in the kitchens. Alaina waited until it was just the two of them before finally allowing her pain at the betrayal to seep free.

"Penny...have you ever divulged information about me to anyone? Are you aware of anyone on this staff who is particularly chatty about my habits?"

The maid's brows furrowed as she shook the wrinkles from Alaina's gown. "No, Your Grace."

"Are you certain?" She leveled a stare at Penny.

The maid cast her eyes down and to the side. "It isn't—that is, it is not uncommon for servants to discuss their employers with one another. It is how we ensure the best work."

"That is not what I mean…but I think you know that." The silence that followed was thick and dark. "It would seem that some words about my activities and habits have been released into the world and made their way back to the duke. This is not a new occurrence either. What do you know, Penny?" Alaina demanded flatly, a single tear breaking free and running down her cheek. It was astonishing that she had any tears left to cry.

Penny shook her head and attempted to deny any wrongdoing. The mottled flush on her fair skin, however, gave her away. "I swear to you that I have never reported to His Grace about your life."

"Then to someone else?"

The flicker in Penny's glittering eyes told Alaina everything. The maid's voice quavered as she spoke, "There was one time shortly after your wedding when I was in the kitchens when the spice delivery came. One of the men noticed I was dressed as an upstairs maid and asked after you because some relative of his worked at the church and heard about the grand event. He wanted to know how the new duchess was acclimating, and he was so kind and so handsome…and I thought nothing of it. I swear that was the only time I've ever spoken of you to anyone."

"I never thought you, of all people, would do that. You were there for me when—" Alaina's words died on a sob, and she covered her mouth with the back of her shaking hand.

Faced with Alaina's obvious struggle, the maid's guilt was released in a great rush of garbled words and tears. Penny fell to her knees and cried unabashedly. "Please forgive me, Your Grace. I—I said only that your husband was a cold man who quit the country without explanation, but I did not doubt that you would recover. I revealed nothing more, I swear it. I am not the one who gabs at the market or barters tidbits of gossip for better deals."

It was becoming clear just how naïve Alaina had been. Her staff had presented a united front against Sterling's intrusion into their household, but that didn't translate to the kinship they felt amongst people of their own class. Her mother had always taught her that all staff gossiped amongst themselves, and she'd been an imbecile to believe otherwise, blinded by the support they'd all provided her in the early, solitary days of their marriage. In sending in his spies, Sterling had successfully found a way into her life. She felt betrayed, but to place the blame solely on her staff's shoulders was unfair. She doubted they would have reported back to Sterling if they'd known him to be behind the questions.

"Please, please do not sack me," Penny begged in a quavering voice.

Alaina heard the words, but her pain was too much to allow her to accept Penny's pleas and apologies at that moment. She needed a little space and time. "Please," Alaina said tremulously. "Leave me. I will bathe alone and dress myself for bed. We will speak in the morning."

Her stomach was too queasy to contemplate food, her heart too heavy to consider facing anyone else that day. Despite her instructions to the contrary, a plate of food was delivered to her rooms. It sat untouched and congealed beneath its silver dome.

Instead, Alaina curled up on the window seat of her bedchamber, staring at the dark seam of the door adjoining her chambers to Sterling's. Maxwell had informed her upon her return to Moton House that the duke had left shortly after their argument. It appeared he was still out.

And so, too agonized to sleep, Alaina there she sat for hours until, suddenly, there was a light.

She'd been momentarily startled by the golden glow, but what really made her heart pound was the quick, rhythmic sound of Sterling pacing like a caged animal, the smack of fabric as he ripped off his coat and threw it at the ground.

Alaina glared at the door, hot tears pricking the backs of her eyes all over again. How could he? How could the man marry her and then leave her? How could he spy on her and then blame her for keeping secrets? How could he think so little of her?

Not for the first time, the nasty thought that—had Sterling not been so selfish—she could have been free to marry another; she might already have a family by now. But then...

Then she wouldn't be *herself*.

She'd spent so many years learning how to break free of the box of obedient wifehood her family had built for her and then Society had reinforced. She'd likely still be trapped there if she'd had a husband watching over her shoulder. Part of her might hate Sterling, but she also hated that, at the heart of it, there was something noble about the reason her husband had left. Of course, he'd gone about it all wrong, but he had been young and foolish. Stupid man. He'd wanted a life with her, but he'd also recognized duty and commitment to the greater good. It was begrudgingly admirable. And, honestly, he had tried quite hard to make things right since his return.

Against her better judgment, Alaina padded to the door and opened it slowly, fully prepared to slam it shut if something heavier than a waistcoat was chucked in her direction.

Sterling whipped around at the sound of the door. His chestnut hair was remarkably disheveled, there were bags beneath his striking eyes and lines bracketed his mouth, his cravat was half-undone, and his cuffs hung loose. A brief moment of tenderness and relief flickered across his face before he hid it, and it struck her like the first licks of fire on a January night; it stole her breath and then made her heart race with wonder and life.

He straightened his shoulders and executed a futile effort to smooth his hair. His movements lacked all their usual grace. She was unused to seeing him in such disarray...

Their argument must have affected him tremendously.

The realization left her feeling at once guilty and powerful, but she clutched her anger to her breast. She could not forget what he'd done; she'd let down her guard once only to find out there had been an even deeper level to his betrayal. She didn't know if she could weather that again.

Without greeting her, Sterling stomped over to his discarded coat and sifted through its silk-lined inner pockets until he found what he was looking for. The garment was then dropped back into a crumpled heap.

He closed the gap between them with surprising swiftness, holding out a small, folded bit of parchment between his two longest fingers. Like a cowed child, he didn't meet her eyes. Several heartbeats passed where they stood like that: Sterling offering her no explanation other than his outstretched hand and Alaina unsure what to do next.

Finally, she plucked the paper from his fingers and retreated a few paces. It made her ache to be too near to him.

"You'll have your wish soon enough." Sterling's voice was rough and raw, unlike anything she'd heard from him previously. He pivoted on his heel and crossed to the far side of the room.

Confused, Alaina hesitated another moment before unfolding the parchment, noting the broken, unmarked black wax seal. Inside, she found rows and columns of strange numbers and runes.

"What is this?" She frowned, turning it this way and that, but unable to decipher it.

"Well, you were unsure if you could believe the truth of my life in espionage…you are holding your proof." He tipped a stubbled chin toward the paper she held. "At least, as tangible proof as I can offer." She caught a sweet waft of brandy as he paced a couple more laps before dropping to the edge of his mattress, scrubbing at his face with his hands and resting his elbows upon his knees. It was the posture of a man defeated, and Alaina didn't think it suited her husband at all.

"What does this mean?" Alaina asked, moving several paces closer. A tendril of alarm began unfurling in her stomach. "What does it say?"

"Essentially, I'm being sent back to the Continent." He spoke without lifting his head. "And you'll be free of my presence once more."

The pregnant silence that followed was unbearable. It ticked on far too long for either of their comfort, but what was there to say? He was right; contrary to the years before, Alaina had spent much of the last several weeks wanting nothing more than for Sterling to disappear and leave her be. Now, after what had lately transpired between them, it was far more complicated.

How had her life become so much more complicated since his return? She'd once been optimistic enough to desire his return to London. Now...

She'd learned Sterling was not who she'd believed him to be. He was vastly more complex than the man she thought she'd married, and yet, he seemed to be his most open, his most vulnerable with her. He'd made it clear that he wanted to be done with being a spy—that he wanted nothing more than a simpler life with her—but this letter in her hand supposedly offered him a chance to disappear once more.

"Do you have a choice?" she whispered.

There was another lengthy pause.

"I have a choice, but I am going to accept the assignment. I meet with my contact in one week and will likely board a ship shortly thereafter, but I'll have other accommodations made until then. I will leave tomorrow, so you needn't finish packing up to stay elsewhere. This is your home and your life; it's far easier for me to pick up and go."

Alaina's heart began racing...but not from excitement. Did he believe himself so disposable from her world that he could walk away without leaving behind a void?

"I'll leave you in peace to live how you wish," he continued. "I promise to bother you no further and swear to you I will send no one to obtain information from your staff. We will return to living separate lives if that is what you desire."

"Is that what you wish?" she asked, surprising even herself.

Another pause as he lifted his head to pierce her with his arresting eyes.

There was obvious pain in his voice when he replied, "The only thing I ask in return is that you let me know if there will be a child."

The note fluttered from her numb fingers, and she pressed a hand to her flat abdomen. Her heart leaped to her throat. Of course, Sterling would wish to know if their actions resulted in a child. He needed an heir. He'd expressed to her how he didn't wish to impregnate her and then abandon her. He'd also made it clear how much he desired to start a family with her. And all of it was crashing down around him.

The look in his eyes broke her beyond what she'd believed possible.

"Is leaving what you want?" she eked out.

"The truth?" Sterling whispered.

Alaina nodded.

"No, I do not want to leave. The thought of it alone feels like a boulder upon my chest. I believed for a brief moment in time that I was finally home, that we could make a life together. I see now that I'd been naïve to believe that and the myriad of mistakes I've made are insurmountable. And now I must go back to pretending to be someone I am not every minute of every day for an interminable amount of time.

"Even here, you now know the truth of who and what I am and have been, yet it is unacceptable. My real self is welcomed nowhere, so I may as well go where I can be of some use, and you can be free to move on. I will not interfere in your Reading Society. I will not be watching over your shoulder. I will send word to my solicitor that you are to be allowed to form a foundation to support the girls' home. I will allow you to be entirely who you wish to be; it is the least I can do."

"Do you really wish to have a life with me?"

"Like an idiot, I'd dared to hope." He was weary and his voice cracked. "Please know, Alaina, that I am sorry. I regret my actions with everything in me and I will regret them until my dying day."

Setting aside her anger and pain and frustration, Alaina approached Sterling where he slouched, dejected. She knelt between his knees and took his hands in hers. They were surprisingly cold.

It finally sank in for her how his time on the Continent hadn't been as carefree or as easy as she and everyone else had been led to believe. It had been eight years of hiding who he was, of wearing a mask and behaving as he was expected to, of being separated from the woman with whom he'd thought he'd share a life. She'd never considered how draining that might be—especially for that amount of time. With her, he'd found solace and freedom he'd not known in so long. Who was she to deny him when his greatest offenses were trying to protect her from the potentially dangerous truth, misguided nobility, and doing what he could to look out for her when he was away? He'd been furious when he thought she'd continued keeping secrets from him, but hadn't she done the same with him?

If she were brutally honest with herself, Alaina had a difficult time imagining Sterling out of her life once more…and it terrified her. Despite her resistance, they had grown accustomed to each other. He'd eventually worked his way into her life with his sweet presence and surprising attentiveness. She wasn't just afraid of being alone again, she feared losing *him*.

They'd each made their share of mistakes and hurt one another, but they'd also done their best to work through it. The road had been rocky, but what Juliette had told her rang in her ears: love wasn't always rational or sane, it made level-headed individuals lose control. Maybe it was her turn again to be a little bit insane.

"What if I do not want you to go?"

Sterling suddenly lifted his head from where he'd been examining their interwoven hands. "What?" he rasped.

"What if," she repeated softly, self-consciously; "I do not want you to go?"

"Why wouldn't you want me to leave?" he asked, his hands tightening on hers until their knuckles blanched. "I left you without explanation and then returned to disrupt your life. I accused you of keeping secrets without giving you a chance to explain—"

"And why shouldn't I want you to stay?" She frowned at him. "Granted, you haven't made the best decisions—especially when it comes to our marriage—but, at the heart of it all, you are brave and caring. You apologized and showed remorse. You told me you loved me. You were willing to sacrifice your own happiness and safety to leave the country to give me my space. I cannot conceive of any solid reasons why you shouldn't stay. As far as I'm concerned, you are a hero, and you've dedicated enough of your life to the service of the Crown…it's time to let someone else do it. We've lost enough time as it is."

The slack expression on her husband's face was blatant evidence of his disbelief. "Are you certain?" he murmured as if barely daring to hope. Her thumb caressed his large knuckle.

"Not that long ago, you swore to me that you would never leave me again. I fear I shall never forgive you if you break that vow. A woman has only so much she can tolerate." She paused for effect. "I have faith that we can make this marriage work…so long as you do not expect me to be an obedient wife…" A wicked smile tugged at her lips. "Or dictate my reading materials."

He stood abruptly, tugging her with him and into his arms. He pressed his mouth to hers, kissing her deeply, holding onto her as if she'd saved his life.

STERLING CLUTCHED ALAINA to him, brimming with joy and relief so fulfilling it nearly choked him. He ran his hands over her, committing every delectable curve and hollow to memory. But, if he had any say in the matter, he'd never leave her side again and would never need to revisit this horrific day.

He fisted the fabric of her nightshift in his hands and created just enough space between their lips to ask if he could remove her clothing.

To his utter delight, Alaina's response was to step back and rip the garment up over her head. He barely had time to appreciate the curve of her hips, the perfect globes of her breasts before her hands began to make quick work of what was left of his cravat and shirt.

Together, they fell back to the bed, a tangle of limbs and desire. Sterling leaned back, his gaze tracing every angle of her face.

"I love you, Alaina," he breathed. "Not a day has gone by where I haven't wished I'd never left you…and it'll be the greatest regret of my life."

Alaina surprised him by rolling him onto his back to straddle his hips. The warmth of her sweet core hovering only inches away from his groin was an intense sort of torture, but he'd have given anything to never have it stop. He would have spoken again, but she silenced him with a finger pressed to his lips and, instead, he settled for kissing the pad of her finger.

"We must agree that we cannot regret the past; it will only be a waste of the time we do have." She leaned forward, her erect nipples grazing his chest exquisitely, making him hiss a breath through his teeth. "For now, you can go on apologizing, or we can start fresh and set about learning more about one another." Her eyes locked onto his. "And I can show you how much I love you, too." Sterling's breath broke and it was a solid minute before he could speak.

She loved him.

All the years, all the mistakes, all the struggles suddenly melted away. It was just the two of them together, prepared to start anew and begin the life they should have had all this time. And they would do it with love.

"Speaking of learning more about one another…" He rolled Alaina beneath him and brushed her golden hair back from her face. "I've heard a rumor that you read some rather naughty books in that society of yours…and I'm dying to see what you've learned."

She flushed instantly, laughing as she wound her arms around Sterling's neck, and he kissed her with all the love he possessed.

Epilogue

STERLING CRADLED HIS infant son in his arms with infinite care. All the while, the squalling babe screamed as loudly as his lungs would allow. Employing a combination of bouncing and rocking, Sterling grumbled, "You've clearly inherited your mother's lungs."

"I take offense to that," came a woman's voice from the doorway.

Sterling turned to find Alaina standing in the doorway between the ducal bedchamber and the adjoining room she'd once occupied before it had been converted into a nursery. Gone was the duchess's furniture, replaced by a bassinet and lace curtains, swaddling clothes, and other items deemed vitally important to raise a child.

True to form, Alaina had eschewed convention for women of her superior rank and insisted that they forgo a night wet nurse. She claimed she'd waited too long to become a mother to simply hand the child over each time he needed feeding, and she was just as capable as any other woman of functioning on little sleep in those early weeks and months of motherhood.

And, as with many things in the year following his return, Sterling had made the concession and deferred to Alaina's wishes.

Now, however, he was questioning the wisdom of it.

He adored his son—was enamored of every little movement or sound the child made—but he missed sleep with a desperate intensity…almost more than he missed sweat-slicked interludes with his wife.

Almost.

Ruefully, he had pondered several times how he'd once gotten more hours of sleep at bacchanalian events in Italy. The amount of screaming and bodily fluids was oddly correlative. He struggled not to shudder.

Alaina floated across the room in her gauzy nightdress and it was all Sterling could do not to seek out the dusky halos of her nipples and the sway of her breasts through the fabric. He was grateful when she retrieved the baby from his arms because the impurity of his thoughts was quickly drawing the blood from his limbs and shooing it elsewhere. He had to force himself to focus on the sweet way Alaina cooed to their son as she curled up on the cushions of her beloved window seat. She proceeded to deftly untie the neck of her nightrail and positioned the babe at her naked breast heavy with milk.

The sight never ceased to move Sterling, his wife holding their son. Motherhood suited Alaina, but it was a far cry from taming her. She was still his beloved hellion and challenged his mental faculties almost daily. The intense swing of her emotions during pregnancy had nearly been the end of his sanity as well as his bollocks, but he wouldn't have had it any other way. Even when they had their spats and arguments, he never doubted her love for him; she loved twice as hard as she fought, and Alaina could hold her own in any ring against even the most vicious prizefighter.

Once their son was situated and suckling happily, little noises of contentment rising from his throat, Alaina settled back and Sterling perched upon a nearby chair to revel in the peace. The quiet was a relief.

"You should sleep while you can," Alaina whispered to him as she stroked their son's downy blond curls. "We have our meeting with the foundation in the morning and you should be well-rested. A drowsy duke is not a sharp duke."

"I will go when you do," he replied in a husky whisper, still unable to tear his eyes away from the domestic sight before him. "Besides, I won't sleep without you there anyway." Alaina smiled warmly at him, melting his insides as the expression normally did. He pulled a chair over to where she sat limned in moonlight and gently propped her feet in his lap. Her moan as he thumbed her high arches went straight to his groin. If Alaina noticed, then she was merciful enough to say nothing.

He had to clear his throat before he could speak. "Are you looking forward to the meeting?"

Alaina's head lolled back against the wall as he continued to massage her feet and her babe suckled at her breast, his pale little hand wrapping around a loose lock of her golden hair. "Of course," she replied with a dreamy smile. "We have been working toward this for nearly a year and it's about time some real progress is made."

After turning down the second assignment on the Continent, Sterling had devoted himself to politics and his seat in the House of Lords; namely championing a cause close to his wife's heart. Together, they now worked to ensure a better system and situations for children in group homes. They made an example of themselves and began investigating more ways to become involved. Their upcoming meeting with their new foundation was one of the final steps in putting together their plan for expanding more orphanages to include schools with more regulated educational standards. They were planning on starting with Mrs. Worthy's Home and School for Girls, the orphanage Alaina had continued to visit on a bi-weekly basis.

The Duke and Duchess of Morton had created a reputation for championing the abandoned and the forgotten. Sterling had assumed more than a figurehead role on the board of the girls' home, and the improvements to the school were promising. Already, the children were demonstrating better reading and writing skills. If they showed an aptitude in a specific subject or trade, then the Morton Foundation would help find them apprenticeships or positions within those areas. They desired above all to give children who had so little support the opportunities fortune had snatched from them.

To say he was excited by how happy this made his wife was an understatement. It was rewarding to see the children thrive, but most of all, he loved being able to help Alaina feel fulfilled and to work on something by her side. In return, Sterling felt as if he was doing something worthwhile. It made him feel like, for the first time, he and Alaina were a team against the world. To have someone at his back was unfamiliar yet comforting in the most primal of ways. He still hated to dwell upon the time they'd lost during their eight years apart, but he recognized that that distance had allowed Alaina to develop into the amazing woman she was.

"I agree," Sterling replied, rubbing his wife's heels with the pressure he knew she liked. It earned him another delicious groan of approval. "It took some doing, but you and Miss Smythe are quite the formidable team." It had been quite the coup, but, with their help and some creative convincing of Mrs. Worthy's grandson and former patron of the girls' home, Miss Smythe was now in charge. Under her careful guidance, the school was flourishing and the girls were thriving. A couple of the older ones had even found secretarial positions thanks to their aptitude for numbers and letters.

"The next step is to implement the efforts in children's homes around London."

"That's my wife—ever ambitious and never satisfied," he groused playfully. Alaina wrenched her foot from his grasp and pressed it into the center of his naked chest so he leaned back in the chair. He tried not to stare at the impossible length of her smooth leg as the hem of her nightrail slid up.

"You say that as if I am a harpy who is difficult to please."

"Well, that is patently untrue." He circled her ankle with his hand and raised her leg higher so he could kiss the inside of her calf. If he caught a glimpse of the gilded curls at the crux of her creamy thighs, then so be it. "I can think of a few ways to please you. Give me five minutes, and I'll come up with a hundred more."

Her blue eyes flashed and she shot him a sinfully wicked grin. "My memory may need some refreshing."

"In due time," he chuckled. Five days, to be exact. Dr. McCullom had advised them to wait at least six weeks before engaging in any strenuous activity or vigorous intercourse. Sterling respected the physician's advice, but that didn't mean he wasn't counting the days like a prisoner waiting to be freed back into the arms of his beloved.

Sterling's hands worked their way up from her foot to knead the lean muscle of her calf. She turned her attention back to their son and stroked his downy head with gentle fingertips. That smile as she held the child was something Sterling would never forget.

He cherished these tender, quiet moments and knew he would look back upon them fondly once the chaos of their life resumed.

Much to his chagrin, Alaina had continued organizing her Reading Society meetings, but he had gotten somewhat used to rooms full of women dancing on furniture and passionately debating literature. Luckily for Sterling, he'd discovered a few more friends of his own in the husbands of those Society members—many of them like-minded men utterly enamored of their unconventional wives—thus expanding upon the camaraderie he had with Sommerfeld. He had a life full of a new kind of chaos and he loved every minute of it.

Alaina caught him staring. "Is everything alright?"

He smiled in reply. "Never better."

Author's Note

Mrs. Worthy's Home for Girls is loosely inspired by The Asylum for female orphans established by Sir John Fielding. Located near Westminster Bridge and the Thames, it offered refuge for orphaned girls who did not qualify for parish support for one reason or another. These girls were taught basic skills they would then be able to take with them into the real world for employment or as housewives. In *Courting the Duchess*, Alaina is determined to ensure the girls who resided at Mrs. Worthy's would be able to read and write at a much greater level than was the norm for other orphanages at the time. Not all homes set their charges up for success and, with the help of Miss Smythe, the Duke and Duchess of Morton vowed to bring about real change to the system.

Ready for more swoon-worthy spies and feisty female leads?

The mysterious Oliver Black meets his match in *Seducing the Spy*, coming soon from DragonBlade Publishing!

Acknowledgments

The seeds of Sterling and Alaina's story were sown long ago, just waiting for their time to bloom. My world of Regency Romance first made its way into the world in 2023 and, by far, my favorite thing to do is sit back and marvel at how it has expanded. I love revisiting characters and having them make reappearances in other stories (so be on the lookout!). Alaina and Sterling's book wasn't my first enemies-to-lovers, but it was certainly my most volatile! I enjoyed writing all the witty banter and how it enflamed their passion. This book wouldn't have been possible without so many people along the way.

I must thank Kathryn for recognizing the passion I pour into my work and allowing me to share it with the world. She and all the amazing members of DragonBlade Publishing have given Sterling and Alaina a home, as well as all the other future members of the Spy Society. Thank you to all the hands who went into making this book what it is; from the gorgeous cover design to the editing, promotion, formatting, etc., this was a labor of love at every turn. I am honored to be a part of this publishing family.

A huge thank you to my readers for following me on this journey and for loving my characters as much as I do. You have embraced their stories and their flaws with open arms and I could not be more grateful. To have something you created out in the world is terrifying; witnessing the love and support for it is humbling. I couldn't do this without you.

Thank you to Amy for being my constant sounding board, letting me bounce ideas off of you at all hours, helping me work through plot points and twists, and remaining my cheerleader even when (I'm sure) you're sick of me, but too kind to say so.

Thank you to my fellow members of the Historical Hoydens for helping me get the spice level where it needed to be for this story. These two *definitely* didn't deserve a tame romance!

Above all, thank you to my family for forever supporting my dreams. Mom, thank you for encouraging my love of reading and cheering me on. Ruta, thank you for your guidance, support, and friendship. To my husband, for always believing I could do it and providing a well of "inspiration" (so he says). To our son, for being so understanding when I worked on a deadline and telling me I look beautiful even in a messy bun and rumpled clothing, bleary-eyed from staring at a screen for far too long. To Dad and Tracey, I miss you both and think of you every day; I know you would be so proud.

About the Author

Kelsey is an Illinois native, author, wife, mother, animal lover, and owner of an obscenely large To-Be-Read book stash. She fostered her love of reading and writing after a heart condition sidelined her childhood. Early one, she learned the joy of living a thousand lives, experiencing hundreds of new worlds, and, eventually, the true pleasure of providing that same escape to others with her writing. Her passions continued to develop long after surgery restored her health and, to this day, it's difficult to find her without a book in her hands. She dove headfirst into the romance genre (perhaps) a bit earlier than the recommended minimum age and became rather adept at disguising her reading material. Once exposed to the glittering world of historical romance, she was forever changed. Her love of writing and all things British translated into her future collegiate studies in both English (with an emphasis on British Literature) and History (mainly British and European). She would go on to earn Bachelor's Degrees in both English and History, as well as a Master's Degree in English. She finished penning her first story fresh out of high school and has never looked back. Her debut novel, *The Baron's Folly*, was published in 2023.

When she's not reading or writing, she's usually watching reruns of her favorite shows, streaming just about any true crime show or podcast; obsessively collecting architectural designs, crafts, and recipes on Pinterest; or sketching, crocheting, cooking, and spending time with her family making the amazing memories she's always dreamt of. She is a diehard supporter of the Oxford Comma and is glued to the TV whenever le Tour de France is on. She is on a never-ending mission to convince her husband that they need pygmy goats, highland coos, and silkie chickens to make their lives complete.

authorkelseyswanson.my.canva.site